THE LAMMAS WILD

Also by Alys Clare from Severn House

A World's End Bureau mystery

THE WOMAN WHO SPOKE TO SPIRITS
THE OUTCAST GIRLS

The Gabriel Taverner series

A RUSTLE OF SILK
THE ANGEL IN THE GLASS
THE INDIGO GHOSTS

The Aelf Fen series

OUT OF THE DAWN LIGHT
MIST OVER THE WATER
MUSIC OF THE DISTANT STARS
THE WAY BETWEEN THE WORLDS
LAND OF THE SILVER DRAGON
BLOOD OF THE SOUTH
THE NIGHT WANDERER
THE RUFUS SPY
CITY OF PEARL

The Hawkenlye series

THE PATHS OF THE AIR
THE JOYS OF MY LIFE
THE ROSE OF THE WORLD
THE SONG OF THE NIGHTINGALE
THE WINTER KING
A SHADOWED EVIL
THE DEVIL'S CUP

THE LAMMAS WILD

Alys Clare

SEVERN
HOUSE

First world edition published in Great Britain and the USA in 2021
by Severn House, an imprint of Canongate Books Ltd,
14 High Street, Edinburgh EH1 1TE.

Trade paperback edition first published in Great Britain and the USA in 2022
by Severn House, an imprint of Canongate Books Ltd.

severnhouse.com

British Library Cataloguing-in-Publication Data
A CIP catalogue record for this title is available from the British Library.

ISBN-13: 978-0-7278-9009-2 (cased)
ISBN-13: 978-1-78029-786-6 (trade paper)
ISBN-13: 978-1-4483-0525-4 (e-book)

All Severn House titles are printed on acid-free paper.

Typeset by Palimpsest Book Production Ltd.,
Falkirk, Stirlingshire, Scotland.
Printed and bound in Great Britain by
TJ Books, Padstow, Cornwall.

In memory of my parents,
who met and married in Cambridge;
with love, as ever.

ONE

The darkness over England was visible to me from some way out at sea.

I was on the deck of a ship, on my way home. It was the summer of 1100, and the month was July.

We had passed a clutch of many vessels, lying at anchor in formations. There was an air of purpose emanating from them: constant, busy activity, shouted orders, and little boats hurrying to and fro from the nearby shore offloading supplies. The signs that something was about to happen were there for anyone to see. But I was probably the only person on the ship that day to see the lowering darkness over the land and sense the powerful air of threat.

I was not like my fellow passengers. I was not even like the woman I used to be. I had been away for almost seven years, and in that time I had changed.

We were approaching the time of the year that I had once known as Lammastide, celebrated early in August, although I now knew it by other names. It was a season of sacrifice and rebirth.

As my long journey up from the south had at last drawn near to the northern coast, I had met with people recently in England. And they spoke of ominous signs and portents. At Pentecost, a village to the west of London had flooded with blood. In another village called Finchampstead – or maybe it was the same village – blood had flowed from a spring for three days and the devil had appeared in the surrounding woodlands in a terrifying range of forms and made dire mutterings concerning the King. There were nervous whispers of disastrous tides and strange images in the face of the moon.

And in an inn where I had put up for the night before setting sail, a fat little monk, hearing I was bound for the land of my birth, had shaken his head and muttered a prayer. 'Something is in the air,' he whispered. Then, leaning closer and enveloping me in a stench of sweat and stale garments, he added in the softest of sibilant whispers, 'Duke Robert's son Richard was killed in the late spring, killed stone dead while hunting in the New Forest!'

He leaned back, his expression a mixture of the salacious and the fearful, clearly expecting me to comment. I was unused to speech, so I merely nodded, tried to look suitably horrified and muttered, 'How terrible.'

I had never heard of this Richard, and I knew little of Robert of Normandy. I had just been travelling through his lands on my way to the coast, but it was long since I had concerned myself with the doings of kings and dukes; since I had concerned myself with those of ordinary people, come to that. Studying the fat monk – and automatically picking up a wide range of information about him from the fact that he had an ingrown toenail and stomach cramps to an awareness of the mean, self-serving aspects of his nature that he was so careful to hide – I realized that I was going to have to re-involve myself with the world and my fellow men and women.

For I had been living far away, in a small community on the north coast of Spain at the foot of the Pyrenees, and there I had been taught how to go through the veil into the other world.

I stood on deck looking ahead as England approached. I made myself move from time to time: small shifts of position, a stretch of the neck and shoulders. These little actions were quite unnecessary, for the years of my training enabled me to stand or sit utterly immobile, barely breathing, for hours at a time. Since returning to the world of ordinary people, however, I had noticed that stillness made them uneasy, as did silence, so I was trying to adjust. To move when I did not need to, to come up with bland remarks and meaningless chat when I was perfectly happy within the peace of my own mind.

I was finding it challenging.

But then very little about this emergence was proving easy.

We docked at Lymington in late afternoon. I had my satchel and my small pack ready and I was one of the first off the ship. I made enquiries and learned that there would not be a boat bound for East Anglia for the rest of that day, but one was planning to sail early the next morning. There were inns and rough taverns where I could have put up for the night, although even the modest cost of the dirtiest of them would stretch my rapidly diminishing store of coins. But I was finding the crowds very disturbing.

Among the vast mass of knowledge and skills I had learned in the Pyrenees was the ability to pick up what other people were thinking and feeling. While it was a crucial ability for someone like me, I was still working on how to block out what was in others' minds when there was no reason for me to know. Which made being among a shoving, barging, angry and dirty mass of humanity extremely trying.

I wanted to feel my homeland under my feet again. Pausing only to purchase fresh bread and a small goat's cheese and replenish my water bottle, I left the port and walked north into the forest that encircled it. Soon I was on quiet rides, and trees in the fullness of high summer gave me their shade.

I walked for a long time. My feet fell rhythmically on the soft ground with a quiet, repetitive thud. There was nobody about. I felt myself slip into the light trance state that I knew so well and, as always, it felt as if I had passed through a doorway into another world. I was still a long way from the fens but I was home, back in the land where I had been born and raised, and my soul was singing.

But then, as the powerful initial joy of homecoming lessened, I began to sense the darkness beneath the light. I had seen it earlier, manifesting itself like a dark cloud over the land. Now that I was walking on that land, the sense of peril was far greater.

There was tension in the air, as if something momentous was being planned; something that offered great rewards but whose execution was dangerously risky.

Violence was hiding in that dark cloud.

I walked on, searching the quiet countryside for somewhere to . . . to hide? But what would I be hiding from? The fact that I could not answer my own question alarmed me, and my unease increased. I spotted a place where a barely distinguishable animal track broke away from the path, leading to a stand of birch trees through which a little stream ran. There was dense underbrush beneath the trees. It looked perfect.

I hurried along the track, brushing aside the ferns and the brambles, and, crouching down, widened the narrow tunnel made by a badger or a boar and followed it until it emerged onto a gravelly little shore beside the stream. The trees grew thickly overhead, their branches weaving together, and I felt safe beneath their protection.

The sun was low on the horizon, and I was more than ready to settle for the night. I set out my cloak and my shawl, washed my hands and my face in the stream, then made myself comfortable on the ground and ate my food, savouring each mouthful. When I had finished, I walked along the stream bank for a little way until I reached a spot where the trees thinned and I could look out at the land all around me.

I stood watching for a long time. The light faded, the sky turned to indigo and the stars came out.

The darkness and the tension were still apparent, but I sensed no immediate threat. The night was warm and still. Comforted, I returned to my little camp and settled down to sleep.

It was deep night when I woke.

If, indeed, I *was* awake.

I lay quite still, feeling the night with all my senses.

Nothing.

I slowed my breathing, waited while my heart rate slowed down, then closed my eyes.

There was a man, in a clearing in the forest.

The man was broad and stocky. His chest was thrown out and his thick legs were planted apart, giving him a swagger. He was bare-headed, his wild hair reddish-fair. His face wore a scowl, as if something disturbed him. His eyes were pale, his gaze intent. He was dressed in garments of good cloth, although he wore them carelessly; his hose were torn and his fine boots caked with mud.

There was an air of restlessness about him. I wondered that he managed to hunt, for it requires a quality of stillness. He had a presence: he seemed to shine.

It was late in the day, the sun going down in the west. The forest felt very quiet, as if it held its breath. The stocky man made a sharp noise; a sound of impatience, as if he was angry because the creatures he sought to hunt and kill were failing to appear before him precisely when and where he wanted them.

Another man materialized on the far side of the clearing, silent, careful, dark of visage. Unlike the stocky man, this one was skilful and knew his craft, for he had appeared out of nowhere: not there one moment, there the next. And, whereas the first man shone, this one almost seemed to absorb the light, clad as he was in shades of dark green, the colours so subtle that they looked as if they had been fashioned out of the forest vegetation. His eyes were the only part of him that moved, and very slowly he turned them on to the stocky man.

Everything was still.

The stocky man suddenly spun round, hearing something, and then his bow was up, the bolt ready, and in a blur and a sudden rush of violence it flew through the quiet air and embedded itself in the shoulder of the stag. But the strike was not fatal: the animal gathered itself and bounded off, blundering and crashing through the undergrowth. The man raised his hand to shield his eyes, for he was staring straight into the lowering sun.

Another stag burst into the clearing, head up, eyes alert. Was it the companion of the wounded animal? Its brother? Sometimes two young males will run together until they begin to compete for the does.

I watched the shining man. He was re-loading, delayed by peering after the wounded stag and now trying to see where it had gone.

But the green-clad man was ready.

I knew what was about to happen. But in a moment of perfect clarity I knew that this was a dream, a vision, and that I wasn't truly present. I was powerless to prevent it. I did not even cry out a warning.

The green man had not noticed that the shining man was

moving. He had stumbled forward for a few crucial paces so that now he was between the green man and the stag.

Why had the green-clad man not noticed? Was the low sun in his eyes?

His bolt flew.

It struck the shining man in the chest.

With a choking gasp, he clutched at its shaft, pulling at it, panicking, crying out in a hoarse shout of pain and fear. The shaft broke off, leaving a short length sticking out of his chest.

He gave a groan. His face was deadly pale.

He slumped forward in a faint, hitting the ground hard and driving the bolt deeper into his flesh. There was a slurp, and a great fountain of blood burst from him.

The bolt had found his heart.

I opened my eyes.

I was lying by the stream, swaddled in my cloak and my shawl, my pack beneath my head. My heart was hammering. It was still dark, but I sensed dawn was near. There was a very faint lightening of the sky in the east.

I am safe, I told myself. I am in my camp, hidden in the forest and alone. I repeated the words several times, and presently I was calm.

I sat up and drank some water. Now there was a band of light above the eastern horizon, and I had rarely been more pleased to see the arrival of the new day.

Restored to myself, I returned to the dream.

It appeared that my sleeping mind had presented me with images of the death I had heard about from the fat little monk. I went back in my memory until I could hear his voice again. Duke Robert's son Richard had been killed, he'd said, in a hunting accident. Duke Robert . . . Yes. Duke Robert was the King's elder brother, nicknamed Short Boots, and he ruled Normandy. I tried to recall the chatter I'd heard on the road and in the inns as I'd neared the coast. Duke Robert had gone on crusade to Outremer, and he'd had to borrow heavily from King William to pay for men, horses and equipment. He had offered Normandy as surety, and the gossip said that King William was furious when his brother returned safe and sound because now Normandy wasn't going to land in his lap without a fight after all and he would have to take it by force if he wanted it.

And this man, Duke Robert, had lost a son in just the sort of fatal accident that I had been shown in my dream. Suddenly I heard the fat monk's malicious whisper in my head: *Richard was a bastard, you know – one of many, they say.* He'd nodded self-righteously, and I'd wondered if he believed that such a violent death was a fit punishment for both the illegitimate son and the unchaste father.

I was reassuring myself comfortingly that this was surely the reason for my troubling dream when a disturbing thought occurred to me.

The fat little monk had said this Richard's death had been in springtime; he'd mentioned it was before Pentecost, which had stuck in my mind because I'd had to think hard to recall when Pentecost fell.

But in my vision the trees of the forest had been in the full-leafed glory of high summer; they had looked indistinguishable from the way my eyes were seeing them at that very moment. They would not look like that in late spring or early summer.

It wasn't a vision from the past but from the future.

I knew I would not sleep again.

I went down to the water, removed my clothes and immersed myself, using some of the precious preparations that I had learned to treasure in the south. I washed my hair, scrubbed the dirt of a very long journey off my body, then put on the freshest of the few spare garments in my pack. I found a patch of sunlight and sat in its warmth until my hair was dry enough to braid, eating the last of my food.

Before I left my little sanctuary, I sat very still for some time and allowed the barrage of impressions I'd been receiving since England came into sight to flow through my mind.

I had long known that peril walked close behind me. In the south, I had made an enemy. She was a woman some years older than me, golden-eyed, dark-haired, watchful. She had disliked me even before we met, and over the years dislike had stretched to embrace resentment, jealousy and hatred. As if life in the south had not been hard enough – the lessons I had learned had come at a very high cost – I had had the malign presence of the dark woman to contend with. Not all the time – I might well have crumpled if she'd always been there – but enough.

I had believed on first meeting her that she was very dangerous. Time turned that instinctive impression into certainty. Although I had left my life in the south behind me now and I knew I would not go back, I was not at all sure the dark woman had finished with me; I knew, in fact, that she hadn't, for all I tried to turn a definite fact into a mere possibility.

It was not that I had actually seen her dogging my steps; I hadn't. She did not need to follow me closely, however, for she knew full well where I was bound. She had been there herself, sent from the south on a mission uniquely suited to her particular talents.[1] Disguised, she had watched from a distance and even spent a winter there, for, struck down by a typical fenland sickness of the lungs, she had been unable to leave when travelling home was still possible. Before she left she had killed. Casually, as if a life mattered nothing as long as she achieved her purpose, leaving her victim lying dead in an alley.

She was a threat, and I sensed her power even though I knew she was not at present near.

And now I was sensing another threat.

I did not know what it was, but there was no doubt it was there. The air carried currents of fear and violence, the earth seemed to give strange little tremors, as if it knew something was going to happen.

I came out of my inner mind and slowly stood up, waiting while my body adjusted itself to the present. I slung my satchel over my shoulder, wrapped my cloak and shawl around me, for the early morning was still chilly, and crawled back through the undergrowth and out on to the track.

I walked hesitantly at first, my state of mind affecting my steps.

[1] See *City of Pearl*.

Then as the sun rose higher and I warmed up, I stopped, took off my heavy cloak and stowed it in my pack. I had left the animal track now and was on the path, and the going was easier. I squared my shoulders, found my courage and strode on.

I was back in England. I was going home.

As the full associations of that simple little word flooded through me, I was filled with joy.

If there was peril in the air, I would try to fathom out what it meant and I would find a way to deal with whatever it was and whatever it might bring. If the dark woman came after me with vengeance in her heart, I would face her and I would deal with her too.

My confidence rose up and I felt invincible.

As I strode back down to Lymington I was singing.

TWO

The sea voyage from Lymington to Lynn called in at many ports on the way but was largely uneventful, with a calm sea and warm, sunny weather. I secured for myself a favoured spot in the shade and was as comfortable as one can ever be spending four days and three nights on the hard deck of a ship. Still hungry for the novelty of my home soil beneath my feet, I went ashore every time we tied up, even if the port was barely worthy of the name and little more than a huddle of hovels.

For the first time in weeks – months, or even years, in fact – there was nothing I had to do. So through all the long days at sea, I settled into my corner, turned my back on my noisy fellow passengers and, my eyes on the lively, sun-spangled water, let my mind and almost all my attention turn back into my own recent past.

I had been living in a small settlement on the north coast of Spain. It lay in a hidden valley between spurs of the coastal mountain range, and access by land was so difficult that contact with the world beyond was almost entirely by sea. Some of the inhabitants endured the difficult and perilous journey through the deep darkness underneath the mountains; they had their reasons, and for them the extreme discomforts and the terrors of those secret passages brought their own reward.

I knew this because I was one of them.

It was via this route that I had first been taken to the settlement.

In winter life was very hard. Snow fell deep in the mountains, and its chill breath seemed to creep down into every corner of the simple buildings where we built our fires and tried to evade it. We felt our isolation powerfully during those months, when few boats put in to the little bay below the settlement and we were thrown back almost entirely on our own resources. We rarely went hungry, for the community traced their presence in the settlement back through countless generations and they knew how to extract enough during the spring, summer and autumn to last through the harshest winter. Everyone worked on the land, and the cultivated strips that had been grabbed back from the steep hillsides were so valuable to the community that they were diligently ploughed, manured, sown, watched, weeded and harvested in order to extract the maximum yield. The women knew how to use the produce to provide nourishing and at times surprisingly tasty food, although as we waited for spring to arrive most of us grew lazy and pasty on too much starch, and I for one grew sick of the sight, the smell and the bland monotony of root vegetables.

The community kept livestock: goats, pigs, five or six cows, and, to keep the stock healthy, every other year they took their females to breed with males of the species in neighbouring communities. I particularly liked the goats, and I discovered that I had an affinity with them. One of my duties was to assist the old man who was responsible for them. His name was Basajaun, he was almost blind and he flattered me and flirted with me as if he was a youth again. With patience at my mistakes, he succeeded in passing on to me enough of his profound knowledge of goat husbandry to make me an adequate assistant.

But I was not in the settlement to tend goats. I was there to receive knowledge of a very different sort.

My teacher was called Luliwa. She was an apothecary and she made her potions and remedies from the plants she grew herself and the ingredients she purchased from the traders who put in at the bay. She was a healer like no other I had ever encountered, including my aunt Edild, who had been my first teacher, and Gurdyman, into whose care I had been transferred once Edild declared she had taught me all she knew. Luliwa had the ability to see right inside a sick person; to follow whatever symptom troubled them right to its roots deep within the body. She opened my mind to the realization that a sore throat and difficulty swallowing, for example, were sometimes symptoms of someone struggling with a situation they did not

want to accept, as if the body was translating this unwilling-
ness into a closing-up of the gullet; that headaches were
frequently the outward sign of profound mental distress;
that a woman could fail to conceive because she did not love
her husband and in some unfathomable way had closed
off her body's reception of the invading sperm.

At first I had felt doubt that quite frequently escalated into
horrified disbelief. As my time with Luliwa went on, however,
I learned to open my eyes and absorb the truth behind what
she was telling me. Then I became humble; ashamed of my
arrogance in thinking I knew better.

Concerning everything that Luliwa taught me, there was
nothing in which my knowledge even began to approach hers,
let alone exceed it.

Because the community was small and we all knew each other,
it was impossible (and probably unnecessary) to try to conceal
the purpose of my presence there. People respected but also
feared Luliwa; she lived apart, in a small single-roomed
dwelling at the top of a steep little track leading up into the
foothills. I did not live with her; it never occurred to me that
I should, for Luliwa was a solitary and, as I grew to know her
better, I felt a strong sense of relief that my own accommodation was down in the settlement. She was a very powerful
presence, and I knew I needed regular spells of time away
from her. I did not care to explore why this was but I suspect
it was because, away from her dominance, my own self could
flow through me once more.

From time to time she shared her house with her son Itzal,
although he was absent from the community far more than he
was present. Sometimes he went off on long and unexplained
journeys by himself, once staying away for almost a year and
returning looking sick, exhausted and very thin, with new
streaks of silver in his long dark hair. Usually, however, he
travelled south, beyond the mountains to the beautiful City of
Pearl, and more often than not I went with him. One such trip
led to a twelve-month absence of my own, during which I
stayed with my dear friend Hanan, received instruction from
a grave and courteous man called Salim but, in the main, spent

my time with the doctor I had met on my very first visit. He was a small, wizened man with dark skin and immaculately white robes and, although clearly well advanced in years, he moved with the impatient bounce of a young man. His name was Fahim, which he told me with a modest smile meant person of profound understanding. He was well-named. With him my travels were not into the world beyond, as in the main they were with Luliwa, but deep down inside the human body and the extraordinary, miraculous secrets it held. As the long days of learning from and working with him ended, I was always left reeling, and Hanan would have to tempt me with food and tease me into laughter to bring me back to the here and now.

As well as her son Itzal, Luliwa also had a daughter, Errita. I had never seen Errita spend even a night under her mother's roof, although on rare occasions she visited during the day. Errita had her own tiny dwelling on the very edge of the settlement, beneath a vast overhanging rock that always looked forbidding and threatening, although that might have been because of Errita's presence. Everyone in the settlement avoided her, speaking to her only when they had to and, I was quite sure, extending even this courtesy out of respect for Luliwa. Fortunately for all of us, especially me, she was away even more than Itzal. When she returned, it always seemed to me that she had descended further into her own dangerous darkness.

Errita had killed. Once to my certain knowledge, and the whispered stories and rumours strongly suggested many more had died at her hands. She dispatched without pause or conscience, for when her own distorted logic told her it was necessary she did not hesitate, giving no more thought to the victim than a butcher slaughtering a pig. She had marked me out as her enemy from the start, and as time went by I understood that her hatred had many and complex roots.

Even back near the start of my long exile, as I had stood on the shore watching the beautiful ship *Malice-striker* sail away north with some of the men I loved most in the world on board, I was looking ahead to the battle with the malign spirit residing inside Errita that I knew was coming.

For the next six years we had faced each other with invisible swords, sometimes one then the other gaining the ascendancy. I had taken so much from her, for as well as everything else her mother gave me, she and I had come to love each other. I believe Luliwa did love Errita, but as time went on I learned to see, like a physical entity, the shield that Errita put up against the tender emotion of maternal love. What enraged her even more, however, was that Luliwa was giving her knowledge to me.

And now, sailing on the calm waters of my native land back to the place that was my home, I was only too well aware that my battle with Errita was not yet over.

The weather continued fine, the gentle winds stayed favourable, and we were making good progress. The ship called in at Dunwich, and I went ashore to buy more food and drink. The port was busier than I remembered from when I had been there thirteen years ago, and, still not used to crowds, I was glad to go back on board, resume my comfortable spot and look forward to the final leg of the voyage as we sailed on to Lynn.

My eyes slid out of focus as I stared back at Dunwich, and all at once the past was more vivid than the present. I had travelled there with my friend Sibert and a handsome young man called Romain with whom I fancied myself in love.[2] Back then I was full of pride in myself, for I had recently discovered certain skills that I possessed and that I thought nobody else did, and I was desperately eager to show them off. We found the remains of an ancient sanctuary built on the sea margins, and what I uncovered there led me to experience for the first time the true power of the forces that exist out of sight and hearing of the world, and I'd been terrified.

I smiled now at the memory. I was still terrified, on a fairly regular basis, but I had learned how to conquer my fear and look beyond it to whatever message lay beyond.

Most of the time, anyway.

*   *   *

[2] See *Out of the Dawn Light*.

We docked at Lynn early in the evening, and I said farewell to the master and his crew. Now I needed to find a craft that would take me upriver to Cambridge. I strolled along the quayside, noting what had changed and what remained the same, enjoying the sensation of firm ground beneath my feet, until I spotted a familiar boat.

It was the one that had ferried Gurdyman and me up from Cambridge seven years ago. *The Maid of the Marsh* looked rather more battered but her master had aged very little. 'You again,' he greeted me with a grin, as if it had been only a week since I'd last travelled with him.

'Me again,' I agreed. 'Are you bound for Cambridge?'

'That I am.' The smile widened.

'Then may I come with you?'

'Glad to have you,' he said.

I spent two nights and a day on *The Maid of the Marsh*, disembarking in Cambridge very early in the morning. Mist was rising off the water as the sun rose and gained strength, and in the hazy light the shabby old buildings took on a mysterious air. I paid my dues and said my farewells, then jumped down onto the quay and set off up the path towards the Great Bridge. There were few people about as yet and I walked slowly, not thinking, simply letting the emotions come and go.

Before I went away, the greater part of my life had been in Cambridge. I had been joyfully happy there, and also heart-broken with grief.

But I wasn't there to indulge in bittersweet memories. There was someone I had to go to see, and sad news I must at long last break.

I walked on. I commanded myself to ignore the strong pull towards the market square and the maze of little alleyways that surrounded it; to one alley in particular where there stood an extraordinary house whose passages and stairs led this way and that apparently at random, so that I had named it the twisty-turny house. It was the house of my teacher and my muse; the man who had taken me off on my long and life-changing journey to Spain and the settlement in the coastal mountains; the man who had given up much of his power so that I could inherit it; the man who I loved almost as I loved my own precious father.

Gurdyman.

I hadn't seen him since he had left the northern coast of Spain on board the *Malice-striker*. We had parted uneasily, for I had learned that our journey together had been part of a far greater plan that he had not revealed to me.

I ached to go to him. I wanted to tell him that I understood now, that I no longer blamed him for what he had done, that on the contrary I knew I had very much to be grateful to him for. I was also painfully impatient to see how he was, for even back then I'd been aware his heart was failing.

Was he still alive?

Yes, I told myself firmly.

I was not the only person in the southern lands who cared about him, and even if I didn't know for sure how he fared, I sensed that those extraordinary men and women with whom my life had become bound up had means of getting messages to each other across the great distance that separated them.

I paused at the place where the quayside emerged onto the road leading down from the Great Bridge, looking left towards the market square.

Just a quick look wouldn't hurt . . .

And then, almost as if the wish had precipitated the action, I was standing outside the twisty-turny house.

The door was closed and there was nothing to say whether or not Gurdyman was within. He must be, I reasoned, he was almost always there and it was still very early. I wanted to go closer, to put my ear to the door, but I didn't. Gurdyman's senses were far more acute than those of normal people and he might very well detect my presence. I wasn't ready to face him quite yet.

But then suddenly the door opened and Gurdyman appeared. He was more stooped than I recalled, and as he carefully went down the steps, he put his right hand on the top of his left shoulder, massaging the spot which always troubled him after a prolonged session bent over his workbench. He had undoubtedly aged, but he was still Gurdyman. Even as he looked around him at the bright day, his expression benign, I drew my presence back into myself and imagined I was merging with the bricks of the shadowed wall behind me.

Gurdyman's bright blue eyes swept straight past me.

He didn't know I was there.

With a shock of mingled delight and dread, I realized that my ability to conceal myself was stronger than Gurdyman's power to make out what was being hidden from him.

In this one small skill at least, it appeared I had now outdone my teacher.

As Gurdyman set off along the alley, he realized that the ache in his shoulder had gone. He had felt, just for a heartbeat as he stood in the doorway, that a skilled and benevolent hand had been easing the stiffness. And he had smelled a very well-remembered smell: rosemary, lavender and pepper.

She had always used those oils when she materialized silently behind him at the end of a long day.

He smiled to himself.

She will come when she is ready, he thought.

I walked back towards the Great Bridge, heading for the house of the person I knew I must see. Ahead and to the right of the road, Castle Hill rose up. Just before it, concealed by the church and the new priory, I knew there was a dark little opening where a narrow path led off.

I had struggled and failed to overcome the impulse to go to Gurdyman's house. Now the urge to hurry on up the road and dive off down that path was even stronger. Without my volition, I found myself walking that way.

The narrow path led to Jack.

Jack.

Of the group of people I loved, to whom I'd said farewell that day on the beach below the settlement, he had been the last.

He had come all that way to protect me, and when he told me so I almost gave up the future that was destined for me and jumped into *Malice-striker* with him.

I didn't.

'I will come back,' I had promised him, 'eventually.'

And now here I was.

I was well aware I was making a mistake, for I had made up my mind and I knew what I must do first. Only it seemed I hadn't, for here I was crossing the bridge, passing the new priory and taking the narrow path. It was bordered on the left by the massive rampart supporting the castle hill and on the right by a stone wall, and was more a tunnel than a path.

I strode on, not allowing myself to think.

The path emerged into an open area bordered by hovels, animal pens, storerooms, some stables and a little church. It had once been occupied by the craftsmen and labourers who had built William the Conqueror's castle. Among them had been Jack Chevestrier's father, and it was the sturdy little house he had built for his wife and child that Jack had restored and lived in.

In my memory the village had been all but deserted. It was busier now. Three or four other hovels were now occupied, and there was the sound of voices. Someone was hammering, and as I stood and watched a small cart drawn by a donkey pulled up and a man unloaded some sawn timber.

I crept further into the village, then concealed myself in a gap between an unoccupied hovel and a stable falling into ruins. From here there was a clear view of Jack's house.

In my memory it had been a safe, welcoming place. Not large: a main room with a hearth, shelves for platters and mugs, offcuts of wood to sit on. A small second room led off this, and in there was a bed. Jack had kept geese, and the first time I went to the house they had set off a ghastly cacophony that had made me jump, and Jack had explained that they were better than guard dogs for informing him when someone was lurking outside.

Now the house looked bigger, and I realized that the old lean-to that stood to the right as I faced the house had been rebuilt. The roof looked sound, the door was of good wood and had an iron latch, and although it was tiny – less than half the size of the main dwelling – it had the air of a place that was very well cared for.

As I watched, the door opened and a woman appeared in

the doorway, looking up and down the path. I drew back, but I was in shadow and I didn't think she could have seen me. I studied her. She was several years older than me, strongly built with a firm bust and a curvaceous figure. She was clad in worn but clean garments, and a folded white cloth covered her thick brown hair. Her handsome face was presently creased in annoyance. She yelled, 'Aedne! *Aedne!* Where are you, you little imp?', and with a burst of laughter a small child of about four or five leapt out from her hiding place behind a water barrel and shrieked in delighted pretend fear as her mother swooped down and gathered her in her strong arms. Pretend fear turned to tears, however, as her mother gave her a sharp slap across the buttocks. 'I've *told* you not to run away like that,' she yelled. 'How can I do all that I must do today and keep an eye on you as well?'

I watched as they went into the house and the door was slammed shut behind them.

What was the woman so busy with? I wondered. But I knew; of course I knew. She would be preparing food. Something tasty and fortifying for a hard-working husband called out at dawn to deal with some emergency to come home to; to share with his wife and little daughter.

I turned away, keeping to the shadows, not wanting anyone to see me there. I felt cold and slightly sick.

I had come back to keep my promise.

But Jack had given up on waiting for me, and his extended house now contained a wife and child.

As I fought my tears I reflected on the little girl's age.

He hadn't waited very long.

As I hurried back along the path, down the road and over the Great Bridge, I understood that there were now two very sound reasons for not letting Jack know I was back.

The first was because, although I had still seen no sign of Errita nor, indeed, detected her presence, I was increasingly certain that either she herself, or some emanation of her, was following or had followed me home from the south, and that her intentions where I was concerned were as far from benign as it was possible to be.

One way to take revenge on those who have hurt us – especially if the wound is by the perceived theft of the love we feel is rightly ours – is to wound not the object of our hatred but someone they love.

If I allowed her even to suspect that I still loved Jack, it would put him in danger. And, while he was robust and strong and perfectly capable of defending himself from a flesh and blood foe, what would threaten him could not really be described as that.

Errita was a storm-created dark cloud flying towards me. At times I could almost see her in the distance. When she finally enveloped me – and I knew it was when and not if – she must not be allowed to discover the identity of the people who were in my heart.

The only way I could face her was alone.

The second reason for not approaching Jack – and it was making my heart hurt as if I'd been punched – was that it appeared he was living his life perfectly happily without me.

THREE

Forcing Jack out of my mind, I took the path leading to the right on the town side of the bridge and marched off along it. I had to find a certain house, and I only had a vague description of its location.

It belonged to a woman called Eleanor de Lacey. She and I had not met. I knew of her because she had been an associate of Rollo Guiscard, and a long time ago Rollo and I had been lovers. He had returned after a very long absence, and for reasons of my own I had agreed to make a journey with him to help him evade a determined killer.[3]

In our final moments together, he had said, 'I have gold. Some you already have, for you hid it for me. There is more. Go and see Eleanor de Lacey. She lives by the river. Tell her I said you're to have it all.'

Gold had been the last of my concerns then, for Rollo had flooded every single particle of me. But that was in the past.

Now I had to find this woman.

I should have gone before, I knew that full well. I had not found the courage, for I had been raw with grief then and I could not face telling her what had happened. I think I felt that sharing the horror with an outsider would broadcast the terrible fact, so that there would no longer be anywhere to hide from it.

But that was then, and this was now.

I passed a row of merchants' houses. One of them I knew, for I had been there with Jack. I shut off the sudden vivid images with the violence of someone slamming a door.

I came to more houses, and then to one small but well-built and lovingly maintained dwelling set a little apart, as if it held itself aloof. There was a sense of peace descending, as if few people passed this way, and the only figure in sight was a

---

[3] See *The Rufus Spy*.

monk striding off along the narrow path. The house had a small extension set into the side of the building over the river, and in it was a window.

It could easily be the place I was looking for, and instinct was telling me it was. If not, with any luck the occupant would direct me to the right house.

I walked up to the door and knocked.

After a brief pause it was opened. A handsome woman of some way beyond the middle years stood before me. She was slim, quite tall, and held herself well. She was dressed in a stylish gown of dark-blue wool. It had clearly been made by skilful hands, for it fitted her perfectly. Her headdress was brilliant white, and her smooth grey hair was drawn back beneath it.

'Yes?' she said. She was, I observed, studying me equally intently.

'My name is Lassair,' I said. I leaned in closer, lowering my voice. 'I believe we have – had – a friend in common.'

Her eyes narrowed. I could almost see her thinking, working out what I meant, and briefly her intelligent face creased in dismay.

'Come in,' she said curtly.

I stepped inside. Her house was immaculate and it smelt of rosemary. She indicated a low doorway, and I went through into the room with the window over the river. 'Please,' she said, and I sat down on the padded seat beneath the window that she was pointing to.

After a moment she came to sit beside me.

Her eyes searched mine. 'Rollo Guiscard?' she whispered.

I nodded. 'I'm sorry.'

Eleanor de Lacey sighed. Then she said, 'I knew about you. Not your identity, for he did not reveal it, merely that there *was* someone. I believe I have been waiting for you.' She paused. 'He's dead, isn't he?'

'Yes. He died some years ago.'

Eleanor de Lacey nodded, her face grave. 'I was fond of him,' she said. 'I saw him only rarely, and usually at very long intervals. But . . .' Whatever she had been about to say was painful; I saw it in her face, felt it in her aura.

After a few moments, she shrugged. 'I am not surprised,' she said sadly. 'Such a long silence told me something had happened. The way he lived his life suggested he would be unlikely to make old bones.'

Mistress de Lacey had taken the news with courage, and I admired her for her pragmatic observation. But I picked up her sorrow. I shared it, and for some time we sat in silence together. It was a tribute, of sorts, to the man we had both known.

Eventually she got to her feet. 'If you are his heir,' she said, 'as I imagine you are, then you probably know I hold in my care possessions of his that are now yours.'

'It's not why I'm here,' I said quickly, 'although he did tell me you had—' I stopped, for suddenly it was impossible to speak of the gold he had bequeathed to me when we had only just been mourning his death.

She leaned down and put a cool hand on my shoulder. 'I am well aware you have not come for the gold,' she said gently. 'You came to tell me he is dead, and for that I am grateful.' She straightened up. 'He told me you were to have it,' she went on. 'I do believe that, in his way and as far as he was able, he did care for you.'

I nodded. I couldn't speak.

She went out through the doorway and I heard her steps on the wooden boards of some adjoining room. Then there was silence: no further footsteps, no sound of some cupboard door being opened, no rustle as a curtain or a cover was moved to reveal some secret hiding place . . .

Then she was back again, and in her arms she bore a sturdy oak chest bound with iron. It was perhaps the length of my forearm and hand, half as wide and half as deep, and it looked ancient. I had seen similar chests in Gurdyman's house, and he said they had been made by the Saxons. From Mistress de Lacey's expression, I surmised it was quite heavy.

She put it down on the floor in front of me.

She pointed to the hasp, fastened with a heavy padlock. A pair of identical apertures were set into it, side by side. 'Two keys are required to open this,' she said. 'I have one, but not the other.' Looking up, she met my eyes. She didn't need to ask the obvious question.

Slowly I shook my head. 'I do not have it,' I said. 'Rollo did not give it to me. He didn't actually give me anything, because—'

But then the words suddenly stopped, because I realized that of course Rollo *had* given me something.

Before I'd gone off with him on his last mission, he handed over to my keeping a leather bag full of gold and coins. He had told me to hide it in the safest place I could think of. 'If anything happens to me,' he said, 'it's yours.'

Sorrow overcame me again, for in that moment he had been smiling, excited at the prospect of setting off together, and the possibility of the dark conclusion to the mission that had come out of nowhere cannot have even crossed his mind.

Once again, I gave the memory its space.

Then I said to Mistress de Lacey, 'He gave me a bag and I hid it for him.'

Eleanor de Lacey smiled sadly. 'That too is now yours, child.'

Yes. 'I will go and fetch it,' I said, already getting up, 'for the key will be inside.'

She followed me as I strode to the door. 'How can you be so—' she began.

I turned to face her. She looked at me for just a heartbeat, then, lowering her gaze, she stood back. 'I see,' she murmured.

I did not know what she meant, but it didn't matter. 'I will come back as soon as I can,' I said, stepping out into the early sunshine.

She muttered something – 'I will be here,' perhaps – but I did not reply.

I set out for Aelf Fen.

For the same reason that I could not seek out Jack, my family were also closed off from me. I did not know how near Errita was – although I was trying to work out a way in which I might be able to discover a clue or two – and I could not risk their safety. For now I did not sense her in the vicinity, so it seemed safe enough to visit my village. At least I could look from afar and ascertain whether everyone was all right. Whether, indeed, they were all still alive, for seven years is a long time and life is full of peril.

I went back to the Great Bridge, crossed over and took the path on the right on the far side. I had walked this way so many times, for it was the road out to the fens. It was still early, although I had already been through so many emotions this morning that it seemed much later. If I kept up a good pace, I would be in the village by mid- or late afternoon.

I had a piece of luck, for a farmer heading for Ely in his rickety old cart gave me a lift as far as the spot where his road diverged from mine. His cart might have been in need of quite a lot of repair but his chestnut mare was fit and lively, and her smart pace cut at least an hour off my journey.

The farmer had more in common with his cart than with his mare. I listened to his descriptions of his ailments and made a few suggestions, and I delved in my satchel to find a remedy for the phlegm that gathered in his lungs. As we talked I recalled, as if from another life, that it had always been my practice to offer my healing knowledge in payment for a ride. It was very pleasing to be doing so again; another reminder that I was home. I purchased some bread, cheese and a punnet of raspberries from the farmer and bade him good day, feeling a surge of affection for him purely because he had treated me as if I was simply the healer girl I used to be.

I was approaching Aelf Fen. I was hot and tired, and I paused to take off my boots and dangle my feet in a slow-running tributary on its way to a wider waterway. As I stood hopping on the spot, replacing a boot, something made me look up.

My father was standing on the bank of the distant waterway. He was half-turned away from me, not looking in my direction, but I would have known him anywhere.

I ducked down below the tops of the reeds, peering through them.

My heart was giving strange lurches, its beat speeding up and then slowing down. My love for him flowed right through me, and in a series of vivid images I saw our past. I wanted so much to break out of my hiding place and run to him that denying the impulse hurt like the clench of a vice.

He sensed something. I knew he did: I could see it in the way he suddenly became tense, as if some unusual sound had just alerted him. Even more, I knew it because I felt him in my mind. I felt his quiet misery at my long absence, his anxiety that I might not be coming back – that I might be dead, even – and, more than anything, his profound love for me. And, shooting through all this like a flash of night-time lightning, the sudden flare of hope . . .

I watched as slowly he turned in a full circle, looking intently all the while. At first there was a bright excitement in his face, but gradually it faded and now he looked so very sad.

I could not reveal myself to him, but there was something I could do. Closing my eyes, concentrating hard, I focused my attention on him. Presently, as if a part of me really had moved right up to him, it seemed to me that I sensed him right beside me.

Slowly, deliberately, I put a picture in his head. It was an image from my very recent past, and I was climbing aboard the ship that took me from the north coast of France to Lymington. I wasn't at all sure that he would recognize the location but it didn't matter. He would see what I was doing and he would know I was on my way home.

Slowly, gently, I withdrew my consciousness from his. I opened my eyes.

He was looking at a spot some twenty paces over to my right. Close, Father, I thought with a smile. Very close. There was such an expression on his face . . . he was smiling, but it was so much more than that. I went on watching him as, slowly, he turned and walked away.

I was almost sure he would not say anything to my mother. But *he* knew.

In that moment of painful love, it was enough.

I stayed hidden in the reeds until my tears dried and I felt strong again. Then I walked on right up to the edge of Aelf Fen and, looking out carefully all the time to make sure nobody was observing, I went to stand in the deep shade of the vast old oak tree that grows on the higher ground behind the village.

I looked down at my parents' house: the place where I had spent my childhood. My father didn't appear, and I guessed that he needed some time on his own before returning to the family. My mother emerged to throw a handful of scraps for the hens. For a moment she stopped, raising her head as if sniffing the air. Then she shook her head, waved an impatient hand in front of her face as if brushing away a persistent fly and went back inside the house.

I smiled with fond affection. My mother is a very literal woman who keeps both feet firmly on the ground at all times. The impatience was so typical of her: if I'd tried to put an image telling her I was coming home into *her* head, she'd have instantly dismissed it as silly fancy and told herself firmly to get on with sweeping the floor.

I stood under the tree for a long time. I saw my brother Haward coming home, and as he approached the door to the little house that adjoins my parents', three – no, four – children came running out to greet him. He knelt down, opening his arms, and the three eldest children closed in for a hug while the fourth tried to clamber up his back. The laughter brought his lovely wife Zarina out of the house, and Haward looked up at her with his love for her clearly painted on his face.

They all went inside. I waited a little longer but my younger brothers Squeak and Leir did not appear. I did not worry that anything had happened to them, however, for I had already read in the other members of my family that all was well.

Or so it seemed.

I moved round to the other side of the oak tree so that I could look down on my aunt Edild's house. For some years I had lived there with her, but then she had married Hrype and I had no longer felt welcome. I had thought that Hrype disliked me; maybe he had, then, but when last we met we had discovered a new affection for each other. Or perhaps it was an old affection reborn, for he had always been kind to me when I was a child.

There was smoke coming from the roof, and a very faint smell of incense on the air . . . I imagined Edild bending over the fire as she made some complicated remedy, concentrating hard on her task. A neat stack of logs stood by the door. As I watched, the door opened and a dark-clad figure reached out to this stack, collecting an armful of logs. Hrype. My heart gave a lurch as I recognized him. I tried to imagine him working on the sawing and splitting like any other husband, but it was hard, if not impossible, to picture him engaged in such a mundane domestic task.

I checked to make sure I was still unobserved, then left the shade of the oak and, swiftly crossing the track that ran along the foot of the slope, hurried onto the marshy ground that separates the village from the water. I was bound for the fen edge, and the little artificial island that my distant ancestors had made on which to bury their honoured dead.

The water was lower than it had often been in the past when I had cause to cross to the island, and, taking it slowly and carefully, I only got wet to my knees. Slowly I paused by each grave, respectfully greeting my forefathers. Finally I went over to the large slab of stone beneath which my Granny Cordeilla lay.

And straight away I saw that there was a new grave right beside her.

I felt a stab of sheer dread.

But then I realized that this was not the grave of my father or any other of my close kin, for I had just reassured myself that they were alive and well.

Then I knew who lay there beside Granny Cordeilla.

When he left me on the shore below the settlement under the mountains, he had understood that I was afraid he would not still be alive by the time I came home. He said, *I cannot say. I shall do my best to stay alive.*

But he hadn't managed it. My grandfather Thorfinn, the Icelander, the Silver Dragon, had come to the end of his long life and he was buried right here, next to my grandmother. The woman he had loved.

I knelt at the foot of the two graves, one hand on each, and for some time I let myself flow into them, sending my love, sharing my memories of them, and I felt them reach out in response.

Then, coming out of my trance, I moved so that I was kneeling at the head of Granny Cordeilla's grave.

I said softly, 'Remember how, before I went away, I left a leather bag in your keeping?'

In my head she said, *Of course I remember, child, I'm not daft and I rarely miss anything.*

I smiled, laughed. 'Indeed you do not,' I muttered, recalling some of the many times she'd caught me in a piece of mischief I thought she didn't know about.

I heard that, she said.

'I need to disturb you again, I'm afraid,' I went on, 'for I am in dire need of money, and also there is something in the bag that I urgently require.'

She didn't answer, which I took for assent.

As I had done before, I got my shoulder to the great stone and edged it aside, just far enough so that I could put my hand in beside her. For a strange moment I thought I felt warmth, but I knew I couldn't have done. My fingers closed on the leather bag and I drew it out.

As I put it in my lap and unfastened the ties my mind filled with Rollo. He had touched these coins, he had bagged them up and given them to me. I sent him my grateful thanks; sent him my love.

I replenished the purse at my belt. Even combining what I took now with what I'd removed before my long journey with Gurdyman, the bag was only slightly lighter. Now that I had travelled so far, I understood coinage better and I realized with a slight shock that there was enough left to live in what to someone like me was utter luxury.

At the bottom of the bag, just as I'd known it would be, was the other key to the padlock.

The evening was well advanced by the time I left the village and set out for Cambridge. I felt like walking all night, for the best memories of my young life in Aelf Fen had been awakened and it was an indescribable pleasure simply to move through the paths of the past. In addition, my senses were alert for any sign of malignancy, either close by or more distant. I still felt Errita's threat, but as far as I could tell she was not yet nearby.

I kept up a good pace for a long time. I had no idea how late it was but it was fully dark, the moon just rising and bathing everything in silvery white. I came to a place where a faint track led down to a stretch of gravelly shore. I knew this place, for opposite the little beach there was an island where a strange old man called Mercure had dwelt. Barely hesitating, I took the track and, finding the raised causeway as easily as if it was a path marked with flaring torches, waded out to the island.

Climbing the slight slope up onto dry land, for some time I simply stood there and let the place impress itself on me.

I expected to feel echoes of horror and grief, but there were none.

Puzzling over why that was, I began to pace slowly all round the island. It was not big, and I felt I knew every part of it. The overhanging trees drooped their branches low over the little area of land, and I was struck with the sense that they were protecting me. Already I felt utterly safe. People didn't come here – they never had done. Even the most adventurous children had kept away.

Mercure had lived here alone for decades and perhaps more. He was a man like Gurdyman, only he had succumbed to the seductive appeal of the dark side of the craft whereas Gurdyman, after one glaring lapse that was only now being put right, had largely managed to resist. The island, it now seemed, had retained a strong echo of Mercure as he had originally been, and allowed his last manifestation to drift away.

I had come back to the place where Mercure's house had stood, with the workroom and storeroom behind it and connected by a covered way. I could see these buildings in my mind, but on the ground there was only the faint shadow of their outline to show where they had been. In the middle of the main room there was a wide patch of bare ground. On a night seven years ago, a great fire had raged there. It had been started by an arrow that flew across from the shore, its blazing point burying itself deep in the thatch.

But the huge intensity of the conflagration had come about because someone else had gathered all the combustible, volatile, explosive materials from Mercure's workroom and piled them on to the fire. It had been a funeral pyre: it had sent the body within it on its way to the spirits in a wild roar of flames that soared up into the sky.

I knew all about the pyre because I had created it; it had been my farewell to Rollo.

After some time it occurred to me that the patch of ground where the pyre had burned looked smooth and flat, as if somebody had raked over it. Intrigued, I knelt down. The moonlight was strong, but nevertheless I relied on touch and not sight, running my palms over the ground in a series of swoops.

I found nothing. No fragments of wood or charcoal, no bumps and hollows where the flames had burned at different intensities into the earth. It really was as if the patch of ground had been carefully tended . . .

Then my right hand came across a smooth mound, perhaps a pace across, where the earth rose up to a low summit. I wondered what lay buried beneath, and who had buried it.

Standing up, I went over to where I had left my satchel and took out the soft leather bag in which I keep the shining stone that was my grandfather's gift to me and my inheritance from him. I sat down cross-legged, spread my skirts between my knees to form a lap and released the stone from its soft wool covering. I had felt its warmth even as I took it out of the bag and now, unwrapped in my hands, it was hot.

I had come to understand the shining stone far more profoundly during my years in the south. I knew now that it was connected in some mystical way with my own deep self; that on many occasions, it shows me what some part of me already recognizes as the truth. You might think this lessens the wonder of it, but the reverse is true. How on earth does it do what it does? I have no idea, and I suspect I never will have.

Now, sitting there in the calm silence of Mercure's island, the shining stone still felt magical to me and I knew it always would.

I held it in my hands, gazing down into its black depths. I let my mind relax; let all thought slip away. Presently there came a flash of brilliant green, then a wide blaze of gold. The stone knew I was there.

I saw a big, broad-shouldered figure tending the very patch of ground beside which I now sat. He was collecting small fragments of bone, and carefully, reverentially, placing them in the hollow he had carved out of the burned earth. He took a long time about it, going over the whole blackened area several times until he was satisfied he hadn't missed anything. Then he built up the mound, tamping down the earth and smoothing it over until it was much as it was now.

When he was done, he stood for some time and I picked up a very faint echo of his prayer for Rollo's soul. There was another thought in his mind . . . concentrating fiercely, I picked it up.

He was hoping that, one day, somehow I would know what he had done.

Slowly I came out of my trance.

Two emotions were uppermost in my mind. The first was regret, for all the time the stone had been showing me what Jack had done – for the big man was Jack, as I'd known it would be – I had caught only the briefest whisper of Rollo. The fierce heat of the pyre I'd lit for him had done its work too well, and he was truly gone.

He was a man of the south; I recalled him telling me his kin were from Sicily. I wondered if he had loved ones who would miss him, who would wonder why he did not come back. Was his mother there in the heat of the south, missing him? Focusing my mind, I sent her a message and told her what had happened and what I had done. Then finally, I sent Rollo my blessing.

As I packed away the shining stone and slowly got up, I understood something: Rollo was gone, utterly absent, and I knew nothing I did would bring any echo of him back. Which meant, I concluded, that we had not been destined for each other.

Tears on my face, I let him go.

As I settled for the night in the shelter of a stand of young birch and alder trees, I thought about the other emotion I'd brought out of my trance. It had been painful and poignant saying goodbye to Rollo, but this emotion was a hurt of a much sharper nature.

I was wondering just how long it was after Jack had come here, buried the remains of Rollo's pyre and sent that thought to me, that he had settled down with the comely woman and they had conceived their child.

In Aelf Fen, Hrype sat on the floor beside the dying fire. It had done its work, and now the stack of items that he had gathered and arranged with such care were no more than ashes.

The little house felt very empty.

But it was not simply because of the absence of everything that had once furnished it, singled it out from every other house and made it home. It had not been the act of putting all of those treasured things in the fire that had robbed the place of its heart. He had felt compelled to burn them – so as to leave the house tidy, so that no one else's hands should touch them, as a tribute of love, he wasn't really sure – and he had set about it as a house-proud woman turns out her house in the spring.

But the task had been an ending and not a beginning; the completion of what had started that terrible night almost a year ago.

Ever since, Hrype had been existing. Sleeping when his restless mind allowed. Eating when his grieving heart did not make the very thought of food make him nauseous. Speaking to people when they gave him no alternative. Walking, walking, long miles every day that took him away from the village and the town for weeks at a time. But he always had to come back.

He waited with agonizing impatience for the day when he didn't have to. When he could set off and turn his back for ever, his precious memories safe within him. He could not go yet; it wasn't time.

As he raked over the ashes and turned his mind to settling for the night, he had a sudden strong sense that the longed-for time was at last approaching.

FOUR

I slept soundly and long. When I woke up, the sun was already high in the sky and it was a glorious morning.

I took my time, bathing, re-packing my bag and my satchel, slowly eating a few mouthfuls of food. Then I crossed over the causeway and went on my way.

I was back in Cambridge by late afternoon. I went straight to Eleanor de Lacey's house.

She opened the door to me and stood back to let me precede her into the room overlooking the river. Her face was impassive and, except to respond to my greeting, she did not speak.

I had the key ready, tight inside my fist. I held it up.

She gave a little cry.

'My instincts informed me that you were who you said you were,' she said with a warm smile that changed her rather severe face. 'I needed to be certain, as I am sure you appreciate, and the fact that Rollo's key is in your possession provides that certainty.'

'Yes, I understand,' I said. 'He— Rollo would expect nothing less.'

Her expression changed and now she looked sad. 'He would not,' she whispered.

I wondered if to tell her about the great scar of the pyre out on the island; about my sure sense that he was gone. I decided it would not help. It was better to leave her with her own memories.

She gave herself a little shake. 'The chest!' she exclaimed, giving me a rueful smile. 'You must be very impatient!'

I smiled but did not reply. Once the impatience would have been burning over me like nettle rash, but Luliwa had taught me that such an expending of unnecessary emotion was wasteful: *It makes no difference at all*, she had said so many times until I finally learned the lesson, *and serves only to make you feel worse.*

Mistress de Lacey had left the room, and now she returned with the wooden chest in her hands. As before, she laid it on the floor in front of me. She reached inside her gown for her key, which she had hung on a fine gold chain. Seeing me looking at it, she said, 'I do not habitually carry it on me. I took it from its hiding place only this morning.'

Bending down, she put her key in the right-hand aperture in the padlock. She turned it and there was a loud click.

She looked up at me. 'Your turn.'

I did the same with the left-hand aperture. There was a second click, and the semicircular loop of the padlock flew out of its housing. I lifted it out of the hasps – it was surprisingly heavy – and opened the latches. Then I opened the lid of the chest and pushed it right back.

It was full of tightly packed leather bags very similar to the one in Granny Cordeilla's grave. There were keys, some on little leather tags. Set among these were a lot of rolled parchments, on some of which I could make out very small, neat handwriting. One had a series of small drawings, each with tiny writing beside it. Others were covered with the same little picture drawn several times in neat squares, and sometimes the parchment had one or two of the squares missing. Some of the documents were clearly very old, for the parchment was deep yellow and the ink had faded to pale brown. It was going to be all but impossible to make out the words. Other documents were sealed, one with a great disc of scarlet wax with a clear imprint and a ribbon hanging from it.

Seeing this one as I uncovered it, Mistress de Lacey gave a gasp. Pointing, her hand trembling, she said in a whisper, 'That is the King's seal!'

I looked at it.

I had known Rollo was an agent of the King: he'd told me so, not long after we met. When he'd helped me up after I'd been hurt and escaped with me over the high walls of an abbey.[4]

---

[4] See *Mist over the Water.*

I'd put my foot in a compost heap, and we had grinned at each other as if it was funny.

I came back to the present. Here before my eyes was the proof. King William had given Rollo this document; he had touched it, signed it, sealed it. I put my fingers on the parchment, and it seemed that I felt a faint tremor from it.

Eleanor de Lacey said shakily, 'So much gold!'

My head shot up and I met her eyes. 'Some of it is surely yours, after all that you did for him, so—'

But she shook her head, her expression indignant. 'I do not want it!' she said sharply. 'I have no need of it.' She stared down into the chest. 'I was only one of his people,' she whispered. 'There are more, perhaps many more, and no doubt each one of them hides a chest like this one.'

I allowed the thought of just how much wealth Rollo had amassed flow through my mind and then leave again. What use was it all when you were dead?

I closed the chest, replaced the padlock and fastened it. Eleanor held out her key. 'This is yours,' she said.

I nodded, putting both keys in my purse.

'What will you do with it?' Mistress de Lacey asked, quite briskly.

I thought about that, especially the tone of voice, and about the fact that she had given me the second key. She could not have made it plainer that she expected me to take the chest away with me.

'I have one or two possibilities in mind,' I replied. It would have been more truthful to say I was trying to work out some possibilities, but I did not want to give her cause to worry about me.

I stood up, picking up the chest, and took a pace or two towards the door. 'Thank you, Mistress de Lacey,' I began, 'I should—'

But she held up her hand to detain me.

'Do not rush away,' she said, and I sensed her relief that I had demonstrated so clearly my willingness to take responsibility for the chest. 'I have prepared food and some wine. Will you take some?'

I realized I was famished. 'Yes, please.'

*   *   *

We sat at a little table she had drawn out from the wall. The food was delicious – little pastries filled with a choice of meat or cheese, a sort of fish paste on warm bread, sweet cakes – and Mistress de Lacey clearly did not stint herself when it came to good wine.

Watching me with a smile as I drank from a beautiful silver cup, she said with an apologetic smile, 'I fear I spoke too hastily when earlier you offered me some of the – er, some of the gold. It was kind, and I should have thanked you, which I do now. But, as you will observe, I am very comfortable.'

She paused, gazing round at the well-appointed, elegant room. 'I was married young, to a much older man; a merchant,' she went on with disarming frankness. 'He was wealthy and successful, but it was not a close relationship.' Again she paused, and this time her eyes seemed to slide out of focus as she thought of her past. 'I am afraid that I did not take to marriage, and I never managed to be more than a dutiful young wife, very thankful when her husband's initial enthusiasm waned and he left her alone.'

Into the slightly awkward silence I said, 'You have no reason to know, but I am a healer and have some experience with young wives and, indeed, women in general. Such a reaction to the – er, the demands of marriage is not uncommon.' Her face creased into a grateful smile. 'Did you have children?'

'No,' she said firmly, and the single word seemed to overflow with her relief. 'My husband died after less than a decade of marriage and I have been alone ever since.'

'Alone and utterly content,' I said softly, and she smiled again.

'How well you understand,' she murmured.

Silence fell again, but it was a comfortable silence. I was still surprised that she should have revealed so much of herself, but it was something I had been noticing as my instruction had gone on and grown more intense: people tended to treat me as a confidante, whether I invited it or not. Almost invariably I didn't.

For some time Mistress de Lacey sat still, gently humming to herself. Then she said, 'Do you know Cambridge?'

'Yes,' I replied. 'I used to live here, although I have been away for some years.'

'The prevailing mood will have changed during your absence, as I imagine you have noticed,' she said.

To be honest, I had perceived very little about the town and its inhabitants since my return, having been totally preoccupied with my own concerns. So I said politely, 'In what way?'

'Sheriff Picot is dead,' she said, and although she spoke with restraint I detected the grim satisfaction beneath the words. 'He was a corrupt man, and most of us believe the town fares far better without him.'

'Dead,' I repeated softly.

Jack had spoken so often of the Picots, and they were not unknown to me. He had recognized the sheriff for the self-serving, cruel bully that he was, and despaired of the state of the town under his rule. As for the sheriff's nephew, Gaspard Picot, he had gone even further down the path to veniality and evil, and Jack had almost perished at his hands before the man himself had died.

Mistress de Lacey was saying something about it not being unusual for the post of sheriff to be left vacant for a few months, if not years, before a new appointment was made. I waited until she had finished, then said, 'So who is in charge now?'

'That fine young lawman Jack Chevestrier has been acting as sheriff,' she replied, her face glowing with approval. 'He is trusted and held in affection by the townspeople, for he is known to be strong but fair. His men support him loyally, which is more than can be said for his predecessor.'

She went on to speak of what was happening in her town, and it was some time before I could listen. Her casual mention of Jack had set my heart thumping, and I felt slightly sick.

Forcing myself to attend to her once more, I picked up what she was saying. I realized that she was intelligent and perceptive; Rollo, as I might have known, had chosen well.

'And you are aware of what is happening in the rest of the land?' she asked suddenly.

'Er – not really,' I said. 'I have been away for some years.'

'Yes, of course, you mentioned that.' She frowned. 'The King, it seems, is uneasy.' She shot me an assessing glance as if asking herself how trustworthy I was.

I wondered how much she knew; even more, I wondered that she could have knowledge of anything at all concerning the King's mood. But then I thought, she was one of Rollo's people. He always seemed privy to an extraordinary amount concerning the state's affairs, so perhaps the important facts were shared somehow among the network of people like him. People like Eleanor de Lacey . . .

She appeared to have decided she could be frank with me.

'King William went on a mission to France last year,' she began, lowering her voice and leaning closer towards me. 'His troops besieged Le Mans in June and he did not return to England until Michaelmas.' She looked at me knowingly, but if there was any significance to these dates, I did not know what it was.

'I see,' I muttered.

Further lowering her voice so that she was whispering, Mistress de Lacey went on, 'They talk of a new crusade, you see, for Duke Robert and the others met with great success in Outremer. They found a land of wealth and plenty, of sunshine, fruitfulness and profound beauty; they helped themselves and they are hungry for more.'

I'd had no idea. But I nodded as if I'd already heard, encouraging her to go on.

'Duke Robert is on his way home from Jerusalem, or so we believe,' she said. 'He'll be married by now, for the betrothal was formalized as he went *out* to the Holy Land. Such an advantageous marriage,' she said with a sly smile, 'for the new father-in-law is wealthy far beyond the dreams of most men and he has been generous with Duke Robert.' She smiled at me encouragingly, as if she expected me to draw some conclusion from this fact.

But I couldn't. 'Really?' I said feebly.

She gave a faint tut; of disappointment, perhaps. 'Duke Robert borrowed heavily from his brother the King to fund his crusade,' she explained. 'He had offered Normandy as surety, and King William thought it highly likely that Duke Robert would be killed, and that Normandy would fall to him without his having to go to war to win it.'

'But he's not dead, he's married and rich and on his way back?'

'Yes!' she exclaimed. 'Already planning a new venture, as I said.' She frowned in disapproval. 'All those Normandy nobles are rushing to mortgage their lands to William now, just as Duke Robert did last time, to fund this mission,' she went on. 'They must all surely be aware of the perils of the long voyage, yet it appears that cupidity outweighs apprehension. They devour the tales of sudden wealth, of glorious sun-drenched lands and castles for the taking, and they demand their share.' She sighed, shaking her head at man's folly.

'And Normandy will not now be handed over to the King,' I said.

'Indeed not,' she agreed. 'The bottomless coffers of Duke Robert's new bride's father have allowed him to repay the loan, and the King has had Normandy snatched from him, or so I imagine he views it,' she went on, 'which perhaps is his punishment for having put so much of his faith in what was only a hope. Therefore he looks for a new land base in France, and there are rumours of a mission to Poitou.'

I remembered the massed ships I had seen as I sailed towards the south coast. 'He is preparing a fleet,' I said softly.

She looked at me very intently. 'You have seen this?'

I nodded. 'I recently crossed from northern France. I saw many ships bustling with activity. I did not know why, until now.'

She didn't ask for an explanation as to why I'd been making the crossing and I didn't give one. Perhaps she assumed that I too had a role of some sort in the King's spy network.

'No doubt Duke Robert has eyes on our ports,' she murmured, 'and is well aware what his brother has in mind.' She hesitated, eyeing me intently. 'The King, they say, is in the vicinity of the New Forest.'

And his invasion fleet lay offshore ready for him to give the word.

I felt a chill of fearful apprehension.

'What will Duke Robert do?' I whispered.

Eleanor de Lacey looked at me, her face expressionless. But she did not answer.

So I said, 'There is much talk of terrifying visions, of omens suggesting a threat to the King. People experience frightful dreams and visions, they see—'

But she gave an impatient shrug. 'Dreams and visions do
not kill.' She shot me a critical look, as if she had expected
better of me. 'What is needed is proof.' She made a fist of
her hand as if to emphasize the word. 'There was word that—'
But then her eyes narrowed and she stopped.

I waited, but she did not go on, instead turning away and
busying herself pouring wine into my cup.

She might have accepted that I had not lied about my identity, but it seemed she was not prepared to risk revealing any
of her secrets.

Darkness would not fall until late, for we were only a month
from the summer solstice. However, the town always grew
quiet as evening turned towards night and it was rare to find
people out and about once the sun had set. Mistress de Lacey
said several times that I must not be seen, for I would be
carrying a wooden chest in my arms and it was as clear an
invitation as any to the felonious.

Mistress de Lacey assumed that I was what I appeared to
be: a young woman, strongly built but a woman nevertheless.
She would think, I was quite sure, that I would be an easy
target, and perhaps her mind was already presenting her with
visions of an attacker creeping out of the darkness, hurrying
on silent feet after his victim, who would be totally unaware
of his presence until the arm round the throat, the knife in the
ribs.

But Mistress de Lacey did not know that I had been altered
by my years in the south. That it was a very long time since
anyone had crept up on me. I would have felt the malice of
any would-be attacker even as the impulse to pursue me first
entered his head.

All the same, when she insisted I wait with her until at last
it grew dark outside, I complied.

'You have somewhere to go?' she asked anxiously as she
ushered me out. She hesitated. 'I have a room where you could
sleep.'

I felt a rush of affection for her. I had been picking up many
things about her, one of which was that she was a woman who
loved her solitude and who far preferred her house when she

was alone within. It had cost her a good deal to offer me a bed for the night, and I was truly grateful.

I shifted the chest so that I was holding it under one arm and put my free hand on her arm. 'Thank you. You are very kind, but I prefer to be alone.' She nodded in quick understanding, one natural solitary to another. 'And I do have a place.'

Her anxiety eased. Leaning forward, she kissed my cheek. 'Go well,' she said softly.

'And you. Goodnight, Mistress de Lacey, and thank you.'

She inclined her head in acknowledgement. As I strode away, I heard the door close and the sound of bolts being shot.

It had not been an untruth to tell her I had a place to go to, although the idea had only latterly occurred to me. As Mistress de Lacey and I had sat in the window over the river, talking quietly over a wide range of subjects that had nothing to do with the matters we had earlier discussed, part of my mind had been mulling over my options. I was still not ready to reveal my presence to Gurdyman, and some impulse that I could not identify was urging me not to take Rollo's chest into the twisty-turny house just yet. I had almost decided that the best – the only – option was to head back out into the countryside and spend another night under the stars, when a much better idea came to me.

The place I had in mind was over on the other side of the main track that went round to the east of the town, out in the fields and beyond the last of the houses. It was not too far, although as I set off on my way towards it, very quickly the weight of the chest began to drag at my arm muscles and I shifted it onto first one shoulder, then the other.

I crept along the darkest, narrowest alleyways of the town, keeping in the deep shadows, senses alert. I heard a patrol coming towards me, and slipped into the profound blackness between two buildings as two well-armed watchmen marched past, talking quietly to each other.

They must be Jack's men, I thought. I recognized one of them, although he had changed in seven years. His name was Henry, and he'd been a thin lad of fifteen when I last saw him.

He had been raised by the monks until he rebelled and ran away, and he'd been a bright, intelligent boy full of ideas. Now he was a man, and his steady, confident step and calm, low-pitched voice indicated he was fulfilling the promise of his youth.

I felt a rush of happiness at the thought that at least one of Jack's band of loyal men was still with him.

I waited until the two watchmen were long gone, then crept out of my hiding place and hurried on.

Not long afterwards, I was approaching my destination. I passed the sacred well, pausing briefly to pay my respects, and then the house was before me.

It was a small dwelling, low to the ground as if crouching down and trying not to be conspicuous. There was a second, even smaller building behind, which had been used as a store-room and workroom. It was deserted; there was a hole in the roof and one wall of the storeroom was curving out at an odd angle. Nobody lived here – I knew that even before I went inside – and from all appearances, nobody had been near since the death of the two occupants.

I had known them both. Morgan had been a strange old man who lived in a world of his own, although on the rare occasions I'd spoken to him, I had found him to be gentle and kind and I had warmed to him. His companion had been a spotty, stuttering lad called Cat, whose nervous yellow eyes had looked out at the world with fear and deep suspicion. Morgan had a secret which I did not learn until after both he and Cat were dead. In fact, he'd probably had a hundred secrets, for he was someone like Gurdyman, like Mercure, and he had walked apart from his fellow men and women.

I was not in the least surprised that the house cried out its abandonment. Its occupants had died savage deaths and people instinctively avoided the spot, no doubt muttering among themselves that it was cursed and haunted. While this was greatly to my advantage now, when I needed somewhere to hide, I was sad for Morgan and Cat. The house was indeed haunted – I sensed their presence even as I pushed the door open and crossed the threshold – but their shades were gentle and I knew they welcomed me.

I left the door wide open to let in the moonlight and set about tidying the room. There wasn't much to tidy, for Morgan and Cat had lived simply. I rolled up thin old straw mattresses in which the mice and the rats had nested and stowed them in a corner. I found a tatty brush and swept the remains of the last fire back within the circle of the hearth. I set cups and platters straight on the shelf. Then I swung my pack off my back and my satchel off my shoulder and laid them down on the clean floor. Carrying the wooden chest, I went through the low doorway into the storeroom.

It was a small, windowless space, and even I, who had known Morgan and did not fear him, felt it resisting my presence. I said softly, 'Please do not shun me. I am not here for any malign purpose, but I am in dire need of a hiding place. I wish to put this chest' – I held it up – 'somewhere that nobody will come looking for it, and I ask that you will permit me to do so and use your power to guard it and keep it safe.' I paused. 'It was given to me out of love, of a sort.' Briefly I saw Rollo, smiling at me. 'It contains more wealth than I ever dreamed of, and you have my solemn word that, whatever I do with it, it will be for the good and not the bad.'

I waited for what seemed a long time, the chest growing increasingly heavy in my arms. Soon I wanted to cry out from the pain of holding it.

Then suddenly the mood in the dark little room altered.

I knew it was all right to go ahead.

The floor was of beaten earth, rock-hard from the long passage of feet. But there was a broad shelf built across the far wall, and the ground beneath was relatively soft. I felt a slight suggestion of moisture as I knelt down and put my hands on it, and I guessed that this was where the damp would creep in during the winter. As I scraped back the surface layer, a faint smell of mould floated out. It was hardly the best place for the wooden chest and its contents, but I had no intention of leaving it there for long. Besides, it was the only patch of floor into which I could dig.

I found a length of wood in the stack set ready for the fire. After a spell of hard digging, I had made a hole big enough for the chest. I put it inside, checking the dimensions. I would cover it and smooth the earth over in the morning, but before I did I would go through the contents again. I stepped back, and in the deepening darkness I couldn't see the chest at all, uncovered though it was. I would check again in the morning, once it was properly buried, although my instinct was telling me the chest would stay precisely where it was until I came back to fetch it, and I had learned that my instinct was usually right.

I went back into the main room, spread out my cloak, wrapped myself in my shawl and rested my head on my pack. I was exhausted, and my arms and shoulders ached as if they were on fire. For comfort, I buried my face in my shawl. My sister Elfritha had given it to me when I left home to look after my other sister, Goda, when she was pregnant with her first child. Goda and I never really got on, but I loved Elfritha dearly. She was a nun, in the abbey at Chatteris. As I rubbed my cheek on the soft wool of the shawl, I felt her near me.

I was blessed that night. It was not only Elfritha who was a close and beloved presence; as I drifted into sleep, I thought I saw Morgan and Cat, sitting either side of the heath, watching over me.

I knew no harm would come to me while I slept.

FIVE

I was awake soon after dawn. I had slept deeply again and I felt refreshed. I had no food left except for a dry rind of cheese, which I ate slowly. I filled my bottle from the sacred well, and the water was very cold and surprisingly refreshing.

I went through the main room into the workroom. I took the chest out of the pit and set it down in the doorway of the main room. I required daylight to go through the documents, but I dared not go outside because I needed to be able to put the chest back in its hiding place very quickly if anybody showed interest in what I was up to.

I took out the two keys and unfastened the padlock. I pushed back the lid, noticing that it had been designed to fold over so that it was level with the top of the chest and form a surface on which to work. It was a beautiful piece of craftsmanship.

I took out every document, unfastening the ties holding them in their rolls. I went through each one. As before, when I handled the one that bore the King's seal, I felt that quivering sense of power coming from it into my hands. The dense script was in an elegant hand, and I admired its beauty even though I did not understand the content: it was in Latin. The few words I did manage to make out suggested it was some sort of agreement between the King and Rollo.

I did not need to know more and the document was making me feel sad. I let it spring back into its roll, fastened it and put it aside.

The remainder of the documents told a strange tale. Many were in a hand which I assumed was Rollo's, and indeed the quick impatience behind those neatly written words put him vividly into my mind. Some of the documents were lists of names and places. On some were written one or more of the names, and beside each name there was a carefully drawn box outlining what seemed to be a collection of facts. One of the documents – a very long one – seemed to consist of Rollo's own interpretation of the King's actions, and there was much reference to his brothers Robert, Duke of Normandy, and Henry, known, as I now learned, as Beauclerc. Rollo's notes said this Henry had landed in a part of Normandy called Cotentin, wherever that was, and in Rollo's view he was more likely to ally himself with William than with Robert.

None of this was of much interest to me, although I made myself concentrate as I looked at each document.

Then I came to one that did spark my attention: it was Rollo's assessment of the strengths and weaknesses of the men and women who formed his network in the east of England, and there were several pages devoted to Eleanor de Lacey.

Most of what he had written was about past events, and in the main consisted of very detailed descriptions of who knew what and how the knowledge had reached Mistress de Lacey. She had been, it appeared, part of the web of information in the area – there was even a diagram that indicated this, with a beautifully drawn crown that presumably indicated the King – and it appeared that she might have been more important to Rollo than I had imagined, for her initials were in the middle of that particular web, which was positioned at the end of a line that angled away from the crown and up to the right. I wondered if the right side of the crown was significant in that it indicated Mistress de Lacey's location, in the east of the land . . .

Thoughtfully I put the documents back in the chest, closed it and fastened the padlock. I replaced it in its hiding place and carefully covered it over, patting and smoothing the earth. I did not think anyone who did not know it was there would find it.

When I had finished, I sat for some time before the hearth, imagining Morgan and Cat beside me and a bright fire burning.

I was thinking about Mistress de Lacey; specifically I was wondering, now that Rollo was dead, if she was still the centre of the region's web; the hub of the wheel.

I waited until it was a reasonable hour to go visiting. Then I stood up, brushed myself down and tidied myself as best I could, re-braiding my hair and replacing my white cap. I picked up my pack and slung my satchel over my shoulder, then set out for the river and Mistress de Lacey's house.

The streets of the town were already busy. I covered my white cap with my shawl, drawing it forward to conceal my face. I let my shoulders slump and my spine curve, and, shuffling my feet, adopted the gait of a much older woman. It is often said that women over the age of breeding become invisible, and I was well aware that nobody was even sparing me a glance.

Which was precisely what I wanted.

The crowds thinned out as I emerged on the far side of the town and headed for the river. Two men and a lad were loading a small boat downriver from Mistress de Lacey's house, but they were too busy arguing over the best way to arrange their cargo to notice me.

I went on.

Mistress de Lacey's house looked just as I had left it last night, but even as I approached the door I knew it wasn't the same. Something had happened: something profound, that had altered the timbre of the air.

I knocked softly but there was no reply; no hurrying feet sounding on the floor. I pushed, and silently the door opened.

As soon as I was inside, I smelt it.

Automatically I closed and bolted the door.

As I did so I had a clear memory of Mistress de Lacey shooting the bolts after I'd left her. I looked at the metal hoops that engaged the ends of the bolts, but they were undamaged: this door had not been forced.

Which meant that she had opened it to whoever had come visiting.

In an instant of horror, I wondered if she'd thought it was me at the door; that I'd changed my mind and wanted to take up her offer of a bed after all . . .

I arrested that thought, for it would do no good. I knew, besides, that I was only postponing the moment.

I forced myself to walk on into the room that overlooked the river.

It had been such a delightful room, filled but not overfilled with carefully chosen pieces. Chairs, a bench, small tables. Lamps. Some precious glassware. A very pretty little sewing box. A tapestry frame, the work half-completed and depicting a jolly hunting scene with trees, flowers and a lively looking deer making its escape by leaping over a stream.

It was not a delightful room any more.

Almost everything was broken. The fine wood chairs and tables were firewood now. The glass lay in shattered pieces on the floor. The tapestry had been ripped across and the sewing box upturned, its contents scattered, its skeins of vivid wools slowly turning the same colour as they absorbed the blood.

There was such a lot of blood.

Mistress de Lacey lay sprawled in front of the window seat. Her pristine white cap was now almost all red, and there was a deep dent in it where the back of her head had been staved in. That was probably the killing blow, I thought.

My professional self seemed to have taken control, which was just as well as the rest of me wanted to scream aloud with horror, pity and grief.

I knelt down beside her, careful not to let my skirts touch the pool of congealing blood. With gentle hands I turned her head and it was as I thought: someone had beaten her before she died.

There were also marks of violence on her hands.

I stood up, my knees shaking.

Slowly I looked all round the room, making myself pay attention, inspecting every detail. It was as I had thought.

So much had been broken, and it seemed to me that someone had been at pains to make it look as though a robber had broken in and been disturbed by Mistress de Lacey, going for her savagely in his panic.

But quite a lot was wrong with that. For one thing, there were items that a robber would surely have taken, even if he was panicking, such as Mistress de Lacey's rings and the long rope of fine pearls, as well as some costly pieces of silver arrayed on a sideboard.

For another, someone had tortured her before they killed her. The usual reason pain is inflicted in such circumstances is to make someone reveal some secret they are trying to withhold.

I had a very good idea what Mistress de Lacey had wanted to keep secret. She had had some hiding place for Rollo's chest, and it did not seem unreasonable to think she had other such items in her possession. And as well as the gold and the coins, assuming I was right and she had indeed been an important figure in the King's network of spies and agents, what other confidential documents did she keep in her care besides Rollo's?

With a soft cry of dismay I realized that poor Mistress de Lacey could not have given up Rollo's secrets even if she'd wanted to, for they were in the chest and last night she had given it to me. She'd had no idea where I was going: all I'd said was *I do have a place*, giving no clue as to where it was.

I was bitterly ashamed of the quick self-serving thought that said *what a good thing you didn't tell her*. Kneeling down again, I put my hand on hers – her flesh was stiff and cold – and whispered, 'I am so sorry, Mistress de Lacey.'

Then I stood up again and backed out of the room.

I could not leave Eleanor de Lacey lying there, perhaps not to be found for hours or days. She lived alone, and the thought of her cooling body gradually succumbing to the processes of decay was simply intolerable. But if I summoned a lawman, which was both my civic and my moral duty, I would very soon be face to face with Jack and I knew I could not bear that.

I arranged my shawl over my head, covering every part of my hair and the white cap. I stood in Mistress de Lacey's cool hall for some moments, thinking myself once again into the appearance and the character of a woman many years older than myself. I felt my body curve into the semblance of age. I even experienced a stab of pain from an aching back.

Then I went outside and carefully closed the door. I made my stumbling way across the fields, grateful there were not many people about. The only person anywhere near was a monk hurrying alone with bent head, lips moving in prayer. The way he strode along was familiar, and I recognized him as the man I'd seen on my first visit.

It was a different matter once I was in the town, where the day's business was already in full swing. Forcing myself not to arouse suspicion by hesitating, I plunged straight into the busy crowds of the market square. As I had hoped, a pair of Jack's lawmen stood at one corner, their posture relaxed but their eyes alert, ready for any sign of trouble but not necessarily expecting any. Unfortunately for them, I was about to change that.

I let myself feel the full distress of what I had so recently discovered. My shock and my tears were not faked; I had controlled my reaction all the time control had been necessary but now I could give vent to my feelings.

The two lawmen turned at my staggering approach. One was young, the other older, and both were well armed and fit-looking. I did not recognize either of them. The young one's expression turned from mildly amused tolerance at a fussy, flustered old woman to concern.

'What's wrong, gammer?' he asked, putting a hand out to take my arm.

I shrugged him off for I did not want to risk being detained. 'Mistress de Lacey's house!' I said in a cracked whisper, my lips drawn in over my teeth to hide them, my eyes round with horror. 'A body, lying by the hearth!'

The young lawman shot a quick look at his companion, then turned back to me. 'You sure now?' he said. 'Not seeing things, are you?' His mouth began to quirk into a smile, but something in my face must have concerned him.

The older man came to stand on my other side. I was instantly uneasy, for they were blocking me in against the wall. 'A body? What, dead?' this second man asked.

'There is so much blood!' I whispered. 'I saw—'

But as the images of what had been done to Mistress de Lacey flashed across my vision, suddenly I felt dizzy and weak, and I thought I might be about to be sick. I took hold of the two lawmen by the shoulder and, my urgency giving me strength, turned them round so that they were facing away from me, back across the square the way I had come. 'Down by the river!' I hissed. 'The house at the end, with the window that overlooks the water!'

The older man was nodding. 'I know it,' he said. Looking at his young companion, he said, 'We should go and see, because the chief will be furious if something's really happened and we didn't bother to check.' Then he turned and I made out the words, 'You'll come with us, gammer, and—'

But he was addressing empty air.

I was already halfway across the square, deep in the crowds, my shawl bundled up under my arm, back straight, head up, walking swiftly like the young woman I was.

I risked a quick glance back over my shoulder. Both of the lawmen looked slightly shocked, as if old women vanishing from beneath their very eyes was both alarming and frightening. But they were well trained, and after pausing only briefly to run their eyes across the busy market, they turned and ran off.

I slipped away and into the maze of alleys.

After quite a lot of doubling back and checking behind me – nobody was following me – finally I made my way back to Morgan's house.

I didn't really have anywhere else to go.

Jack Chevestrier stood looking down at the body lying beneath the window. He had commanded the young lawman to wait outside. 'Did you go into the room?' he had demanded as he and the youth had hurried out from the castle.

And the young man – his name was Cal, he was one of Jack's newer recruits and had already demonstrated that he had wits and kept his head when matters turned nasty – had said with faint indignation, 'Course not, chief.'

Jack trained his men well.

'I could see that she was dead,' Cal had continued. 'She—'

But Jack had stopped him. 'Thanks, Cal, I'll look for myself.'

Cal had nodded. Another lesson learned, Jack had thought.

Now he bent down and put his hand to the exposed nape of the dead woman's neck. As he had expected, she was cold. It appeared she had been slain during the night.

He removed the blood-soaked cap. He had to pull it quite hard to unstick it from the congealing blood. The back of the head had been crushed: there was a depression almost the size of his fist. The blow would have felled an ox. He turned the head to the side to study the face. The nose was broken and had bled profusely. There were huge bruises on the left cheek and the left side of the jaw, and the lips had been driven against the teeth. One of the front teeth was broken.

She had been beaten hard before she died.

He knew that because of the blood and the bruises. He had been told that once the heart ceased to beat, the blood was no longer driven to flow round the body. He did not understand this – it made no sense – but the person who had told him was wise in the ways of the human body and to be trusted.

For a moment he almost thought she was there kneeling beside him, so vivid was she in his memory.

He pushed the thought of her to the back of his mind. It seemed to have taken up residence there.

'Her name is Mistress de Lacey?' he called out to Cal. 'You can come in now,' he added.

Cal came into the room, his face expressing his reluctance. He stared at the body and the wide-spreading blood, paled, then stood up straight and said with only a faint tremor, 'That's what the old gammer told us.'

'Tell me again exactly what she said.'

'"Mistress de Lacey's house, a body, lying by the hearth." Then she said there was so much blood and that the house was down by the river with a window overlooking the water.'

'But then she vanished?'

Cal looked embarrassed. 'Well, I know I *said* she vanished, chief, but I know she didn't, not really, because people don't.' He frowned hard. 'I reckon Penn and I were preoccupied with deciding what to do and she just slipped away.' He lowered his eyes. 'Sorry.'

'There were two of you,' Jack pointed out mildly. 'Another time, try to keep your eyes on your witness and don't let them go till you tell them they can.'

'*Witness?* You're saying you think she saw—'

'I'm not saying anything, Cal. She found the body. She may have been the first person to see it since the killer left it. She may have seen the killer. She may even *be* the killer, although from your description I doubt it.'

'Why?' Cal asked.

One of the things Jack liked about him was his curiosity. He never minded asking a question, and when it transpired that the answer was so obvious he should have worked it out for himself, always joined in the laughter.

'Kneel down – not on the blood, over there – and I'll explain,' Jack replied. 'Look.' Silently he pointed out the blow to the back of the head, the broken nose, the split lip, the extensive bruising. 'Those injuries required force, and you said your old woman was bent and trembly.'

'I did, that's right,' Cal said softly. He was looking intently at the injuries, and already his revulsion was being replaced by an inquiring, interested intelligence.

'She was beaten before she was slain,' Jack said.

Cal thought for a moment. 'It's a nice house,' he said. 'She had some pretty things. D'you reckon someone wanted her to say where she hid her money bags?'

'It's quite possible,' Jack agreed. 'What do you think we ought to do next?'

'Have a look round and see if anything's been taken.' But almost immediately Cal saw his error. 'No, not that, because if it's missing we won't know if it was there in the first place.' He thought for a moment, then his expression brightened. 'We could check to see if anything that could have been stolen wasn't!'

'Good. Off you go, then.'

Cal looked slightly frightened, then very eager. 'Me?'

Jack made a show of looking all round the room. 'I don't see anyone else.'

As Cal's footsteps rang out on the stone flags, Jack got up and lowered himself down onto the window seat. Noticing a shawl folded up beside him, he spread it out and placed it over the corpse. Soon he would send Cal back to the castle to fetch men and a trestle, and they would take the victim away to prepare her for burial.

Mistress de Lacey, Jack thought.

What do I know about her?

For some moments nothing came to mind. Then, like a very faint whisper, he recalled someone murmuring the name.

And, although Cal had not mentioned it, he knew her first name had been Eleanor.

He closed his eyes, not consciously trying to remember, simply letting the name echo in his head and waiting to see if anything else followed. Where had he been when he heard it mentioned? Had the voice been a man's or a woman's?

But nothing emerged.

Presently Cal returned to report that he'd found a very well-concealed hiding place behind a piece of panelling in the scullery, that it looked as if it had been opened recently because there was a fresh scratch across the flags where a piece of grit had caught underneath the panel as it had been dragged aside, but that the aperture behind it was empty.

'But something had stood on the floor until recently,' he added.

'Explain,' Jack said.

'The floor was dusty except for a space about this big.' He gestured with his hands.

'Something has been removed from its hiding place,' Jack said.

'That's what I thought, chief.' Cal frowned. 'D'you think the killer took it?'

'I have no idea,' Jack replied.

Cal's frown deepened. 'Perhaps the killer knew this box, or whatever it was, was somewhere in the house and that's why he . . .'

He didn't go on. But then, Jack thought, he didn't need to.

It was evening. The body had been taken away, the house thoroughly searched, Big Gerald and Young Henry had been detailed to clean up the room, and Jack was doing a last check before locking the house.

He had asked his men if they knew anything about Mistress de Lacey, and nobody had anything to tell him. He had called upon her nearest neighbours in the grand merchants' houses some way along the river, but nobody admitted to knowing anything and it seemed she had lived a quiet life of utter respectability. The men and women he spoke to all said much the same: she was courteous, she'd help you out if you asked

her, she'd nod a good day and a how d'you do if she passed
you on the way to market or you stood near her in church,
but that was all.

For the time being, the reason why this elegant, comfortably
well-off and reserved woman should have been beaten and
killed remained a complete mystery.

Jack locked up and put the key in the purse at his belt.

He headed off across the fields towards the town, for he
had a destination in mind. Something was nagging at the edge
of his mind . . . there was something he'd said he would do.
He thought back through the long day and it came to him:
this morning Leveva had told him the wooden frame of Aedne's
little cot needed a repair and, in a hurry, he'd said he'd see to
it when he came home.

He paused for a moment. Should he carry on into town or
fork left and go back to the village?

He went on.

Leveva was more than capable of picking up a hammer and
banging in a couple of nails, he reflected. It wasn't how he
would fix the cot, but it would suffice.

He made himself turn his thoughts away from Leveva. There
were matters on which he needed to put her right, but for now
he had other things on his mind.

'Come in,' Gurdyman said, standing back and holding the
door open.

'Am I disturbing you?' Jack asked.

'Not in the least. I was sitting out in the courtyard enjoying
a mug of ale in the beautiful evening light, and I would
welcome your company.'

Gurdyman kept a permanent supply of very good ale. Going
ahead of him, Jack went along the dark passage and out into
the little courtyard, open to the sky. He sank down onto a
bench and, as Gurdyman handed him a pewter mug, drank
a third of it.

'You needed that,' Gurdyman observed, smiling.

'I did.'

Gurdyman sat down in his big chair, drawing a rug over
his knees. 'Anything I can help with?' he enquired.

'No. Yes,' Jack muttered.

Gurdyman waited.

'I've just been dealing with a body.' Briefly Jack gave the details. 'It seems to me that I have heard her name before, but I cannot think where or how.'

There was rather a long silence.

Then Gurdyman said softly, 'Eleanor de Lacey had dealings with Rollo Guiscard.'

The name cut through Jack as if he'd been stabbed.

'*Rollo*,' he breathed.

'I am sorry that the mention of his name causes you pain,' Gurdyman began, 'but—'

'It doesn't,' Jack said roughly.

Gurdyman made no comment to the denial, merely raising his eyebrows. 'As you may be aware,' he went on, 'Rollo had a network of local agents who, or so I construe, kept their eyes out for anything that might be of interest to him. I believe he kept a supply of money with them, so that when he was in need, wherever in the country he happened to find himself, there would be someone fairly close at hand to supply the funds with which to acquire what he wanted.'

'And Mistress de Lacey was one such person?'

Gurdyman nodded.

'How do you know?' Jack exclaimed. *How did you know when I didn't*, was what he wanted to say, for he had a fair idea of who it was who had provided the information, either wittingly or, because this was Gurdyman, more likely unwittingly.

But Gurdyman just shrugged.

Impatiently Jack said, 'One of my men found a hiding place at the house. Until recently an object like a box or a chest had stood on the floor but it's gone.'

'Taken by the killer?' Gurdyman asked, then, before Jack could answer, he added softly, 'But how could you know?'

'I don't know, but I assume so. It was a clever hiding place, and Cal wouldn't have spotted it but for the mark on the floor where the panelling had been dragged aside.'

'So possibly Mistress de Lacey was forced by her visitor to give up the secret of the contents . . .' Gurdyman frowned thoughtfully. 'There is, of course, another possibility.' He looked up expectantly.

Jack put up his hands in surrender. 'I don't possess your sort of mind, Gurdyman, and I'm tired. It's been a very long day and I ought to be back in the village mending a cot, so why not just tell me what this other possibility is?'

Gurdyman smiled apologetically. 'I am sorry, Jack. But I do not wish to discuss this now, for the idea is newly formed and I need to think about it.'

'Is it going to help me resolve this business?' Jack demanded bluntly. 'Because if so, then you—'

'I too am tired,' Gurdyman interrupted. 'As yet the idea is, as I just said, vague and unformed. We shall speak of it again tomorrow.'

Jack drained his ale and put the mug down on Gurdyman's little table. 'Thank you,' he said. He reached down and briefly put a hand on Gurdyman's shoulder.

Then he strode off down the passage and let himself out into the alley.

I settled down for a second night in Morgan's house. As always seems to be the way when you have been travelling for a long time, anywhere you stay more than a night very quickly begins to feel like home, and thus it was with the old place. I had spent the remainder of the afternoon on more tidying and cleaning, and I'd discovered a tightly rolled straw-filled mattress out in the storeroom. I had been hit with a wave of musty air as I unfastened the ties, but a day spread out in the sunshine had done much to improve the smell. I'd managed to raise the door on its hinges enough so that I could shut it and shoot home the rusty bolt. Not that I felt I was in danger of being surprised by an intruder; it just felt reassuring to have a closed door between me and the night.

With my newly replenished purse I had been able to treat myself from the market, and that night I ate well on good fresh bread, a delicious hard cheese studded with raisins and nuts, some slices of ham and some little cakes with blackberry conserve in their soft centres. I had also purchased a thick wool blanket and a little feather pillow, which now lay ready on the mattress. When I lay back on my makeshift bed, sipping at the cold well water in my flask, I felt like a queen.

I was tired, but the images of the day were far too alive in my head for me even to think of trying to sleep. No matter how hard I tried, it was proving impossible to banish the pictures of Mistress de Lacey lying dead on her floor. I wondered what was happening now, whether the body had been removed, whether she was being treated in death with the dignity she had displayed in life.

But I knew I must banish those thoughts too, for they led straight to Jack.

After some time, I sat up and took the shining stone out of its bag.

It was perhaps a reflection of my exhaustion, but for a long time nothing at all happened. I did not mind. I began leaning gently to and fro so that the light altered and caught a variety of flashes of colour in the stone's black depths. It was soothing, and I felt my eyes going in and out of focus.

I was not sure how long I sat like that but it felt like a long time.

And then all at once the stone changed. The solid black broke up and images appeared.

I saw Errita.

It was no surprise, for a part of my mind was permanently thinking about her, seeking after her, wondering where she was, how close she was to me and what she was up to.

Now she emerged out of the shining stone so clearly that she might have been standing in front of me.

We were facing each other and the air bristled and prickled with our animosity. She shouted something but I could not hear. She grabbed me by the upper arms and dragged me towards her, and I cried aloud in fear.

For we were in a high place and peril was like a third person up there with us.

I looked behind her and saw the low-lying land spreading out all around. It was night-time, and the moonlight glistened on a little river. The air was warm.

She was pulling me towards her as she backed away from me, towards the terrible blackness behind her.

Where were we?

We must surely be back in the coastal mountains that ringed the settlement. The high, dark passages that tunnelled through the rock had sometimes emerged suddenly into the open; you would be trudging along, head down, bent with weariness and longing for rest, and all at once feel the night air on your face. Then you must always stop dead, for quite often the path would have a sheer drop on one side. A single unwise step would send you flying through the air to a gruesome death a very long way below.

Errita wanted to kill me, and my deep mind had set that scene in a place known to both of us.

The image was fading now, and I realized I had stopped trembling.

I waited for a time until I was fully back in myself. Then I held the shining stone to my forehead for a moment, melding us together, and put it away.

I lay down under my shawl, closing my eyes and hoping sleep would eventually come.

So Errita wanted to kill me.

Well, I already knew that.

I tried to calm my mind, for I knew I was exhausted and my body desperate for repose. I sensed I was far from my usual self; that the long journey and everything that had happened since I had returned to the land of my birth had set me awry. And then there was the growing threat of Errita . . .

I told myself firmly that tomorrow I would rest. I had battles ahead, and I could not fight them with any hope of victory if I was weak and undermined by my own dread.

Rest.

It was a lovely thought.

Very soon I felt myself slipping into sleep.

SIX

Jack was awake very early and back at the castle as the sun rose.

He nodded to the guards at the first gate, exchanged greetings with the pair manning the outer end of the high, narrow walkway leading to the upper-floor entrance to the castle itself.

The interior was dark, the air chilly, even on a July morning. It was the chill of fear, and it lingered even though Sheriff Picot was dead.

Jack went into the anteroom where the men grabbed food and drink between patrols. A group of half a dozen of them stood round a basket of fresh bread, cramming chunks into their mouths. 'Morning, chief,' a lean man mumbled, grinning and displaying half-chewed food.

'Morning, Ginger,' Jack replied. Turning to a slim man with watchful dark eyes, he said, 'Anything to report, Walter?'

'No, chief. We passed the house by the river several times, and Young Henry here stayed there hidden behind a tree keeping his eyes peeled – or I hope he did,' he added, glancing at a bright-faced man. He was in his twenties now, but they all still called him Young Henry; he'd been a boy when he first worked for Jack.

'I did!' the young man said with a grin. 'Barely blinked the whole time.'

'But you saw nothing?'

'No, chief,' Henry said.

An older man with a sallow face helped himself to more bread, then said, 'Body's been laid out like you said and it's been taken to St Bene't's crypt.'

'Thank you, Luke,' Jack replied.

Luke grimaced. 'Wasn't me did it.'

'Payment as usual for your cousin and her daughter,' Jack said.

Luke nodded and bit into the bread.

Jack went through a doorway into an inner chamber. Once the heavy wooden door with its iron studs had always been closed. But that had been in Picot's day, and now it had been pinned back against the wall. The room had been cleared of the late sheriff's possessions, and the enthusiasm with which Jack's lawmen had broken up the heavy old chair and the table Picot used to thump when he was angry – which was almost all the time – and hurled them on the bonfire had said a great deal about their feelings for their late commander.

Jack mildly regretted their fervour now, for there was nothing in the room but a rickety bench beside the hearth. But the room was useful as a space apart, and he had got into the habit of going into it when he wanted to think. He usually stood by the thin arrow slit that gave a view over the outer gate below, looking over it to the town beyond the Great Bridge. His men appeared to understand that when he was standing there he wanted some peace and quiet.

He stared down at the river. Along the quays, the day's business was just beginning. The town beyond still appeared quiet. His eyes on the distant tower of St Bene't's, Jack thought of the woman whose body now lay in the crypt and wondered yet again what she had known that someone else had wanted her to reveal; wanted it so desperately that they had beaten her brutally to persuade her to talk.

He thought again about her hands. He'd assumed at first that the damage – the bruising, the torn nails, the crooked index and little fingers that told of breaks in the bones – had been part of the persuasion. He now believed these had been defensive injuries, and imagined her on the ground, hands up to shield her face as her attacker raised his weapon to hit her again.

Weapon . . .

What had her killer used to bludgeon her? A stool, a solid iron pan, a cudgel or a heavy piece of wood that he'd brought with him? There would have been a lot of blood; there *was* a lot of blood. He had seen it and smelt it.

A thought occurred to him.

He went back into the antechamber. Most of the men had

gone – Jack had been so deep in thought that he hadn't heard them leave – but Big Gerald and Henry were still there and two newcomers had arrived.

'Any of you know where Cal and Penn are?'

'Penn's gone off duty and Cal's down in the yard,' Young Henry said promptly.

As Jack hurried off, he reflected that he would have put a modest bet on it being bright, ever-observant Henry who came up with the required information.

Cal was fastening a small pack, clearly about to leave.

'A moment, Cal, please,' Jack said. Cal looked up at him, apprehension very evident on his expression. 'It's all right, I'm not here to give you a bollocking.'

Cal blew out his cheeks in relief. 'How can I help you, chief?'

'Tell me everything you can remember about the old gammer.'

Jack didn't think he needed to specify which old gammer, and he was right. With barely a pause, Cal closed his eyes – perhaps the better to picture the scene – and said, 'Me and Penn were on the corner of the market square. This old woman came hobbling up. She was crouched over, she limped as if the way she was walking – hurrying, she was, and all bent over in an arch – was making something hurt. She wore a heavy cloak, and she had a cap and a big shawl arranged over it, both drawn forwards over her face. She didn't have any teeth, and she mumbled a bit when she told us about the body, so it was quite hard to make out what she was saying.' He paused, opening his eyes briefly to look at Jack.

'Good. Go on.'

Cal closed his eyes again. 'She had this big, voluminous cloak, as I just said. I thought she was fat – you know how old women spread a bit – but, come to think of it, she might have been carrying a bag under it.'

'What colour was the cloak?'

'Can't say, chief. It was some dark shade, and well worn. She was weeping!' he exclaimed suddenly. 'I just remembered.'

'Good,' Jack said again. After a moment, when Cal did not go on, he said, 'Did you see her arms and hands?'

Cal closed his eyes again. 'Yes, but only for a moment. She came towards us with her hands spread out, as if she was going to clutch at us, but then . . .' He paused, frowning. Looking at Jack, he said, sounding puzzled, 'Then she put her hands up to her face, like women do when they're distressed. Like I said, she'd been weeping. Then she sort of tucked them inside her shawl, clutching it to her as if she was cold.'

'And did you notice anything about her hands?'

Cal looked anxious. 'Like what?'

'Were they clean or dirty?' Jack paused. 'Was there blood on them?'

Cal's worried expression cleared and he smiled. 'Oh, no, chief. I'm sure I'd have noticed.'

'I'm sure you would too. Thank you, Cal.'

Dismissed, Cal gave him a quick nod and trotted away.

Jack stood still, thinking. He'd wondered if the old gammer had gone right into the room where Mistress de Lacey's body had lain, or whether she'd simply seen the corpse from the doorway or even through a window. If there was no blood on her hands, then it did at least suggest she hadn't touched the body.

The old woman had snagged his interest, although he couldn't have said why. There was surely no imperative reason for him to find her; she'd discovered the body, rushed to report it to someone, found the two lawmen, Cal and Penn, told them what she'd found and then hurried away. There were many reasons for her haste, Jack reflected: she had undoubtedly been shocked and terrified at finding a bloodied dead body, desperate to get herself safe within her own four walls and bar the door. Her distress would be the greater if Mistress de Lacey had been a friend, which was surely likely because people didn't usually call on complete strangers. She might have been reluctant to spend too long talking to a couple of lawmen, if, say, she had relatives or friends involved in dubious activities. If she herself engaged in business best kept from the eyes of the law . . .

Jack shook his head. He resolved to forget about the old

gammer, although even as he did so, he had a feeling it wasn't going to be as easy as that.

He glanced up at the sun. It was still early. He stood frowning in thought, wondering if Gurdyman was ready to discuss his thoughts on the death of Mistress de Lacey and if it was too soon to go and badger him. Sensing someone come to stand beside him, he turned.

'Henry,' he said. He smiled, for not only was the young man a hard-working and intelligent member of the team but in addition almost always cheerful and optimistic. 'What can I do for you?'

'More what I can do for you, chief,' Young Henry said. He was looking at Jack apprehensively.

'Well?' Jack prompted. Then, realizing he'd sounded curt, added, 'It's all right, you're not interrupting some profound and productive train of thought. What is it?'

'I've seen someone near Mistress de Lacey's house,' Henry said. 'Couple of times now. Well, three times, because last night when I was on watch he passed one way and then went back again.'

'And you think he might be our killer?' Jack demanded.

'*No!*' Henry looked horrified. 'Sorry, chief, I should have explained. I know him, see, or at least I know who he is, and it's likely he goes that way frequently. He's a monk, lives in the little community up the river to the south of the town, and he cares for the girls with the babies who stay in that old wreck of a place near Margery's.'

Margery was an enormously fat woman who ran a brothel on the quay. She was shrewd and tough, in character forceful enough to make sure no trouble broke out in her establishment. It was said she took good care of her girls and her women, some of whom had been with her for years, which, Jack always thought, spoke for itself. He knew the place nearby that Henry referred to: it was a disused and dilapidated warehouse that had stood for too long out in the fenland damp without anyone bothering to maintain it, and a year or so back it had become an unofficial refuge for women on their own who had a baby or infant and no one to support them. Sheriff Picot had done everything he could to close the place down, even sending a

band of men to burn it and telling them not to be too fussy
over making sure first that it was empty. The men had been
led by Walter, however, and they burned down the vestiges of
a ruin of a shed that stood nearby instead.

'He cares for them?' Jack said. 'In what way?'

'Takes them food, listens to them, helps them if they're
sick,' Henry replied.

'What's his name?'

'Brother Aleric. He's around your age, maybe a bit older,'
Henry went on, starting to answer Jack's next question before
he'd asked it, 'he's thin – lean-faced, spare and rangy – and
dark, with deep-set eyes. He's a good man, chief,' he added
earnestly.

'So you're not suggesting he's involved in the murder,
merely that he might have seen something that might be
useful?'

'Yes, chief. He passes by Mistress de Lacey's regularly,
like I say, and I thought we could—'

But Jack didn't let him finish. Grabbing his arm, he led the
way across the courtyard.

'Where do you think he'll be now?' he asked as they stepped
out onto the road.

'Monastery, most likely,' Henry said instantly. 'Early
devotions, then whatever it is they do in the morning. Quite
often he doesn't get away to the refuge till around noon.'

They had reached the Great Bridge. To the left was the quay
and Margery's; to the right the river wound away to the south.
'Come on,' Jack said.

Brother Aleric must have finished his devotions and his chores
early that day, for as the low buildings that constituted the
monastery loomed up ahead, Jack and Young Henry saw a
monk walking fast towards them.

'That's him,' Henry said, but Jack had already surmised as
much. He stopped, standing on the narrow path with Henry
just behind him as the monk strode towards them. Brother
Aleric had his head down, and he was frowning slightly. When
Jack said, 'Good day to you, brother,' the start he gave as his
head shot up suggested he had been deep in thought.

'Oh! Good day,' he replied. Looking from Jack to Henry, he smiled. 'Henry. You are well?'

'I am, Brother Aleric, as I trust you—'

Breaking into the courtesies, Jack said, 'Brother, Henry tells me you regularly walk up and down this track as you go between the monastery and the refuge?'

'I do.' Brother Aleric was watching him with interest.

'And you pass Mistress de Lacey's house.'

The monk nodded.

Jack could tell from his expression of polite enquiry that he did not know what had happened. 'I regret to tell you that Mistress de Lacey is dead,' he said.

Dismay flooded Brother Aleric's narrow face. 'But she was by no means old, and I thought—' he began. But then, understanding, he nodded, paling. 'Not a natural death,' he said softly, 'for I know who you are, and I do not think you would be here speaking to me purely because a woman had died through accident or because of some sickness.'

'She was murdered,' Jack said.

Brother Aleric's eyes closed and for some moments his lips moved in silent prayer. Then, looking at Jack, he said, 'I am deeply distressed by this news.'

'You knew her?'

'I would not say that, no. I knew who she was, we nodded a greeting to each other if she saw me go by, and last year she gave me a bundle of blankets for the women in the refuge. Not many of our fine upstanding townsfolk are so generous towards those less fortunate than themselves,' he added, and Jack observed that there was no suggestion of judgement in his expression.

'It appears she was killed some time during the night before last,' Jack said, 'and her body was discovered by an old woman who hurried to the market square and notified the lawmen on duty there.'

Brother Aleric stared at him but did not speak.

'We do not know if the old woman had business with Mistress de Lacey, or whether something alerted her to the fact that not all was as it should be – a door half-open, for example – so that her curiosity led her to go into the house to investigate.'

The monk nodded. 'If she was concerned, she was right to check.'

Jack had the strong sense that Brother Aleric had just uttered a mild reproof, reminding Jack that seeing whether a woman living alone had come to harm should be viewed as an act of charity and not simple nosiness. 'I do not believe this old woman killed her,' he went on bluntly – the gentle criticism had stung – 'but I should very much like to speak to her.'

Brother Aleric spread his hands. 'I cannot help you, for I do not know her.'

'You pass by frequently,' Jack pushed on. 'Have you noticed anyone else in the vicinity of Mistress de Lacey's house?'

The monk stood quite still, eyes glazing slightly, and Jack hoped he was thinking and hadn't returned to his prayers. Eventually he said, 'I saw a man on the path two days ago, or it might have been three. About your age' – he looked at Jack – 'but much slighter in build than you, and dressed in dark garments. It was evening, and he was walking away from the house towards the Great Bridge. Now I cannot say he had been visiting Mistress de Lacey—' He frowned. 'But there was something about him that made me aware of him . . . Yes!' His expression cleared. 'I thought I saw him step out onto the path from the undergrowth beneath the trees by the river,' he went on eagerly, 'and I averted my eyes because I thought he had probably been in there because – er—'

'He'd gone for a piss,' Henry supplied.

'Quite so,' Brother Aleric agreed with a faint smile. 'No reason why he shouldn't, of course.'

'Will you show us the spot?' Jack asked, and Brother Aleric nodded. He led them back along the path until they were some half a dozen paces from the dead woman's house, then pointed towards a group of young alder and hazel trees, around which the greenery grew thickly. The monk stopped and silently indicated.

Jack walked slowly up the path a few paces and back again. He studied the riverbank, and the position of Eleanor de Lacey's house upon it. There was a faint line of trodden grass and bent bracken, and Jack followed it deeper into the undergrowth. It curved to the left round a tree, then to the right, and it opened into a small clearing overshadowed by thick foliage and barely high enough for a man to crouch. He could hear the river close by, running swiftly just beneath the bank.

Jack crossed the four or five paces to the far side, and through a dense clump of bramble, he made out a wall. He pushed on through the tangle of barbed stems, his forearms quickly scratched and bleeding, and pulled apart the leaves.

He was face to face with the side wall of Eleanor de Lacey's house.

He looked down and saw that he was standing on a spot where the grass was flattened and bruised. It was releasing a sweet smell into the warm air. Tree branches had been bent out of the way to roughly head height.

And just over to his right, a little below his eye level, he could see through a narrow window straight into the room overlooking the river in Eleanor de Lacey's house.

The spot which Brother Aleric had just identified was the perfect place for someone to conceal himself if he wanted to keep an eye on the house and its occupant.

Jack backed out through the brambles and the undergrowth and emerged onto the path. He caught Young Henry's eye and nodded.

Brother Aleric, observing the look, said tentatively, 'I believe I have something more to tell you.'

'Yes?' Jack turned to him.

'I – er, I am afraid that I am not as observant as perhaps I should be,' the monk confessed. 'I spend much time apart from my brethren, you see, and while my abbot accepts my absences because he knows where I am, what I am doing and that I am about God's work, nevertheless he does insist that I say the daily offices, even when I am alone and walking to and from the refuge. Hence I am often in communication with the Lord and my eyes are turned inwards to God rather than out towards the world.' He gazed at Jack out of bright and candid blue eyes.

'I understand,' Jack said.

'But now that I have recalled seeing the man emerging from the bushes,' Brother Aleric went on, 'it has reminded me of something.' His face was full of happy expectation, as if he couldn't wait to tell Jack the welcome news. 'That time wasn't—'

'It wasn't the only time you saw him,' Jack said.

'Yes!' Brother Aleric said, and he looked so disappointed at being denied the pleasure of the helpful revelation that Jack wished he'd held his tongue.

Brother Aleric, sensing himself dismissed, hurried on his way to the next of his morning's tasks. Noticing Young Henry watching the departing figure, Jack said, 'You might have another word with him. There must be more he can tell us and I think he's more likely to respond to you than to me.'

Henry turned clear-sighted eyes to him. 'He was doing his best, chief,' he said. 'I'm not sure he likes the law much. He and his brother monks had a very poor opinion of Sheriff Picot.'

'Did anyone have a *good* opinion of him?' Jack muttered.

Henry grinned. 'What do you want to know?'

On the point of telling him, Jack said instead, 'What do you think?'

'Er . . . I imagine you'd like a description of this lurking man, details of when Brother Aleric saw him before, if he noticed him coming or going from here and if so, where he came from. Or went.'

Jack nodded towards Brother Aleric, who was now hurrying as if desperate to make up for lost time. 'Off you go, then. Find out everything you can and, if you manage to uncover any interesting trails, see where they take you.'

Looking as pleased as if he'd just been promised a pint and a good pie supper, Young Henry sprinted off along the path.

Jack set out across the fields in the direction of Gurdyman's house.

'I have nothing certain to tell you, only conjecture,' Gurdyman greeted him as he led the way along the cool passage to the little open courtyard.

'Your conjectures are as good as if not better than most people's firm opinions,' Jack replied.

Gurdyman nodded an acknowledgement. 'Sit,' he said. Pouring ale into a large mug, he handed it to Jack. The ale was cool and welcome.

With a grunt, Gurdyman resumed his own seat. 'I believe that in order to understand why Mistress de Lacey was slain, we must first consider what we know of her.'

'She was a local agent for a man we know to have been a spy for the King.'

'Indeed. We further know that she kept a supply of coin for him; that presumably she also provided local intelligence.'

'She has neither given him access to his own money or passed on any useful information for the last seven years.'

'No, not since Rollo Guiscard was killed,' Gurdyman agreed. 'Can she have known he was dead?'

Jack thought for a moment. 'Not many people knew,' he said. 'You and I did.' He stopped.

'Hrype knew, and I suspect at least one other person in Aelf Fen.' He paused, clearly waiting, and when Jack still did not speak, he said very softly, 'Lassair knew. Rollo died in her arms.'

Abruptly Jack slammed down his mug of ale and leapt up, striding across the courtyard and standing in the doorway.

He sensed Gurdyman's eyes on him. Not wanting his reaction to spark some comment, he said quickly, 'Eleanor de Lacey was obviously a clever woman, or else she wouldn't have been working for Rollo. I imagine she must have realized Rollo wasn't coming back.'

'And what do you think it was she did for him?'

Jack shrugged, fighting to hide the emotion stirred up by Gurdyman's reference to Lassair. Slowly he sat down again and picked up his ale.

But Gurdyman was intent on answering his own question. 'Rollo could not be everywhere at once, and it is logical to assume he used his local people to keep him advised of any information they thought he should be aware of. Which leads to the further assumption that they had some way of contacting him. Not directly,' he went on before Jack could speak, 'but possibly via a chain, or perhaps *network* is a more fitting word.'

'If secrecy was important—' Jack began.

'Of course secrecy was important,' Gurdyman muttered scathingly.

'—then surely these agents wouldn't know about each other.'

'I have known of such a means of transmitting secrets,' Gurdyman said slowly. 'A long time ago, and far to the east. In a network of perhaps a hundred, each man would have a single contact. Thus even were he to be captured and taken for questioning, only one name could be extracted from him. When this next man was questioned in turn, he would only have one more name to reveal. It is a slow means of discovering information and identities, which of course works to the advantage of those guarding the secret.'

'Not the ones who are taken,' Jack said softly.

Gurdyman did not reply.

After a few moments, Jack said, 'So what information do you think Mistress de Lacey was compelled to pass on, if indeed that's what she did and her murder was somehow connected to this secret and its transmission? It can't have been that Rollo was dead, for that surely is old news?'

'I agree. I am at a loss, however, to suggest anything else. So far,' he added, so softly that Jack barely heard.

'And who did she pass it to?' Jack went on. 'Are there other people like her here in the town?'

'I cannot say for sure,' Gurdyman replied. 'Putting myself in Rollo's position, however, I would have preferred, for the sake of maintaining secrecy, to have but one agent in any one town. I further imagine that—'

But suddenly Jack had heard enough of Rollo Guiscard for one morning. Impatiently he drained his mug and stood up. 'I must go,' he said shortly. 'Let me know if you make any progress.'

Gurdyman nodded. 'I will.'

He listened to the echoes of the street door slamming. Jack had shut it rather forcefully.

Reflecting that Jack might have said *when* you make progress rather than *if*, he smiled softly.

This matter would give up its secrets: he was confident of it. He needed time alone, the world shut out, and then he would summon the concentration to slip into the inner places and the answer would be revealed.

For now, something else was filling his mind.

He had the strong sense that Mistress de Lacey had been prompted to act in some way by something that had just happened; perhaps she had been wondering whether to do so but had not yet decided. And then all at once she had made up her mind, set out on her mission and walked, or ridden, off to wherever she needed to go to pass on her message and hadn't noticed she was being followed . . .

But it was all conjecture, just as he had told Jack.

It was this unexpected event that had intruded into Mistress de Lacey's quiet life that was obsessing Gurdyman, and he had the strangest feeling that he knew what it was.

For he too had experienced an intrusion, of a sort.

Three days ago something had happened that he had not experienced for seven years; he had felt an easing of a long-endured pain; he had thought he'd smelt that very familiar mix of lavender, rosemary and pepper.

He closed his eyes.

Just as he had thought then, he said softly to himself, 'She will come when she is ready.'

SEVEN

I woke, heart pounding, from a dream of horror.

It was the forest scene again, and the man with the crossbow bolt in his chest. This time, the blood that burst out of him soared up in a great arc and drummed down onto the ground . . . a pool, a lake, overflowing its banks so that a stream, and very quickly a river, surged over the grass.

And then in the way of dreams all at once the scene had altered. Now the man lay face-down on a rough cart, and even as I watched, it seemed to me that the shining quality he'd had, the luminosity that spoke of some interior light source, was steadily fading. The cart lurched and bumped along over the rough track, making the body bounce up and down. The man had been poorly positioned on the filthy planks so that one shoulder, his neck and head lolled over the side. His hair was dull now with the mud and the dust, his bright clothes bespattered.

And from his chest, where that terrible wound was, the blood that had soaked into his tunic was drip, drip, dripping onto the road as the cart rumbled on its way.

I made myself breathe slowly and deeply. I sat up, turning my face to the east. I stared at the first tiny arc of the sun as it climbed up over the horizon. Still more than half in my dream world, I wondered where the trees had gone, and why there were walls around me, and then I thought, *Of course, I'm not out in the forest, I'm in Morgan's house.*

I tried to put the dream – or the vision, if that was what it was – to the back of my mind. I tried to bury it with thoughts of how I would plan this new day. Normality was out of reach, however, for I had the strongest sense that the world had gone wrong, that some malign intent was pushing back the light, that the wildness of the Lammas force was pulsing unchecked through the land and cowering everything and everyone before it: silent and unseen, its progress could only be detected by the devastation it caused . . . And in this new abnormality the images in my awful dream had too much power and they were too strong; and now, as well as seeing that dripping blood, I could hear its steady beat.

And it sounded as if it was coming nearer.

I felt like screaming.

But then I thought I saw a figure in a robe straighten up and stand before me, between me and that ominously approaching sound, and I felt Morgan's presence right there in front of me and I thought I could actually see the light from the raised outstretched hands push back the dark cloud that had begun to flow inside the dwelling.

And then it was gone.

I lay back in my bedding, relief flooding through me. I whispered, 'Thank you,' and I thought a quiet voice said in my head, *You are welcome. Now, make a little fire – it is early yet, nobody will see – and prepare a hot drink and nourishing food.*

I wondered if it was Morgan's voice. It was precisely the advice I would have suggested for someone who had just suffered a severe shock, so perhaps it was just some aspect of me.

It was still very early, even after I had eaten and drunk, made quite sure my fire was out, tidied my bed away and straightened the room. I went to fetch water from the sacred well and, after apologizing to the resident spirits for such a mundane use of their gift, I stripped and had a wash. Cleanliness had become such an ingrained habit in the south, particularly in the City of Pearl, that now I resented the days when I was not able to wash before I set about my work.

When I was done, I stood for some time in the doorway, looking out first towards the river to my right and then ahead to the town. Smoke was spiralling up into the pale sky from some of the houses as the early risers set about preparing food and drink. The streets, however, would still be all but deserted: the time was right for what I was proposing to do. What I must do, and today, for I had frittered away much of the previous day on small domestic tasks – going through the supply of remedies I always carry in my satchel, mending my worn garments, washing my spare linen – for I had been keenly aware that I needed the quiet hours to restore me after my long journey and the shock of finding Mistress de Lacey's body. With all my housekeeping tasks complete, I had chosen a corner of Morgan's old workroom and, sitting cross-legged on the floor, stayed there quietly for a very long time with the shining stone in my lap, not trying to read it, not even looking closely into it, simply feeling its presence as if it was an old friend. It had been surprisingly comforting; as indeed, I realized as now I stood in the very early morning looking out at the new day, the entire day had been. But that was yesterday and this was today, and I knew I could stand apart no longer.

I went back inside the house, picked up my satchel and slung it over my shoulder and, gathering my courage, set out. I was fighting myself, for I wanted to stay just where I was, in the safety of Morgan's house. But another, stronger emotion drove me on: guilt.

It had taken me a long time to fall asleep the previous night, and I'd known it wasn't because of my restful day. I had been thinking of Mistress de Lacey; how I had liked her at our first meeting and quickly come to understand that she and I were going to be friends. How I'd sensed that somehow we were already close because of Rollo. He had been her friend and he had trusted her; he had once been my lover and I had grieved for him. He had entrusted his chest of secrets, gold and coins to her until I turned up to collect it.

I had tried to keep at bay the unwelcome and deeply distressing thought that her death was connected to Rollo's chest, but I no longer could. Had someone perhaps known of her connection to him? Known that she kept money for him; known, or guessed, that she and the other men and women like her might very well know rather more about the profound and secret matters of the land than was usual in decent law-abiding citizens? I wanted to convince myself that I was wrong, that I was seeing conspiracy and a trail of dark dealings where none existed, but I could not.

And what was haunting me as powerfully as that awful dream was the possibility that Eleanor de Lacey's murderer had come for the chest. Had demanded to know, with increasingly brutal insistence, where she had hidden it. Had perhaps found the secret place, wherever it was, only to discover it was empty. And then he – of course it was a man – wanted to know where it was now.

But Mistress de Lacey could not have told him even if she'd wanted to, because she didn't know.

The track and the riverbank beside Mistress de Lacey's house were deserted, and I had seen barely a handful of people as I skirted the town, and only in the distance. I slipped into a gap between two hazel bushes and, screened by the foliage, waited and watched.

Presently I saw a figure emerge from the undergrowth on the far side of the house, stepping down onto the track as it curved away towards the Great Bridge. A man, slim, only just filling out from his skinny boyhood: it was Jack's Young Henry. He approached the house, walked slowly up and down a few times, tried the door, presumably to see if it was locked – it was – and then simply stood there staring at it.

I wondered if he too felt guilty that a dignified old woman who lived a self-contained life and was no trouble to anyone should have suffered such a death. Did he have reason to? Did he—

But that speculation was interrupted because just then a hurrying figure came along the path from the left, head down as his long strides ate up the ground. Nearing Mistress de Lacey's house, he slowed, as if the house itself was exerting a force on him. Making sure I was well hidden, for he was only a handful of paces away, I studied him closely. He was a monk, a young man still in his prime, lean to the point of thinness but healthy-looking; the cropped hair around the bald crown was dark, as were his deep eyes under the frowning brow. There was an intensity about him – his wiry body and his quick, economical movements spoke of someone driven to get on with the task and not waste God's precious time – but I also sensed a wellspring of kindness and solicitude.

All at once his intent expression lightened, and he said, 'Good morning to you, Henry! You are abroad early?'

Henry spun round, jerked out of his reverie. 'I might say the same of you, Brother Aleric,' he replied.

'The hour is not early for a monk,' Brother Aleric said. 'I am very glad to find you here,' he went on, leaning closer to Henry and lowering his voice, 'since it saves me having to seek you out.'

Young Henry's head went up like a hound scenting the trail. 'You have thought of something else?' he demanded.

'I have. Not about the man I saw lurking here, but trying to dredge up everything I could bring to mind about him reminded me of something else. Some*one* else, I should say.'

'Another man watching Mistress de Lacey?' Young Henry grabbed the monk's arm.

Gently Brother Aleric removed it. 'No need to restrain me,' he said mildly, 'I shan't run away. I'm trying to help.'

'Sorry.' Young Henry blushed.

'There *was* someone else, and I only saw him the once. But this was not recently – perhaps a month ago, maybe a little less. When the days have a set pattern, as do those of my brethren and myself, they do rather tend to run into each other,' he added apologetically.

'Go on,' Henry said. 'What did this man look like?'

'He was old – considerably older than the lurking man – and somewhat bent and weary-looking. He had ragged grey hair, and his skin was yellowish. He was dressed well enough in clothes that had probably cost a fair sum many years ago, although they had been *very* well-used and were worn and patched.'

'You're very observant,' Henry remarked.

Brother Aleric gave a modest shrug. 'No more than anyone else,' he said. 'I'd had the chance to study the man, you see – he'd been walking along ahead of me for perhaps a quarter of a mile, having joined the riverside path by crossing over the fields from the road that leads south to Trumpington.'

'What did you—' Henry began, but the monk spoke over the interruption.

'I noticed him, you see, because he paused only briefly to knock and then went inside straight away, not waiting for Mistress de Lacey to admit him. I thought it was odd – furtive, perhaps – especially given the hour. I remember thinking it

was too early to go calling, and I wondered if I should make
sure Mistress de Lacey was all right, but then I heard voices,
hers and, I presumed, his, and she did not sound distressed or
frightened. So I hurried on my way.' He glanced at the sun,
steadily rising over in the east, and added in a rush, 'As indeed
I must now, for already I have delayed too long.' Breaking
into a run, he called back, 'Good day to you, Henry!'

Henry raised a hand in response.

For some moments he stood perfectly still. I was too close
to risk moving, for he would have heard. I had cramp in my
right leg, and the urge to relieve it was growing unbearable.
I focused my attention on Henry, hoping it would take my
mind off the pain.

It was clear he was thinking hard. I wondered if he was
trying to remember something. Perhaps the description of the
old man had set off a memory? His jaw was set and he looked
grim, but there was the light of excitement in his eyes, and
even as I watched, he nodded as if having just come to a
decision, then, turning his back on the town and the Great
Bridge, he strode off down the path.

It didn't need any particular degree of perception to deduce
that he had a lead to follow and had just made the first move.

I was tempted to follow him, but a stronger instinct was
telling me otherwise. Not stopping to reason it out, I made
sure my hood was drawn forward so that my face was
in shadow, then stepped out onto the track and, gathering up
my skirts, ran after the monk.

I caught up with him as he approached the bridge.

'Good day, brother,' I said.

The start of surprise told me he had indeed been as deep
within his own thoughts as I'd imagined.

'Oh! Good day to you, madam,' he replied politely. 'May
I help you?'

The monk and the healer's first instinct, I reflected.

'I heard about poor Mistress de Lacey,' I said, 'but there is
little news other than the fact that she is dead. I was acquainted
with her' – this was true enough, but I still felt that I was
misleading him – 'and I wondered if you pass this way often
and if you can tell me any more about—'

It was all the invitation he needed. 'I do indeed pass by the house very often, twice a day at the least, in fact, and the man who acts as our sheriff nowadays asked me precisely the same question!' His face was alight with excitement, as if being questioned by a man of the law was a thrill in his quiet life. Then, his expression straightening, he added, 'Not that I was able to be as helpful as I should have liked, for this is a terrible business . . .' He stopped. 'Will you walk with me?' he asked. 'I am in somewhat of a hurry, for there is a sick young woman I am trying to help, and—'

'In what way sick?' I interrupted, falling into step beside him.

'She is very young and she has recently given birth,' he replied gravely. 'She is unwed, barely more than a child herself, and I fear very much that conception was the result of brutality.' It was, I reflected, a discreet yet powerful way to describe rape. 'She has—' But then, perhaps belatedly realizing such a frank conversation with a stranger was unwise, he stopped.

'I am a healer,' I said. 'Please do not think I am suggesting you are not competent to treat this young woman, but if I can help in any way, I am happy to do so.'

He stopped, looking at me with a slight frown. 'You are versed in the practices pertaining to the care of women and their babies?' he asked, and I could see the hope in his eyes.

'I am,' I said.

Now, for the first time, he smiled: a wide beam of a smile that changed his face and spoke of a vast relief. I sensed that he had been struggling for some time to try to offer advice and treatment in a case that was beyond his skills, and that to have someone come running up behind him and offer to help without being asked might even be an answer to a prayer.

Before I could allow the self-congratulation to take hold more than it had done already, I said, 'Lead the way, and as we walk, tell me a little about her. Is she—'

But he held up a hand. 'I am sorry to interrupt, but you should know that she is not my only patient. There is a place – a refuge – down on the quay where young and desperate women know that they can go, where there is at least the hope of a meal and where, most importantly, they can lie down to sleep at night behind a locked door. Many have babies and children, and the world is a cruel place.'

'Is this refuge run by your order?' I asked. I had never heard of it; it must have been established during the years I had been away.

He shook his head. 'No, although we support it. We take food when we have it to spare, and some of the more charitably minded townspeople give us cast-off clothing, blankets and the like for us to pass on to the women. I am permitted to visit regularly and administer remedies.' He shot me a hopeful glance. 'Can *you* prepare remedies?'

Suppressing a smile, I said, 'Oh, yes.'

He nodded. 'I am Brother Aleric,' he said.

'I am Lassair,' I replied.

I had been about to give a false name, but all at once it seemed important to be known as the person I truly was.

We strode on; Brother Aleric, I noted, moved as swiftly and easily as his athletic appearance had suggested. The upper part of my mind was engaged in discussing the relative merits of some of the most popular remedies with my new companion, but underneath I was once more feeling guilty, although now the emotion came from a different source.

The monk hurrying along beside me was radiating joy at having found someone to help him; to provide the skills he lacked and so badly needed. He was filled with gratitude and benevolence towards me; he had already said I must have been sent from God, and I'd been hard put to stop his effusive thanks.

He believed I was going to the refuge with him purely to help, but it wasn't true. I had a secondary motive, which in fact was as compelling as my healer's wish to treat and support those in need.

I had made myself a safe place to hide out at Morgan's house, and for the time being it was serving me well. But I had already been anxiously asking myself what I was going to do if and when – and surely it was when – I was discovered. Where else could I go?

If I was the answer to the monk's prayer, then he was also the answer to mine. The refuge on the quayside would provide me with a second place to live unobserved, and I wasn't going to hesitate in accepting the gift.

Amid my other, more pressing concerns, I had become increasingly disturbed by the sense that Errita was near. There was nothing definite: I hadn't seen her, and as yet the threat of her was still fairly weak.

But it was getting discernibly stronger.

For the whole of that long morning, I barcly gave a thought to my many anxieties. Brother Aleric stayed long enough to introduce me to the large, tough-looking, tawny-haired woman who was in charge – her name was Fritha, and she greeted me with such a penetrating look that it was as good as a challenge – and then to take me to where his young mother lay with her new-born daughter, after which I assumed he concluded his business and returned to his monastery.

I was too absorbed to notice.

My new patient was indeed barely more than a child, just as Brother Aleric had said. She had a girl's body still, and I was surprised that she had been sufficiently mature to have conceived. The birth must have been arduous, and there was damage that clearly still caused much pain. She was also very worried because she didn't think the infant was feeding properly but did not know what she should do. As I began to treat her and to instruct her, I sensed her fear-born resistance slowly melt away, to be replaced – or so I fervently hoped – by trust.

She told me her name was Mattie.

When I had finished with her, we both turned our attention to her baby, who was crying strongly now because my ministrations to her mother had delayed her feed. I taught Mattie just as I'd taught so many new mothers, and after a while the baby girl was suckling strongly and Mattie was beaming.

I caught a movement out of the corner of my eye and looked up to see Fritha standing beside the door.

'You're good,' she said curtly.

I didn't reply.

'Child all right?' she asked.

'From the power she's putting into her yelling,' I muttered, 'I'd say she's fine.'

Fritha came to crouch beside me. Together we watched as
Mattie put her baby to the other breast and, thankfully, the
temporary piercingly shrill yell of protest quickly stopped.

'Want to treat a few more?' Fritha spoke laconically, as if
my reply was a matter of indifference.

'May as well,' I said, in much the same tone.

I might have been wrong, but I thought I heard her laugh
softly.

The refuge might have been housed in a dilapidated, over-
crowded hovel of a place that wasn't too clean and undoubtedly
had an infestation of rodents, but as soon as I began to meet
its inhabitants I knew it was a good place.

It looked as if it had once been a warehouse, and there were
big double doors on the side facing the river where cargo
would have been loaded and unloaded. They were very firmly
closed, with a bar slotted into iron hoops to ensure they stayed
that way, and the only entrance was through a narrow door at
the far end of the long building. There was a little recess just
inside the door which appeared to be Fritha's special place.
A ragged curtain could be drawn across the entrance, and the
space contained a palliasse with folded blankets and a pillow,
as well as a wooden stool. From my brief acquaintance with
Fritha, I guessed she guarded the door, and the women and
children within her domain, with the ferocity of a lioness.

The remainder of the structure consisted of a long central
passage with flimsy plank walls along each side. The left-hand
area was further divided by shoulder-high partitions into a
series of small rooms; on the right there was what seemed to
be a communal dormitory that ran the length of the building.

There were perhaps eighteen or twenty women living there,
their ages ranging from fourteen or fifteen up to around sixty.
Many had babies and infants with them; one woman had five
children under six, and she was pregnant with a seventh.
'Widowed,' Fritha said succinctly when she saw me looking
at the woman, adding with a harsh grin, 'At least there won't
be an eighth.'

I tended another four patients that morning: a woman with
a fever and a pounding headache, a young boy with a badly

sprained ankle, a child of five with a harsh cough and a baby with croup. These were all ailments for which there were ready cures, and I carried the ingredients I required in my satchel. While I was gladdened because I'd been able to help, part of me was deeply sad that these women and children had been suffering so much when it was so easy to ease their symptoms. *Easy if you have a coin or two to purchase the remedy and the knowledge of how to apply it*, I heard a voice say in my head. It was that of Fahim, the doctor who had taught me so diligently in the City of Pearl. *I already have the remedies*, I replied silently to him, *and thanks to my aunt Edild, to Gurdyman and mainly to you, I have the knowledge.*

It had been one of his fundamental beliefs that those who had the ability must help and instruct those who did not. As I worked, sensing his presence and hearing his voice in my head, I sent him my gratitude that the number of those he had instructed in his long life had included me.

'Coming again?' Fritha asked shortly as I packed my satchel and prepared to leave.

'Yes,' I replied.

She met my eyes. Hers were tawny like her hair, and fringed thickly with reddish lashes. She stared at me intently for a moment, and I sensed her mind trying to see into mine. *You cannot*, I said to her, and she flinched even though I hadn't said the words aloud. She backed away slightly, and I smiled at her.

I think I knew, even then, that in time she would become my confidante; perhaps even my friend.

I strode back along the quay and up the steps to the Great Bridge, then turned down to the left and on into the market square. The stalls were busy with people purchasing food for their meal, and I joined the queue at the hot pie stall. I also purchased bread and a piece of ewe's milk cheese, some onions and a little woven basket of raspberries.

I knew I should go straight back to Morgan's house. For one thing, I was hungry, and the delicious aroma of the pie was making my mouth water. For another – and this was far more important than hunger – I had resolved not to be out in the open any more than was essential, for many people in the town had known me before I went away and I didn't think I'd changed very much. Not on the outside, although the inner changes were profound.

I stood at the corner of the square wrestling with myself, then abruptly turned into the lane that leads, via many turns and double-backs, to Gurdyman's house.

I wasn't going to go inside. I was not ready to announce my return; if he hadn't sensed it for himself – and I had an idea that I couldn't keep it from him for very long – then I wasn't going to tell him. But I missed him. I missed many people, and being among the townsfolk in the market served to remind me painfully of the fact.

I missed Jack. Oh, dear God, I missed Jack.

But I didn't let myself dwell on that.

I was just going to go and stand in the alley outside the twisty-turny house that used to be my home and . . . and what? Remember happier times? Wish that Errita and the threat she posed to those I loved didn't exist and I could fling open the door, fly down the steps to the crypt, give Gurdyman a huge hug and shout joyfully 'I'm back'?

All of those things.

I crept along to the overshadowed corner where I'd hidden before and simply stood there, looking at the heavy old door, thinking of the man inside. Of the life that once was mine.

I should have hurried away but I didn't. I went on standing there.

And then the door opened and someone came out.

It wasn't Gurdyman.

It was a younger man, clad in a black cloak with a high collar. Given the warmth of the day, he seemed overdressed. He had dark blond hair, long and lifeless, his face was deathly pale and his eyes were deeply shadowed with greyish circles.

Although he looked so different, I knew who he was and my heart gave a painful lurch at the change in him. Was he ill? Oh, Lord, had he been visiting Gurdyman because he had some dread disease and hoped his old friend could help?

But I'd seen him back in Aelf Fen, I thought wildly. I'd

stood looking down at Edild's little cottage and seen the smoke that told of a cooking fire, and I'd tried to imagine him chopping logs. Yet here he was, thin, gaunt, hollow-cheeked and his eyes deep with suffering.

He had already left. He was striding away down the alley as if hellhounds were after him.

I guessed where he was bound for, so it didn't matter if I lost him in the crowds in the marketplace, but I set off after him anyway.

And, keeping my head and face carefully covered, I followed the tall black-clad figure of Hrype through the maze of alleys that surrounded Gurdyman's house.

EIGHT

'd thought I knew where Hrype would be going but I was wrong.

He emerged onto the main road that runs south-east to north-west around the northern side of the town, and as I expected, he turned left towards the Great Bridge. I lagged back as he strode across it, for although there were quite a few people about, he would have spotted me out on the bridge if he'd happened to turn round. I let him get ahead, then hurried after him.

I caught up to within fifteen or twenty paces of him on the track that leads to the fens. I was just thinking that I could relax now and not bother about keeping him in sight since I knew the way to Aelf Fen as well as he did, when he came to the spot where the track to Ely branches left and the one to Aelf Fen turns right, and to my great surprise he turned left.

So he wasn't going home . . .

I believe I knew even then that something was wrong. I ought to have been thinking to myself that Hrype went everywhere; that he had always been a roamer, venturing all over the fen country and, in his younger days, a great deal further. His jade rune stones came from far away to the east, where his ancestors had travelled and traded, and I had long suspected that Hrype too had wandered those distant roads and waterways. So why, as I watched him stride off, did I *know* that this was more than answering the summons in the blood to be on the road again?

I went after him.

I am not sure when he realized I was following him. Probably far sooner than I thought, and certainly well before the moment when he stopped on the middle of the path and said, without turning round, 'If you're coming with me, Lassair, we may as well walk together.'

Slowly I advanced until I was standing right behind him. The sense of foreboding had grown with frightening speed, and it was all but unendurable now.

He turned round.

I stared up into his haggard face. Despite the fact that he'd been walking fast, he was deathly pale. I felt waves of deep distress and profound pain emanating from him, and the dull glaze over his silvery eyes horrified me: it was as if his inner light had gone out.

And here he was, walking as swiftly as he could away from the village that he looked upon as home . . .

I knew what was wrong.

My legs were suddenly so weak that it was all I could do to stand up.

I said, barely managing to form the words, 'She's dead. Isn't she?'

He nodded, a new wave of grief sending his face into a brief spasm.

But I was in Aelf Fen only four days ago! I wanted to cry. *I stood looking down at her cottage and I saw the smoke rising, smelt the sweet smell of incense! I saw you fetching wood!*

And then I thought, *But I didn't see Edild.*

I ought to have known. I'd been away for a long time, and life was fragile: I was a healer, and all too well aware of that. Had I truly believed I would return to my home and the people I loved and find everyone and everything just as it had been when I left?

If I had, how wrong I had been.

My grandfather Thorfinn was dead. Jack had not waited for me but was now happily settled and his wife had produced a child.

And I'd lost my beautiful aunt.

'When did she die?' I said when I could speak.

'Almost a year ago.' His voice was expressionless, and I thought perhaps he could only say those terrible words if he held his emotions in a grip of iron.

'*How?*' I couldn't imagine what had killed her, for she was a relatively young woman still, healthy, with the skill to treat sickness and injury.

Hrype was silent for a long time and I thought he wasn't going to answer. But then he said, in such a low voice that I strained to listen, 'There was a baby. But something went wrong. Both of them died.'

It was as ironic as it was tragic. My beloved aunt Edild, who had helped so many new lives into the world, tending and comforting their labouring mothers, had been unable to save herself, and neither could anybody else.

A year ago I had been in northern Spain, in one of the more intense phases in my long and arduous training.

I felt the tears coursing down my face.

'You could not have helped, Lassair,' Hrype said, misinterpreting the tears.

I shook my head. 'That's not what I was thinking.' I did not explain, but my gruelling years in the south had beaten out of me the arrogant belief that my skills were so much in advance of anyone else's that I could save lives where nobody else could.

His face softened a little. 'What, then?'

'I'm just so very sorry that I didn't say goodbye to her.'

That I didn't have the time to tell her how grateful I was for all that she had taught me. For her care of me.

To tell her that I loved her.

He must have picked up the words I couldn't speak. He put his arms round me and drew me to him, holding me tightly. I couldn't recall him ever having done so before – not since I was a child, anyway – but now it was an extraordinary comfort. I didn't speak, neither did he; we just stood there, and I felt our grief unite and blast up into the bright sky, seeking the spirit, the soul, of the precious woman we both loved.

'So you're back,' Hrype said some time later.

'I am.'

He stared down into my eyes. 'And you bring a dark shadow with you,' he said very softly.

I looked round wildly. 'How do you know? Is she—'

He smiled grimly. 'She's not hiding in the undergrowth behind you, Lassair. You would have picked up her presence long before now if she was. But I didn't imagine she would

have simply let you walk away when you set out for home.'
He paused. 'Besides, I can see part of her spirit self in you.'

I had long feared that she had put something of herself into
me, as I believed I had into her, but nevertheless it shook me
rigid to hear someone else say so.

After a moment I said, 'I have not revealed my presence
here to anyone – not my family or my village friends, not
Gurdyman, not—' I couldn't bring myself to say Jack's name.
'If I do, if Errita sees me with them, she'll pick up how much
I care for them, and she'll harm them' – she would kill them,
without a doubt, but I couldn't say that either – 'in order to
punish me.'

'That is illogical,' Hrype said coolly. 'Errita already knows
of your connection to Gurdyman and . . .' He paused, glanced
at me and went on, 'And to the others of us who came to the
south to seek you out.'

'I know,' I said. 'I felt her eyes on me, penetrating inside
my mind, back there in the settlement by the coast. I knew
what was in her thoughts even back then, and that was long
before—'

*Long before I discovered the full depths of the deeply
disturbed, malicious, vicious spirit that dwells inside her,* I
almost said.

But it was probably better not to.

'You have long been in conflict with her.' It wasn't a
question; Hrype knew.

'Oh, yes.'

I could have told him how hard she fought to prove her
force was stronger than mine. To demonstrate that even with
the knowledge and the skill and the frightening power that
Luliwa and Gurdyman had passed to me in retribution for the
harm they had done and the innocent lives they had squandered
between them, still I was the weaker one.

But I wasn't.

For the sake of her mother Luliwa whom I loved, I had
held back when Errita summoned her dark skills to attack me.
I fended her off, saving myself largely from harm while trying
not to hurt her. There had been times I had almost given in
and let loose, however . . . The night when she left me walled

up deep beneath the mountains, buried by a sudden roof fall, when, having finally managed to extricate myself, I had raced after her and held her over the precipice, my hands, arms and shoulders trembling with the strain. I had *so nearly* let go. The day when she challenged me to drink a potion she'd prepared, telling me that if I was truly as powerful as everyone said, it would bring about disturbing hallucinations but would not do lasting harm; she did not reveal that she had put poison in it, but I knew and she hated me even more. The time she evaded my watchfulness and finally managed to slip a deadly preparation into something Luliwa had cooked for me – a batch of the little orange-flavoured biscuits she knew I loved – knowing full well that, loving and trusting Luliwa as I did, I would not suspect. I had very nearly died that night, for the terrifying and agonizing convulsions as my body tried desperately to void itself of the poison had almost driven me to crawl up the mountain path and throw myself to my death. I had fought off the temptation by bringing to mind the faces of those back home whom I loved and who loved me. Including that of the grieving man now standing beside me.

Hrype kept silent as these memories ran through my mind. Seeming to pick up the moment I gained control and shut off the stream of images, he said, 'The root of her hatred is jealousy. You are loved and she is not. She knows this and it makes a constant knife in her heart. And what pains her most deeply, of course, is that her mother loves you, yet she finds her own daughter very hard to warm to.'

I looked at him in surprise. 'You were only there in the settlement briefly! How do you know all this?' But before he could answer, I muttered, 'Gurdyman told you.'

'Yes.'

We stared at each other.

'Where are you going?' I asked presently.

He turned to look away up the track. In that moment he looked utterly bereft. He shrugged. 'I'm not going anywhere. I'm just walking.'

Away from Aelf Fen and from all the places he associated with Edild, I thought. People grieving for someone they loved adopted one of two alternatives, I had noticed; those with the luxury of choice, anyway. Some stayed just where they had always been, comforted by the presence of the one they had lost, taking simple pleasure in doing the same things, handling the everyday objects they once shared. Others could not bear to be in the familiar setting when the beloved person they'd lived there with was no longer present.

I might have guessed that Hrype would choose flight.

I looked up to see him staring at me. 'I am waiting, Lassair, as I have been ever since Edild died.'

'For what?'

He didn't answer, but a strange expression slowly spread across his face. 'Think,' he said very softly. When I didn't speak, he added, 'I do not believe I shall have to wait very much longer. *Think,*' he said again. 'What major change has just happened?'

After quite a long time I thought perhaps I knew. I hesitated to give my answer – I'd long had the sense of my own importance crushed out of me – but finally I didn't think there was any alternative.

As I prepared the words, I knew I was right.

'You've been waiting till Gurdyman can set out back to Spain,' I said, 'back to the City of Pearl, where he wants to end his days.' I met Hrype's eyes, and for the first time I saw a shimmer of light in them. 'You're going with him, and you won't come back.'

And he nodded.

I thought again about what he meant by this major change that had recently happened. I went through the alternatives: he was surely not referring to Edild's death, for he'd said that was almost a year ago. Errita was coming to the fens, as we both well knew, but I didn't think she was actually here yet . . .

It looked as if I was going to have to risk his scorn and speak my conclusion aloud.

But then, with a quiet exclamation of impatience, Hrype said, 'Gurdyman cannot leave his house empty; cannot abandon his life's work; cannot simply walk away from all the elements of himself that he has expended down in his crypt. Not until there is someone there to take his place.'

Slowly I nodded, for it was indeed as I'd thought.

Gurdyman was ready to leave and sail south, and he was only waiting for me to present myself as his replacement.

My legs began to shake.

It was a frightening prospect.

'You are ready,' Hrype said. 'You would not be here otherwise, for your path has long been leading here. You know this, Lassair!' he said forcefully when I didn't reply.

I met his eyes, holding them, for I did not want him to look away.

'Perhaps so,' I said. 'Perhaps, too, you are encouraging me, boosting my belief in myself, because you long to be on your way and you will not leave until Gurdyman goes with you.'

I saw the swift flash of guilt in his eyes as he wordlessly acknowledged the truth of this. And then instantly a deeper guilt flooded through me, for he was my friend, I had known him all my life – although not always liked him – and he was lost in grief.

It really wasn't a time for unkind accusations.

'I am sorry, Hrype,' I said.

He nodded. 'You are right, of course.'

'Even so, I should not have spoken hurtfully.'

He smiled very briefly. 'When did you ever hold back from speaking a truth?'

'Perhaps I should know better now.' He didn't reply. 'I will go to Gurdyman soon,' I said. 'I cannot promise more than that.'

He shrugged. 'Then that will have to suffice.'

I stood watching as he walked away. For someone who wasn't going anywhere in particular, he was moving fast. He was, as he'd said, waiting. It probably didn't much matter to him *where* he went.

When he was out of sight, I stood for some time sending my thoughts and my love to Edild. Then I turned and made my slow way back to town.

It was difficult to say for certain just when the dread began to creep over me. I was approaching the town now, nearly there . . . I'd been meandering along, enjoying the pleasure

of the sunshine on my face, thinking of nothing much beyond
that there promised to be a glorious sunset and I would have
another fine, still, warm night in my borrowed lodgings. I tried
to rest in these quiet moments whenever I could, for these
brief respites from my anxieties and my griefs – the loss of
Jack and now the news of Edild's death – were essential if I
was to maintain my strength and my resolve.

The first hint of what was about to happen was that I started
to feel cold. For no reason, for although it was now early
evening, the ground held the heat of the long, sunny day and
I'd been walking for miles.

I shouldn't have felt even mildly chilly, yet now it was as
if there was snow on the ground and the air all but frozen, so
that it was hard to breathe . . . for a frightening instant, I
thought I saw my breath in a pale cloud, as it is on the coldest
of days.

I shook my head violently, and the image dissipated.

I walked on, trying to look everywhere, so alert for what
would happen next – for something would, that was sure – that
my muscles ached.

I saw a group of people on the path in front of me.

Something about them was familiar.

Something about them was very, very scary.

I made myself go on.

Then the scene behind the people on the path changed. I
was on the track leading towards the Great Bridge now, with
the castle looming up on my right perhaps a quarter of a mile
away, the priory under its shadow. Familiar sights, that I had
seen so often over the years that I barely noticed them.

Which is perhaps why it took me some moments to realize
that neither the castle nor the mound it stood on nor the priory
beside it were there. Instead the group of people – a lot closer
now – stood on the edge of a dark stretch of water fringed
with dead reeds. A greyish miasma floated up out of the water,
and already I could detect its charnel stench.

And I was right back in a childhood nightmare.

I'd been about five years old and someone had been telling
a frightening story about figures rising out of the flooded
fen; the living were very afraid of them but, thinking they

recognized some of the faces, they hurried towards the mother, the father, the child or the dear friend they believed they saw coming towards them, outstretched hands appealing desperately for help.

But when they got right up close they saw they were mistaken.

Every single beloved face altered before their eyes. Flesh seemed to slither away as if it was melting in some fierce undetectable heat. Noses became bony holes. Lips seemed to be eaten away, leaving a mess of blood and yellow rodent teeth. Eyes that had once looked out brightly on the world were covered with a filthy slime which, perhaps most horrific of all, none of the figures even tried to blink away . . .

The dream had hit me with full force that night, and my child self had been so terrified that I'd soiled my bed. My parents could not comfort me, and they'd had no choice but to let me sleep between them in their bed for the next week. It would have been longer – I was still very frightened – but my mother said briskly that enough was enough and I must find my courage. She was probably right, but it was hard. My father, understanding rather better, took to going all round the one room of our little house with me each night before I was put in my bed, opening every box and chest, picking up every object so I could peer behind it to make sure there were no ghosts lurking. He made me laugh, bless him, holding up a battered old pan and banging it with a wooden spoon, yelling, 'Be gone, whoever you are!' at the top of his voice.

Standing there all those years later, facing the same ghastly figures and feeling the same dread, I conjured up my father's strength and love and, taking a deep breath, bellowed out his words: '*Be gone, whoever you are!*'

I thought for a terrible moment that they weren't going to obey. They kept advancing towards me – they weren't walking, they were not moving at all, yet somehow they were coming relentlessly nearer – and I clenched my fists. I forced myself to stare at one single figure – it was a man, or I thought it was, with a skull for a head and mere vestiges of flesh on the face, eyes wide open and filled not with a coloured iris and a black pupil but just a blank white mist . . . yet he *saw* me, I knew he did, he—

And suddenly I knew what was happening.

Furious with myself because this wasn't the first time and I ought to have realized straight away, I let the relief flood through me and felt my agonizingly tense body relax.

'You are not real,' I said in my normal voice.

I went on staring at the man with mist for eyes and he began to melt away.

His companions disappeared more quickly, and soon they had all gone and I could once more see the castle and the mound.

Strength was returning, and my legs were no longer shaking. I started to walk, slowly at first and then gradually getting into my usual stride. Soon I was at the bridge, and I crossed over and went through the alleys into the market square. The stalls were busy with customers hurrying to purchase food for the evening meal, and I treated myself to a feast, for I'd realized I was famished.

I drew up my shawl and made myself unobtrusive, then slipped away and hurried across the fields past the sacred well to Morgan's house. I closed and fastened the door, made myself comfortable and ate every scrap of food. I washed my platter, then my face and hands.

When the room and I were tidy and clean, I sat down cross-legged on my bed and drew out the shining stone.

As if it had been waiting for me with growing impatience, the images flashed out at me as soon as the stone was free of its soft covering. And right there, staring up at me as I'd known she would be, her face twisted with malevolence, was Errita.

'You don't forget, do you?' I said to her. 'Do you store up everyone's weak spots in that clever, cruel mind? Do you use people's own terrors as a weapon against them?'

She did; I knew she did.

It wasn't the man with the mist in his eyes that she'd used against me before; it was Rollo's death, and my agony as I understood I wasn't going to be able to save him. It had happened early on in my training, and Luliwa had taken Errita and me and her son Itzal deep into the mountains to teach us the power of sound in the trance state. Luliwa had praised me; commended me for listening and doing what she said rather than believing I knew better. She had cast a glance at Errita as she said that, and we had all noticed. Errita had taken her revenge with that vision of Rollo dying as we'd made our way out from under the mountain: at the place of greatest peril, just as we were negotiating a narrow and difficult pass with a sheer drop on one side. It was perfectly clear what she had hoped would happen. But it didn't.

I had no idea how she'd found out about my childhood nightmare, and it didn't really matter. She had used that weapon now – squandered it – and it would never have power over me again.

Looking at her face in the shining stone, I concentrated on turning her malice back at her. And, at first almost imperceptibly, her image began to break up. I increased my focus and bits of her seemed to blow away, like clouds before a rising wind.

Then she was gone.

I sat for some time, the shining stone resting in my relaxed hands, its surface as blank as my calm mind. Then I wrapped it and put it away.

I should have felt elated.

I didn't.

My thoughts filled with memories of Edild, and I gave into them, let them run and felt the tears flow. I thought of Hrype, grieving, waiting for the one thing that would give him solace but unable to hasten it because its timing was not in his hands. I thought of my father, whose sister Edild had been, and I tried to send him comfort.

Presently I dried my eyes, told myself it was enough.

My grief was spent, for now. But as it faded into the background, another thought took its place.

Errita had made her first assault. It had been awful, but ultimately unsuccessful.

But she was not a woman to give up.

I sensed the benevolent, protective power of Morgan's house, wrapping around me like a soft blanket. Did the old magician know what was happening? Know what threatened me and, recognizing that it was evil, put out a counterforce to defend me? It was a good thought, and I sent out my thanks.

But even if I was right, the protection would only work here in the house that had been Morgan and Cat's, and my battle with my enemy would be enacted elsewhere. She would use everything she could against me. I knew I must maintain and strengthen my resolve to keep right away from Gurdyman and Jack. Now that she had shown herself, it was more vital than ever.

With growing apprehension, I wondered what Errita would try next.

NINE

I t was late in the evening, and Jack was on his way to the
tavern on the quay before heading home. The sun had gone
down in a spectacular display of radiant pink and yellow,
and he paused for a moment on the bridge to admire the last
of the brilliant light. Then he strode down onto the quayside,
hurrying now. He wanted to speak to some of the close circle
of his most loyal lawmen – Ginger, Luke, Big Gerald, Peter,
Young Henry – and check if there was anything to report on
the murder of Mistress de Lacey.

Equally and perhaps more crucially, he hadn't eaten all day
and only had some brackish water to drink. Magnus kept a
good barrel of ale, and his pretty wife had a light hand with
a pie.

The inn was not very busy. A couple of boatmen were eating
something that smelt very appetizing over in a corner, and
Jack, encouraged, asked Magnus for the same. Shortly afterwards, carrying a mug of ale and a portion of fragrantly
steaming pie, he went over to a bench just inside the door
where Walter, Ginger and Big Gerald were sitting, heads close
together, pulled up a second bench and sat down.

Other than a nod or a brief word of greeting, the three of
them left him alone while he ate. When he had finished, he
pushed the platter aside and said, 'Two days now since Mistress
de Lacey's body was found. We've no idea who killed her,
although you only have to step into the marketplace to hear
any number of rumours. She was comfortably off and aloof,
people say, so probably someone knew of her wealth and killed
her for it.'

'I've heard that story,' Ginger said. His lean face creased
into a frown. 'It's usually told with the distinct implication
that if rich widows who prefer their own company get brutally
slain, they've brought it on themselves. Can't see the logic,
myself,' he added, the frown deepening.

'People are frightened,' Big Gerald said. 'Some old gammer was saying the Night Wanderer's back, and *he* did it.'

'I overheard someone whispering that she was someone of great importance and had vital information that her killer tried to beat out of her,' Walter said quietly. He glanced at Jack. 'Reckon word got out about her injuries, chief.'

Jack sighed. 'Unfortunately it wasn't one of us who found the body,' he replied. 'Who knows how many people that old woman spoke to? I'd imagine she'd have had them waiting on her every word with a tale like that to tell.'

'There's no sign of her,' Walter said, anticipating his next question. 'Penn and Cal have been looking, and they've described her to the rest of us as best they can, but as Big Gerald here said' – he flashed the large man a quick smile – 'one old woman looks pretty much like any other, and it's not as if Penn or Cal got a good look at her face.'

'I would like to know what she was doing, calling on Mistress de Lacey early in the morning,' Jack said. 'As we've just been saying, Mistress de Lacey was a woman of means and status, neither of which describe the old woman, from what we're told.'

'Was she a servant? Or someone who did regular work for the mistress? A sempstress, a laundress?' Ginger suggested.

'If she was,' Walter replied, 'it's likely she'd have had regular comings and goings at the house, and someone would have spoken of her. But nobody's mentioned any callers, except that monk that Young Henry found who told him he'd spotted a man hanging around watching the house.'

'He told me too,' Jack said. 'I was with Henry. The monk – Brother Aleric – claimed he'd seen this man more than once.'

'Are we thinking he's the killer, then?' Walter asked, his voice low. 'But why?'

Jack looked up, glancing around the inn to see if anyone was near enough to overhear. The two boatmen had gone and now there was nobody in the inn but the four of them and two young lads chatting to Magnus. Leaning in close – the others did the same – he said, 'There is something I should tell you. As yet it is only a theory, which is why I didn't share it with you straight away. But another day has passed and it remains the only theory, so you should hear it.'

'Go on, chief,' Ginger muttered. 'We're listening.'

'Eleanor de Lacey acted as a local banker and observer for a man, now dead, who—' He tried to think of a way to describe Rollo Guiscard's role; not easy, when he had no very clear idea. 'Guiscard watched out for the King's interests, I suppose sums it up,' he went on. 'It seems he had a web of men and women like Mistress de Lacey who kept their ears and eyes open and passed on anything of interest. They also guarded money for him, in order that he should have funds available nearby wherever he was in the country. Or that, at least, is what we believe.'

'When you say *we*, chief,' Big Gerald ventured, 'that's you and who else, exactly?'

Jack looked at him. Big Gerald was not the brightest of souls, and the challenge of trying to explain Gurdyman to him both quickly and in terms he would understand was beyond Jack just then. 'Someone who knew this man Rollo Guiscard,' he said, and Gerald nodded, apparently satisfied.

'So . . .' Ginger was frowning again, but now there was the light of sharpened interest in his eyes. 'So do we think this killer was after the money?'

'For sure, no cache of coins was found,' Jack said, 'so it's possible.'

'But there's something that's potentially even more valuable than gold,' Walter said softly. 'Secrets. And particularly secrets that concern the King.' He dropped his voice so low for the last two words that he was mouthing rather than speaking them.

Ginger was shaking his head. 'Is it likely that a wealthy widow living a solitary life tucked away in a house beside the river in an out-of-the-way town should *have* such secrets?' he protested in a hiss. 'Even more relevant, who's going to know she's got them and turn up to try to beat them out of her?'

Jack nodded. 'You argue well, Ginger,' he said. 'Especially,' he added, 'since I should also tell you that Rollo Guiscard died several years ago, so if Mistress de Lacey was holding secrets for him, they are by now rather old ones.'

Big Gerald was watching the swift exchange with his mouth open. Walter, eyes narrowed in concentration, said, 'That hiding place behind the panel that Cal found – it was big enough for a decent-sized chest.'

'It was,' Jack agreed. 'And there was a shape outlined in the dust to indicate that a chest had indeed recently stood there.'

'So the killer's now got it?'

'Either that,' Jack replied, 'or it had already gone, and Mistress de Lacey died because she couldn't give it up to him.' He went on trying to make her tell him where it was, he thought, and she couldn't, and so she died.

The thought made him very sad.

'Why would you think that, chief?' Walter demanded. 'And who took it?'

But Jack could give no explanation. It was, as Walter's deeply sceptical expression was implying, an unlikely and pointless piece of speculation.

And it would be impossible to have explained to these three good, loyal and hard-working men that the idea was nothing more than a gut feeling; that he had no more reason to believe it than they.

But that it simply wouldn't go away.

Ginger broke the slightly awkward silence. 'Young Henry's been keeping a close eye on Mistress de Lacey's house,' he said. 'I saw him late yesterday evening and he said he was going to stand watch overnight.'

'He was also going to speak to the monk again,' Jack added. 'We both thought he might have more to tell us.'

'Anyone seen him today?' Walter asked.

'If he was up all night on watch, he's probably been home for a sleep,' Big Gerald observed.

'True,' Walter acknowledged, 'but he won't still be asleep now. He'd have gone home for a nap and then come back on duty.' Nobody spoke. 'Wouldn't he?'

Jack stood up. 'I'm off home,' he said. 'I'll call in at the castle on the way, see if he's about, or if anyone knows what he's up to.'

Walter put a hand on Jack's arm. 'He's a bright lad, chief,' he said. 'Very likely, if he's discovered something he thinks might lead us somewhere, he'll have hared off on his own to follow it up, just for the pleasure of coming back with a crucial piece of information and sitting smirking while we all tell him how clever he's been.'

'You're right, Walter,' Jack replied. And I told him to do just that, he remembered. *If you manage to uncover any interesting trails*, I told him, *see where they take you.* 'All the same, if he hasn't turned up by morning, we'd better see about looking for him.' Looking at each in turn, he added, 'Good night to you all,' and strode out of the inn.

I heard Jack say *I'm off home* and the words shot me into action. I'd been crouching in the deep shadow of a stack of empty barrels beside the inn for quite some time. I'd been listening intently to the lawmen's quiet talk just the other side of the ancient wattle and cracked old daub that formed the wall, my ear to one of the larger cracks. I'd been careful and I knew nobody could see me, curled into my tiny hiding place like a new-born kitten, and as I began to move, every limb ached with cramp.

I limped and staggered down the side wall of the inn until I could peer round and see the door. I was just in time to see Jack emerge.

I watched him walk away.

He was clearly in haste, and I told myself it was because he urgently wanted to find out if Young Henry had turned up at the castle.

And not because he had a comely wife waiting at home with a tasty meal and a welcoming bed.

It took a while to convince myself, and I didn't manage a very good job.

When Jack was just a figure in the distance, I set off after him along the quay, heading for Morgan's house and my own lonely bed. There were few people about, and those who were displayed not the slightest interest in a solitary woman huddled in a shawl. It was safe to dive into what I so much wanted to think about, for my feet knew the way back.

I had been on my way back from the refuge. I'd tried to

settle to a quiet evening after I'd dried my tears and put the shining stone away, but it had proved impossible. I knew I wasn't going to sleep, and I tried to think of some distraction. Almost immediately, I'd thought of Mattie, out at the refuge on the quay. I'd said I would return, although I hadn't said when; why not right then?

It had proved a good decision. Mattie was in pain, and I'd been able to provide a specific to help her sleep. I'd also treated a baby only a few weeks old with a violent outcrop of sores all over his poor little bottom, and shown his very young mother not only how to apply the soothing ointment I provided but also how to keep his skin clean, so that the rash and the sores didn't occur in the first place. I sensed Fritha's eyes watching me as I treated the baby, and as I stood up to leave she came with me to the door.

'You're troubled,' she said quietly. 'Not like them in there' – she jerked her head in the direction of the women and the children, now settling for the night, 'but then there's more than one sort of trouble.'

I turned, meeting her eyes. 'How true,' I said.

She studied me. 'You're welcome here, any time,' she said curtly. Then, as I stepped outside, she closed and barred the door.

As I walked away, I sensed it was an offer she very rarely made.

Heading off along the quay, I'd been very well aware of passing by Magnus's inn. I knew it was where Jack and his trusted circle regularly convened at the end of the day, for I'd been there with them. Drawing level with the partly open door, I'd heard his voice. *No cache of coins was found*, he said, and I knew instantly what he and the others were talking about. Then he mentioned Rollo's name, and that was when I knew I had to stay and listen. I couldn't stand there by the door, so I'd slipped along the side of the inn and found my hiding place.

Now, striding along the quay, I tried to summarize in my mind what Jack and his men knew and what they thought was happening. They too believed, it seemed, that Mistress de

Lacey's killer was after Rollo's chest of coins and parchments; they imagined he'd made her tell him where it was and that was why it was now missing. But Jack had another idea . . .

How did he know?

The question screamed inside my head.

How did he even begin to guess that Mistress de Lacey had been unable to give up the chest because it was no longer in her house and she had no idea where I'd taken it?

I did not dare speculate about an answer, so I turned my thoughts instead to Young Henry. There I had the advantage over Jack's men, for I had seen him that morning. Heard him, what's more, as he had that intense conversation with Brother Aleric. As he learned of this second man seen in the vicinity of Mistress de Lacey's house . . . I summoned the words from memory.

He was bent and weary-looking. He had ragged grey hair and his skin was yellowish.

And Brother Aleric had clearly been surprised that this old man, dressed in good clothes tattered and worn from long use, had gone calling on a respectable and well-to-do widow very early in the morning and not only gained admittance but apparently been welcomed like a friend.

So who was he, this weary-looking man? He'd walked up from the Trumpington direction, according to Brother Aleric, who'd noticed him cut across the fields from the road south to jump down onto the riverside path.

I brought to mind the little I knew about Trumpington. It was a small village some four miles to the south of Cambridge, and people said there had been a settlement there from time out of mind because there was a ford over the river; not that the Cam amounted to much more than a brook down there, although even a brook is sufficient to wet you thoroughly if you try to cross it other than by bridge or ford.

This man, then, lived out of town; if indeed he had his dwelling there and hadn't just happened to be on the road. He was apparently a friend of Mistress de Lacey, however, which suggested acquaintance, which in turn suggested proximity.

I was on the road leading south from the Great Bridge now, and presently I took the path across the field that led to the

sacred well and Morgan's house. It would be good to be safe
within its sanctuary, for my mind was whirling with faintly
understood ideas and I knew I was not keeping a lookout for
danger as well as I should. I hastened my pace, and soon I
was inside the house, the door closed and fastened.

Once snuggled up in my bed, my thoughts returned to what
I had just overheard.

Jack's band of men seemed to believe that Mistress de Lacey
had been killed because her killer wanted the chest; Rollo's
chest, now in my keeping and buried only a few paces away.
Jack had other ideas, but I knew I couldn't let myself think
of what they were and how he came to have them.

I had also intuited – although I was not entirely sure how
– that Mistress de Lacey might have had some very important
secret information she felt compelled to impart to others in
Rollo's network; to perhaps just one other . . . She had spoken
to me of the King, I now recalled, and the memory struck me
with a force that quite surprised me, for in the wake of her
death much of what had led up to it was now vague and misty.

She had told me of the King's plans to lead an expedition
to Normandy, where he needed to establish a base . . . no, not
Normandy; she'd said Normandy was now denied to him
because Duke Robert was on his way back from Outremer
and, because he wasn't dead after all, his brother the King
was no longer going to have the dukedom meekly handed
over to him. The expedition would be to somewhere else . . .
Poitou, that was it. I'd told her how I'd seen the fleet assembled
off the south coast, and her eyes had lit up with interest. We'd
spoken of dreams and portents, visions of blood and some
rumoured threat to the King, and she said with some impatience
that dreams and visions didn't kill, and that proof was required.

Then – oh, yes, this was it, I had it! – then she said, *There
was word that* . . .

But she did not finish the remark.

What did she mean? She'd sent a message, perhaps, to
another of her network? Or – and it struck me this was far
more likely – was it that she'd *received* some message?

Suddenly there was a vivid picture in my mind.

I saw a fire blazing in a clearing in woodland. It looked

like a bonfire. Many little snakes of flame were running out of it, burning trails in the grass, and someone, or something, was patiently and efficiently stamping each one out, making sure the wild flames of the bonfire did not spread out of control to somewhere they were not wanted. Somewhere they would be very, very dangerous . . .

And I knew what it meant.

It was putting into my mind the idea of a secret: a secret that must be kept safe at all costs, so important that those whose duty it was to guard it sought out every place, every person, from where and from whom they feared it might escape.

And stamped on those who might reveal it, crushed them dead, like the unidentified boot extinguishing the errant, dangerous flames.

Had the message come to Eleanor de Lacey via the weary-looking man with the worn-out clothes that had once been so fine?

Young Henry had listened intently as Brother Aleric told him of this man. Did he too, then, identify the old man as somehow important to Mistress de Lacey? Relevant, perhaps, to her brutal death? Not because he was her killer, but because he knew her, knew her secret business? Was *part* of that clandestine business, privy to these dangerous secrets?

Did this ragged-looking old man now know, then, that whatever he had told her had led to her death? *Had* it? Or was all of this speculation purely that, with no foundation in reality?

I didn't know; couldn't know.

But there was something I could do to help me along the road to finding out.

I had overheard that conversation on the path by Mistress de Lacey's house. I knew what the monk had told Young Henry; I had observed the expression on his face and seen the direction he took when the monk departed.

He'd been heading for Trumpington.

I was the only one who'd seen him go, and so it was up to me.

Tomorrow I was going to follow him.

TEN

The long hours of sunshine began early at this time of year. The walls and roof of Morgan's old house were riddled with holes and gaps, allowing the low sunbeams to spear their way inside, and once more I was awake soon after dawn.

I took my time, following my morning routine with concentration and deliberation, as Luliwa had taught me to perform every task. I tried to let the various jobs absorb my whole attention – something else that Luliwa insisted on – but my mind kept escaping and leaping ahead to what I was planning to do.

It was quite a relief finally to close the door and set off.

It was a fine morning for a walk out of town. It would be hot later, if previous days were anything to go by, but for now the air still held some of the night's coolness. Remembering exactly what the monk had related to Henry, I made my way round the northern end of the town and across the fields to the riverside track, joining it some way to the south of Mistress de Lacey's house. I turned left, and presently reached a spot where I could see the road that led south out of the town, now only a short way distant across the field.

The bent and weary-looking man whom Brother Aleric had seen going into Mistress de Lacey's house very early one morning had crossed the field round about where I now stood, I guessed. There was a faint track through the dry grass, and it looked as if this was a regularly used short cut. I took it.

The road leading south was almost as devoid of traffic as the riverside path. I saw a couple of horsemen up ahead, travelling quite fast. Then an ox cart came round a bend and out of the shade of a stand of oaks, lumbering its slow way towards the town and the market. Without really thinking about it I decided I would rather not be seen, so I jumped down off the road and slipped into a little copse of young hazels, where I crouched down until the cart had gone by.

The sun was considerably higher in the sky by the time I reached Trumpington. I didn't think I had been there before, although it was possible I had because I'd treated people in and all around the town during the years I'd lived there. Nothing looked familiar, however, so I found a vantage point on a low rise beneath a stand of apple trees and for some time simply stood looking around.

The little settlement consisted basically of the road south and a wide brook, which at this point ran over pebbly shallows into which two lines of huge, flat stones had been laid to allow pedestrians to cross dry-footed and carts to negotiate the water without their wheels becoming bogged down. Beyond the ford there was a rambling set of buildings, the largest of which was an inn. A stable block extended out to one side and a series of other, smaller structures on the other, none of which was in very good repair. I could hear the squeals and snuffling of pigs from somewhere close by, and I guessed there was a pig pen behind the inn.

Opposite the inn there was a series of dwellings, some in good repair, others not, and I heard the sound of raised voices from the one nearest to me. A woman yelled to someone to shift his backside and get out of her way, a man shouted a crude insult back at her, she yelled at him again and there was the sound of a slap, followed by a shrill scream and the all too recognizable sounds of an angry man bellowing his rage at the nearest target.

I didn't think this particular man sounded like Brother Aleric's worn and yellowish-skinned old man, but I watched the door anyway to make sure. Presently it was flung open and a red-faced bull of a man emerged, well-built, strong-looking, in the act of turning back to shout a last insult. My pity for the recipient was mitigated slightly, however, because a pair of hands appeared in the dark doorway hefting a heavy pan, which she proceeded to thump down on the man's head. Before he could retaliate – I was getting the feeling that this sort of fight was a regular occurrence – she had the door shut and the bolts across and was screaming at him, *'And don't you dare come back till you've learned some manners!'*

I waited until he was a mere distant figure striding away

into the distance, shoulders hunched, head hung, the picture of frustration and fury. Then I made my way down to the ford, crossed over and approached the first of the dwellings. It was as yet the only one from which there had been any sign of life, if you discounted the pigs, so I thought I might as well start there.

I knocked gently on the door. In moments it was flung open even as an angry voice shouted, 'I thought I told you not to come back until – oh.'

I saw straight away that this was not the big man's wife but his mother. The thin hair under the tightly bound head cloth was pure white, the brownish skin of the bony face was heavily scored with wrinkles, the mouth had caved in where teeth had been lost and the nose curved out in a hook that seemed to be trying to meet up with the out-thrust chin. The well-worn, dark garments hung upon the skinny body, and the hand that gripped the edge of the door was like a claw. For all that, however, the eyes were bright blue, alert and intelligent, and now fixing me with an aggressively enquiring expression.

'Who are you?' she demanded.

'I'm—' I almost told her my name but I held back. There was no knowing who she might tell. 'I'm a healer,' I said.

'Don't know what you think you're doing at *my* house, then,' she grumbled. 'Make my own remedies, see, always have done, like my mother and grandmother before me.' She briefly straightened her bent back as she said these proud words.

'I haven't come to offer you a potion,' I said, adding with craven obsequiousness, 'Not that you look as if you need one!'

She narrowed her eyes. 'Don't you give me any of your flattery, girl!' she said sharply, but I thought I saw a smile twitch at the corner of her mouth. 'What do you want?'

'Your help,' I said promptly.

'My help?' She looked pleased. 'Better come in, then. But don't you go imagining you can rob an old woman on her own, because I have my trusty frying pan to hand and I know how to use it!'

I know, I thought, *I saw you.*

The room was tiny and crammed with a lifetime's

belongings, but it was as clean as Mistress de Lacey's very different house. One small window set high admitted a meagre light, but the old woman now flung the door wide, and the sun poured in.

'So you're after my help,' she repeated as she nudged me towards a three-legged stool and sat down on its pair. 'What with?'

'I'm looking for someone, and I believe he comes from here,' I replied.

'Who is he and what does he look like?'

'I don't know who he is, for I've only heard him described by someone else and they didn't provide a name.'

'Go on, then!' she said impatiently. 'Give me this description! I know everyone hereabouts, I've lived here all my life and that's very nearly four score years, so if anyone's likely to recognize him, it's me.'

'He's—' I'd been about to say he was old, but I realized this could be a mistake, since he was surely not as old as this old crone and if I described someone younger as old, it might annoy her. I was getting the distinct impression she was someone who became annoyed rather readily. 'He's older than me but younger than you,' I said instead, 'with long, tatty grey hair and yellowish skin, his back is bent, he has a weary look to him and his clothes were once fine quality but are now worn with age.'

The old woman had begun nodding shortly after I'd embarked on the description. 'Sounds like Stephen,' she said. 'Specially the garments. We all reckon he was a nobleman who upset someone he shouldn't have and ended up ruined.' She nodded to herself, her face grim. 'He's lived around here for years. Scrapes a living doing odd jobs at the inn, and, to speak fairly of the man, he does them well and he doesn't complain, not like some.' She glared down the road in the direction her son had taken.

'Is he a sociable sort?' I asked, thinking of Mistress de Lacey and her preference for her own company.

'*Sociable?*' The old woman cackled. 'Not him. He lives in a lean-to at the end of the chicken run – that's in the field behind the inn – and to the best of my knowledge, he's the only person to have set foot through the door since he took up residence and he doesn't talk to his neighbours if he can help it.'

'And he spends his days here, in the village? Carrying out these odd jobs for the innkeeper?'

She shook her head. 'Oh, no, now that's not right.' She sent me a scolding look, as if I'd been deliberately trying to mislead her. 'I couldn't tell you how he spends his days, and that's the truth. When he's here you see him in the inn yard or out heaving buckets of swill into the pig pen, that sort of job, but as often as not he's *not* here, if you take my meaning, or if he is, he's shut away in his lean-to and no one knows *what* he's up to.'

She was, I thought, making this Stephen sound mysterious. I wondered whether she had good grounds to, or if it was simply a woman living a monotonous life in a small community making a lively story out of very little.

'Could you show me where this lean-to is, please?' I asked politely.

She looked sharply at me. 'Want to go there, do you? See for yourself? Check I'm telling you the truth?'

'I don't doubt it,' I replied, 'but—'

'What do you want with him, anyway?' she demanded, suspicion narrowing her eyes.

My usual response to that question is *He owes me money*, which satisfies most people, but I didn't think it would serve here, for this quick-witted old woman would surely not be able to imagine what could possibly have incurred the debt, a recluse like Stephen being hardly likely to consult a healer. 'He went to see a friend of mine and I want to ask him about her,' I said instead.

'Why can't you ask this friend instead?' the old woman demanded.

I met her eyes, not looking away. 'Because she's dead,' I said.

The woman didn't flinch; perhaps when you're nearly eighty years old death has lost its power to frighten you. 'What happened to her? Did she fall sick? Take a tumble?' she asked.

'She was killed.'

Now she paled a little. 'And you think Stephen—'

'No, I don't think he killed her,' I interrupted. 'In fact I'm almost sure they were old friends.'

'And you've come to break the news to him?'

I would have done, of course, but that hadn't been my first concern. 'Yes,' I said, 'but I also want to find out if he can think of any reason why she was killed.'

The old woman looked at me for some moments. Then with surprising agility she got to her feet, gave me a curt nod and said, 'We'd better go and ask him, then.'

I really didn't want her with me when I located him, but it was going to be difficult, if not impossible, to shake her off, so I accepted the inevitable and followed her out of the door, across the road and round the back of the inn buildings, then along a beaten earth path that led across the corner of a field towards an enclosure for hens. Built against one side was a wattle-and-daub lean-to. It was a small structure that looked barely wide or deep enough for a tall man to lie down in, although both the walls and the reed thatching looked in good repair.

'Keeps it neat and tidy, does Stephen,' the old woman said approvingly, noticing me looking. 'Wouldn't necessarily expect a man of quality fallen on hard times to have the skills you need to look after yourself and keep a clean house, would you? But then he's far from stupid, is Stephen, and there's much more to him than meets the eye, as I've always said, and in addition I reckon he's—'

But I was never going to know what else she reckoned.

Because as she spoke the words she was tapping on the door, and even as she did so opening it, pushing it hard as it scraped against the bare earth floor and a tiny gap grudgingly opened up.

And as soon as it did so, a great swarm of flies flowed out like a filthy black cloud. A wave of stench accompanied them and the old woman and I fell back, grabbing at folds of our clothing to cover our noses and mouths. I could hear the old woman gabbling a prayer, crossing herself over and over with her free hand, the words distorted by her distress so that they were barely comprehensible.

'We must look inside,' I said firmly. 'You can stand back if you wish, but—'

She gave me a look so ferocious that no words were needed to convey the meaning. Before she could shove me out of the way, I pushed again at the door and this time, after a brief resistance, it opened and I fell inside, the old woman at my shoulder.

He was lying on his side diagonally across the floor, his long frame curled in on itself, legs bent, arms crossed over his chest. He had been dead for some time – several days, I thought – and the flies that we had disturbed had been busy. Some of his flesh had also fed the mice and the rats, and one eye socket was empty.

I crouched down beside him. The horror of his death and the awful smell combined to inform me that I could not endure to be in there for long, and so I did a very swift check of the body – hands, arms, legs, face – and, as I had thought I would, found the same sort of injuries that had killed Mistress de Lacey.

It was not the moment to speculate on what had happened here. There would be time for that later, when this poor, pathetic corpse had been taken away, laid out and buried. I stood up and staggered out through the door, to find the old woman had preceded me and was now standing bent over, hands on hips, taking in deep breaths of the good, sweet air.

'That's him? Stephen?' I asked presently.

'It is.' The words were a gasp.

He was without doubt the man Brother Aleric had described. Every detail tallied, from the straggled grey hair to the fine leather of the ancient boots.

I put out my hand, and to my surprise the old woman grabbed it. I hadn't expected her to display this sign of fallibility, and the gesture had been for my sake rather than hers. She met my eyes, and hers held compassion.

'No way to end your days,' she commented.

'No.'

'You've come from town?' She jerked her head in the direction of Cambridge.

'Yes.'

'Good. I hear there's a lawman in charge there now who's an honest man – not something you expect in one of that kind – so will you make sure he knows?'

'I will.' I would not be telling Jack myself – I didn't even allow myself to think about doing that – but I'd find a way to pass the news of the death to him.

The old woman turned and, letting go of my hand, headed off back up the path. 'Shall I see you home?' I asked.

She snorted. 'I don't need seeing anywhere!' she said sharply. Then, relenting, she gave me a faint smile. 'Anyhow, I'm not going home, not straight away. Someone'll need to tell Harold, see – Harold's the innkeeper – and it had better be me.'

'Shall I come with you?'

Now the smile was wider. 'No, my lass, because Harold will flap about like a frightened girl and he'll exclaim with horror for the remainder of the morning, and you need to be on your way back to town to find that lawman.' She gave me a gentle push. 'Off you go, now!'

I went on just standing there staring at her for a moment – I was strangely reluctant to move away from her fortitude and her plain down-to-earth practicality – but I knew she was right.

'Goodbye, then,' I said.

And she gave me an approving nod to send me on my way.

It was only when I was halfway back to the town that I remembered I hadn't even asked her name.

Before I went into the marketplace, I adopted my old woman's guise. I stood behind one of the stalls at the edge of the square – it was not long after midday and the market was heaving with people – hoping that I'd be able to spot a lawman other than the two to whom I'd reported finding Mistress de Lacey's body, and I kept out of sight as I looked all round. Then I saw one of Jack's close associates, a lean man with a ready smile known as Ginger, who was leaning against the side of a building and chatting to an older man lounging beside him. They were both grinning, as if one of them had just said something funny.

I pulled my shawl right forward to shade my face, bent my back a little further and hobbled towards them.

The corner where they stood was busy with the hurrying crowd, so I reckoned I ought to be able to tell them quickly about the body and then melt away. I very much hoped so, anyway.

I crept right up behind Ginger.

'There's a dead man called Stephen in a lean-to behind the inn at Trumpington,' I hissed, right in his ear, 'and he was the man seen visiting Mistress de Lacey early one morning.'

Ginger spun round to stare at me, mouth open in shock. '*What?*' he cried. He reached out his hand and grabbed at me, his fist closing on the cloth of my sleeve, but I gathered my strength and jerked it as hard as I could out of his grip, then turned and fled into the crowds. I heard feet pounding after me and I thought he, or maybe the other man, was about to catch me, but then there was a loud cry and the sound of bodies crashing to the ground. I risked a very quick look behind me and saw the older man lying beneath a very fat woman, struggling to shove her off him and get up, while Ginger elbowed onlookers roughly aside and yelled at them, '*Get out of the way!*'

I fled.

I headed off into the maze of alleys around the square, doubling back, turning this way and that, and finally emerging on the south side of the square across the road from St Bene't's church. I crept into the churchyard and headed over to the tangle of undergrowth on the far side, where I crept into its shelter and sank down on the bare earth, my knees drawn up, resting my head on my folded arms, while I got my breath back and my alarmed heartbeat slowly returned to normal.

I raised my head and straightened up, looking from my shady corner out into the churchyard. I stared up at St Bene't's, at its tower soaring up into the clear blue sky. The bright light threw the openings in the uppermost storey into blackness, and for a strange moment I thought I saw someone up there, their back to the opening, spine bent in a curve – and leaning outwards. I blinked, anxious for this person's safety – I couldn't see if it was a man or a woman – and the image went away.

I thought I should get back to Morgan's house. The day was now well advanced, I had walked a long way and I had

barely eaten. I didn't feel like food now but I would have to
force myself, for although today had delivered enough in the
way of troubling sights and I wanted nothing more than to
hide away and turn my mind inwards, I would have to go out
again as soon as I'd eaten because I'd promised to go and see
Mattie and her baby this afternoon.

I got up and, careful to look all around me, set off to skirt
the market and emerge on the far side of the town, from where
I could then hurry back to my sanctuary.

I wondered if Ginger and his companion had told Jack about
the body yet. To distract my mind from the horrible after-
images of that poor man, I tried to think what the second
lawman's name was, but after a few moments I concluded that
I didn't know him. As well as Ginger there was Walter, Big
Gerald, Young Henry—

Henry!

I'd gone out to Trumpington because that was where *he* had
gone, looking for the old man who had called on Mistress de
Lacey. But then I had talked to the old woman and we'd
discovered the body in the lean-to, and all thoughts of Young
Henry had fled from my mind.

I hurried through the narrow back ways, head down, all
my thoughts on Henry. Was I right in thinking he'd gone to
Trumpington? Had he too come across Stephen's body?

If he had, then I'd found no sign of him, either on the road
there or in the village. And I didn't think my old woman could
have encountered him, because if he had knocked on her door
as I had done and asked about Mistress de Lacey's early visitor
– who I now knew to be Stephen – then wouldn't she have
said so? Wouldn't she have exclaimed in fascinated curiosity,
*Now that's very odd, you're the second person to ask me about
him in as many days!*

Very alarmingly, she hadn't.

ELEVEN

It was not until the middle of the afternoon that Jack finally had the time to turn his thoughts to Young Henry's whereabouts. His day so far had been fully taken up with a wealthy nobleman who had believed himself to be a close friend of the late sheriff – although Jack and everyone else within the castle could have told him Sheriff Picot did not understand the concept of *friend* – so that when the man's favourite mare had apparently gone missing, he had refused to budge from the doorway of the castle until Jack organized a search. When the horse turned up unharmed, having made her way through a gap in her enclosure, the man snorted as if this was entirely Jack's fault and stomped away without a word of thanks.

In haste now, suppressing his fury at the wasted time, Jack spoke to those of the town's lawmen who were in and around the castle, asking them all if anyone had seen Henry. Nobody had. Impatient with the repeated shakes of their heads and the mutters of 'No, chief, sorry,' Jack flung himself out of the door and down the steep steps to the courtyard below, to bump into Ginger and Peter running towards him.

'She's done it again, chief!' Ginger cried, red in the face and breathless, bending forward with his hands on his knees.

'Who? What?' Jack snapped back. 'Come on, I'm in a hurry!'

'We were on duty in the market square,' Peter said as Ginger whooped for breath; Peter was an upright, fit-looking man who always seemed to walk as if he was bouncing, and he had survived the sprint from the marketplace to the castle somewhat better than Ginger. 'We're just standing there, chatting, watching the crowd, when this old woman comes up and says as how there's a dead body in a lean-to out at Trumpington, in a field behind the inn, and—'

'Name of Stephen,' Ginger gasped out. 'The corpse, not the old gammer.'

'This old girl, she says this dead man's the one seen visiting the *other* dead body – that woman in the house by the river – although she doesn't say how she knows, and me, I'm doubtful she—'

'Mistress de Lacey,' Ginger said, straightening up and apparently beginning to recover. 'She was the dead body in the house by the river, and this old woman in the marketplace said the man out at Trumpington was the same one that went calling on her.'

Once again, at the mention of this mysteriously well-informed old woman, a soft chord seemed to ring out in Jack's head.

'We'll check,' he said shortly. 'Ginger, go down and arrange a cart and horses. Peter, stick your head inside the guardroom and if Cal and Penn are still there, tell one of them to come with us.'

And, not very long afterwards, Jack was riding ahead down the road to Trumpington with Ginger driving the cart trundling behind him and Cal on the narrow bench beside him; Ginger and Cal had each described their respective old gammers as best they could, and it seemed at least possible it was the same person.

But it was equally possible, Jack thought morosely as he led his little procession down the road, that it wasn't. One woman or two? he wondered. And why was something about her proving so troubling to him? He had the two descriptions now, surely that ought to help? It didn't, and all that filled his head were more questions: who is she? How did she come to discover two bodies? Were they slain by the same hand? If so, what was the link?

His mind was still throwing up increasingly unlikely answers when they rode into Trumpington. A man was standing outside the inn, and from the sense of agitation emanating from him, clearly waiting for them. There was a stooped old figure with bright eyes standing beside him, and she greeted them with an accusatory 'About time too!'

'You're the innkeeper?' Jack demanded, dismounting and handing his horse's reins to the man.

'That I am, and—'

'I'm Agathe, I was the one knew where he lives!' the old woman cried, elbowing the innkeeper out of the way. 'She came asking, see, and I recognized him from the description – I keep my eyes open, see, and I know what goes on – so I says, I'll show you where he lives, and I led the way behind the inn and across the field, and then when we pushed the door open this great cloud of flies came out and we—'

But at that point her stout courage wavered and she went pale, swaying slightly. The innkeeper tried to put out an arm to save her, but he was encumbered with Jack's horse and it was Cal who leapt to her aid, putting his arms round her and gently lowering her to the ground as her eyes rolled back in a faint.

'See to her, will you?' Jack said. Turning to the innkeeper, he added, 'Now, where's this lean-to?'

Some time later they had the corpse on the cart, covered with a worn blanket which, although it hid the sight of the dead man from the curious, did little to disguise the stench. Cal, who had apparently been watching from inside the inn, came hurrying out to join them as Jack mounted up and Ginger clambered onto the cart.

He gave the blanket-covered shape a glance and quickly turned away. 'You got it, then,' he muttered.

Neither Jack nor Ginger bothered to reply.

As the cart trundled back to town, Cal broke the silence to say musingly, as if in answer to a private thought, 'Yes, it *was* odd, when all's said and done.'

'What was?' Jack turned in the saddle to look at him.

'The old woman. Agathe.'

'Was she all right?' Jack realized belatedly he ought to have asked before.

'Oh, yes, right as rain. I took her inside the inn and said I'd fetch her a mug of water but she was having none of it and she told me strong liquor was the cure for shock, specially for someone as old as her.' He chuckled reminiscently.

'And why was that odd?'

'Oh, no, it wasn't that – it was something else.' Cal frowned thoughtfully. 'I thought it'd be helpful if we each described our respective old women – you must remember, chief, the one who told me and Penn about the first body and the one who approached Ginger and Peter today?'

'I remember,' Jack said, suppressing a sigh; did Cal really think his memory was so feeble?

'Anyway, like I said, I thought I'd tell her what *our* old gammer looked like, then *she* could describe the old woman who came asking about the dead man, who was with her when she found the body and who then must have hurried into town to tell Ginger and Peter about the *second* body, and—'

'Yes, I understand,' Jack interrupted. 'So the fact that strikes you as odd is somehow connected with this old gammer who keeps finding corpses?' As if, he added to himself, that was not odd enough in itself.

'*Yes*, chief!' Cal said with barely disguised amusement, as if it was Jack who was being slow on the uptake.

'Go on, then,' Jack said resignedly.

'Well, I said tell me about this old woman who came looking for the man – the man who turned out to be dead,' he added helpfully, 'and that was when she said it!'

Holding on to his patience only with difficulty, Jack said, 'Said what?'

'She said – and it was really scathing, like when my mother's getting into her stride with nagging me – she said, "She wasn't *old*!"'

Back at the castle, the body was removed from the cart and taken to a cellar, where it would await the ministrations of Luke's female relations and be prepared for burial.

Putting the matter to the back of his mind – for even more of the day had gone by and still he had done nothing towards his main goal – Jack said briefly to Walter that he was going to go looking for Young Henry and swung out of the castle before anyone could stop him.

Outside on the track – *free*, he thought with relief – he thought back to the last time anyone had seen the young man and realized with dismay that it was not since the evening before last.

Where was he?

What had he been doing, and what had driven him on to do whatever he did next?

He was interested in the monk, Jack recalled, and believed he knew more than he'd already revealed. What was his name? Brother Aleric, and Young Henry said he wanted him to describe the man he'd seen lurking round Mistress de Lacey's house.

And I told him to follow any interesting lead, Jack reminded himself again.

Had Young Henry done just that? Discovered something that was more than interesting but also important and somehow dangerous? And was that why he was now missing?

Jack forced the thought aside. Undermining himself with fears for Henry's safety – and guilt that if he was in danger then Jack himself had sent him there – was not going to help either of them just now.

Brother Aleric belonged to the community on the riverside, a short way out of town to the south of Mistress de Lacey's house. Increasing his pace with every stride, Jack headed off that way.

The monastery was comprised of four low, unadorned buildings set out to form a square around a central enclosure. Within there was a small chapel and, standing on tiptoe to look over the wall that stretched a short distance on either side of the gate, Jack could see a run of modest outbuildings and shacks, some of which had a clear purpose such as the wash house and the bakery and some of which appeared to house animals.

He bunched up a fist and hit it lightly on the gate. After quite a long pause, a little window opened within the door and an elderly face appeared. 'Yes?'

'I am sorry to disturb you if you were at your devotions, brother,' Jack began courteously.

'I was not,' the monk interrupted in a reedy old voice. 'Too late for nones, too early for vespers. What do you want?'

'I wish to speak to Brother Aleric.'

'You cannot,' the monk replied with a definite note of triumph.

'It is important, and I am—'

'You're about to tell me you're a man of the law, I don't doubt, and that you have the right to demand to speak to whomever you choose, but it won't help in the least,' the old monk said, and he was grinning toothily now at his own humour. 'Brother Aleric is not here but has gone to take a basket of stale bread to those women in that refuge of his. Undoubtedly you will find him there.'

The little door was slammed shut and Jack heard the bolts shoot across.

Fritha welcomed me at the entrance with her usual paucity of words; not much more than a grunt and a 'Brother Aleric's in there.' She clearly thought I'd come to see him, perhaps believing we were better acquainted than we were; we had arrived together the first time I came, I recalled, and he'd introduced us. She was indicating a long room with a table and benches. 'He's brought bread and he's handing it out. Mattie's where she was before.' She nodded towards the room where Mattie was living. I thanked her and went on into the refuge.

I didn't seek out Brother Aleric but went straight to Mattie. I found her in good heart, considerably happier than on my first visit. The ointment I had given her was healing her fast, and, much more crucial to her peace of mind, she had listened and watched so intently when I'd explained how to breastfeed that now her baby girl was visibly thriving and Mattie no longer suffered what every woman I'd ever treated for it described as the excruciating pain of overfull breasts.

I was about to leave her and her child to each other and go to see some of the other women when I heard a man's voice from the outer door, speaking to Fritha.

The man was asking about someone . . . yes. I heard him say he was a lawman, he wanted to talk to Brother Aleric and it couldn't wait. But I hadn't needed that clue in order to identify him.

Mattie could obviously see my distress. Her eyes rounding in alarm, she hissed, *'What's wrong?'*

'I have to hide!' I hissed back. I looked around wildly at the rows of beds and the clutter of their occupants arrayed all around them. 'But there's *nowhere* . . .'

'Yes there is,' Mattie said firmly. Getting up, her child relaxed and droopy-eyed held tight to her chest, she grabbed my arm with her spare hand and pulled me across the room to where a ragged curtain hung over a narrow recess, so dark in colour that I hadn't noticed it against the even darker wall. Pulling it aside to reveal a bowl of water and a bucket half-filled with pungent liquid, she grinned and said, 'Women who've just had a baby often need to piss in a hurry – didn't you know?' Her smile widened. 'It's better all round if we don't do it on the floor.'

I slid into the recess, careful to avoid the bucket, and she let the curtain fall.

I leant into the corner formed by the rear wall and the side wall, my heart pounding, desperately hoping I'd be able to calm my breathing before anyone entered the room.

I was not sure if in fact he did come in; I could hear him talking to Brother Aleric now and to my alarmed ears it sounded as if they were very near, but they might have been out in the passage. Perhaps it was just that theirs were the only male voices in a dwelling full of women and children and therefore stood out, but I heard every word Jack and Brother Aleric said.

'You spoke to Young Henry again, didn't you?' Jack asked the monk.

'I did,' Brother Aleric replied, already sounding alarmed. As well he might, for I'd picked up Jack's anxiety – bordering on desperation – even from where I stood hiding.

'He thought you might have more to say about the man you saw hanging around Mistress de Lacey's house, didn't he?' Jack demanded.

'Yes, precisely that, but as well as that, I remembered some-thing else – some*one* else, I should say – and I told him about that – him – as well,' Brother Aleric said, his words spilling out in his eagerness to help and, I could not help thinking, to supply the information Jack was after and stop the interroga-tion. Smiling with fond memory, I thought, *He never realizes how threatening he can sound.*

'Another person?' Jack seemed to hurl the words at him.

'Yes, another man, and this one came visiting very early in

the morning. I followed him as he came across the fields
from the Trumpington road and joined the riverside path ahead
of me, and I watched him as he went to knock on the door.
It seemed to me that Mistress de Lacey perhaps expected him,
or at least knew him and was not at all alarmed to find
him there, for she did not hesitate to let him in.'

'You said all this to Henry?' Jack barked.

'I did indeed.'

'And how did he reply?'

'Oh, he was interested – very interested,' Brother Aleric
stuttered, 'and he encouraged me to describe the man, which
of course I was more than willing to do, and I told him the
man was quite old, that he had a stooping sort of posture, with
long, straggled hair and the yellow skin that speaks of ill
health. Oh, and that he was dressed in what looked like good
apparel that had been worn for far too long.'

For some time after he had finished, Jack did not reply.

'Did I – have I been of help?' Brother Aleric ventured
timidly.

'You have, brother,' Jack said heavily. 'I am sorry that I
must repay your assistance with ill news, but the man is dead.'

Quite clearly I heard Brother Aleric gasp.

Then Jack spoke in a softer tone, and I could no longer
resist. I pulled back the curtain just a very little, making enough
of a gap to put one eye to, and stared out.

Jack and Brother Aleric were standing in the open doorway.
Mattie had the second bed along, so I was separated from
them by only a few paces.

It was the closest I had been to him since I got home
and I could not tear my eyes away from him. I stared at him
hungrily, and in that instant the fact that he was lost to me
seemed to break my heart.

I was too busy trying to cope with the pain that I missed
what they were saying.

When I was able to listen again, I realized that Jack was
talking about me.

'. . . an old gammer wrapped in a shawl, her face covered,
and twice now she's approached my men to tell them where
to find a body,' he was saying. 'Do you recognize anyone you

know from this description? Anyone with a tendency to go poking around finding the bodies of the recently deceased?'

'No,' Brother Aleric said, 'I cannot say that I do.'

'You?' Jack demanded, and for an awful moment I thought he'd seen me spying on him and was asking me.

But, 'No, nor I,' Fritha said, and, opening the gap a tiny bit more, I saw she had gone to stand beside Jack and Brother Aleric. 'But then,' she added, 'old women tend to wrap themselves up in similar garments and they all tend to look the same.'

They went on talking, but they were moving away towards the door and I could no longer make out the words. I let the curtain fall back into place.

It seemed a very long time afterwards that it was pulled aside and Mattie's face appeared.

She looked at me worriedly, holding out her hand as I stepped over the bucket. 'I didn't tell,' she said earnestly. 'I reckon you have your reasons for keeping out of a lawman's way.' She glanced down the passage, in the direction Jack had taken. 'Even if like everyone says he's a good one,' she added.

I knew I should find the strength to resist but I couldn't stop myself.

I gave Jack time to get right away, then I went softly and carefully along the quayside, keeping to the shadows, and turned to the right up onto the Great Bridge and across it towards the castle. I slipped into the narrow little passage that led off the road beneath the castle's skirts, senses alert, constantly expecting some sound to set me fleeing.

But all was quiet.

I emerged into the workmen's village and, once again keeping to the shadows between and behind the old ruined dwellings, made my way to where the section of now-restored cottages stood. Finding a gap between two empty dwellings from which to look out at Jack's house, I leaned forward until I could make out the details.

The woman was standing outside and she was cross; that was apparent from the way she was standing. She was staring up and down the track, first this way and then the other, then repeatedly dipping back inside the newer half of the dwelling, from which I could smell a wonderfully savoury smell. She was, I decided, a woman with something tasty suspended in the pot over the fire, and she was impatient for her man to come home and share it. I heard a small child's voice call out querulously, and the woman replied with a few harsh words that stopped the complaint dead.

I couldn't stop watching her.

Then suddenly her face changed and a broad smile of welcome spread across it. Spinning round, retreating even further into the shadow, I saw Jack coming striding into the village.

I slipped deeper back into the space between the two abandoned dwellings. Further, further, for I didn't want to see any more; couldn't bear to witness the moment when the two of them hurried towards each other and their eyes lit up with quiet joy at the happy thought of the evening that was now before them. At the prospect of the night.

I hurried through the wild spaces behind the ancient settlement, wading through hip-high grass, stung by nettles, snagged by long trailing ropes of bramble that seemed determined to hold me back. I blundered out in the open to find myself some way downriver, east of the castle, the quay on the opposite bank now petering away to nothing.

I stopped, irresolute.

Morgan's house was across the water, but unless I was prepared to swim, the only way to get there was to return to the Great Bridge, cross over and cut out across the fields to the sacred well. Such was my state of mind that I seriously considered swimming.

But sense persuaded me. I turned to the right and trudged off towards the bridge.

My profound distress made me vulnerable, however. Not only was I shivering, although the night was not cold, but in addition I was beset by a parade of the sort of devils and demons I thought I'd left behind in fearful childhood. Mysterious rustling sounds in the undergrowth turning into bat-high shrieks that pained the ears. The sounds of waterfowl that became the scathing cackling of witches. Bramble thorns that were the long, thin, horny nails of black creatures out of the fen. And, not one to leave such an opportunity unused, here was Errita, her face full of hatred and malice as she pushed it into mine, her strange yellowish eyes narrowed into slits of glittering gold, her teeth turned to fangs tipped with blood.

I was well aware that she wasn't really there. That the awful image was a product of my own mind and my deep distress. Yet when she started shouting at me – yelling as loud as a thunderclap, *I know! I KNOW!* – I was driven to put my hands over my ears.

Jack was trying to suppress his irritation. She had hold of his arm, and was virtually forcing him to go inside and sit down. 'It's *good*!' she said, more than once. 'Savoury! Tasty!' The words came punching out of her lips as if she was hitting him. 'I saved up the finest ingredients and I made it specially, because I know how hard you work, and for such long hours, and don't you deserve a good meal when you finally come home?'

He looked down into her eager face, gently removing her strong fingers from his arm. He paused for a moment, then said quietly, 'Yes, Leveva, I'm sure it's truly excellent, and you must have spent a lot of time preparing it. But you should not have waited because I'm not staying, I have to go out again.'

Her expression changed, just for an instant, and the anger showed. Then she was smiling again, persuading, desperate to please. 'Just a quick bowlful!' she said. 'Surely there is time for that?'

'No, really, I'm not hungry and—'

'You should *tell* me if you don't want feeding!' she hissed, her mood changing again and this time the fury gained the mastery for a little longer. 'I've worked all day, if you count having to go out early to acquire the best cuts, pushing and shoving a path through those stinking, sheep-like townspeople, and—'

He spoke across her. It was the only way to stop her, and just now he was in a hurry.

'Eat it yourself, Leveva,' he said shortly. 'Even better, give it to Aedne. She's always hungry, she needs it far more than I do.'

Then he turned and strode away.

By the time he had fetched his horse and was at last on the road, evening was drawing on. The road leading south out of the town was overshadowed here and there by trees, heavy with the foliage of high summer. The night felt full of foreboding, and Jack had to fight to keep his over-alert senses from picking up sounds and sights that weren't really there. In a brief moment of weakness he wished he didn't have to do this; that he could turn round, stable his horse, go back home and . . . But home was all wrong now, and he did not know how to put it right.

Besides, he knew he would despise himself if he didn't carry on. It was he who had told Young Henry to follow up on the information Brother Aleric had provided, and in any case Henry answered to him and, like all the others, he was Jack's responsibility.

So what did Henry do? Where did he go? Jack wondered, trying to counteract his increasingly dark suspicions with logic. Brother Aleric told him about this early visitor who seemed to be a friend, or at least someone who was expected and was quickly ushered inside. The monk described him and said he'd come up from Trumpington. So Henry decided that was where he should go to try to find him.

Did he find him? Did he locate the bent old man in the once-fine clothes while he was still alive? Or had he already been slain by the time Henry found him? And why was he killed? To extract vital information from him? Or because Mistress de Lacey had passed some secret on to him and so he had to die, just like her, before he told anyone else?

But what if he had already told someone? What if Young Henry had sought him out, his bright, intelligent face shining like a light in the dimness of that little lean-to, asking the right questions, persuading the old man that it was safe to speak because Henry represented the law? And then did the old man – tired, perhaps, weary of being afraid, of constantly having to worry about his safety – spill this dreadful secret that was worth killing for to the kind-hearted, decent young man who had come asking about it?

Jack had unconsciously increased his pace, and now the horse was cantering, strong legs flying over the miles.

Or did Henry arrive *after* the old man was dead? Did he find the body while the killer was still lurking, still watching? Did Henry challenge him? Try to apprehend him, take him in to face justice?

And did the murderer kill him? He'd already killed two people, would he baulk at another one? Especially if his orders were to make sure this secret was kept at all costs?

'*What was it?*' Jack shouted into the night.

There was no answer.

He tethered his horse by the water trough beside the hen enclosure – the fowl had been shut up for the night – and then commenced on a slow, steady and thorough search of the land in the vicinity of the lean-to behind the inn. But it became clear nobody had hidden a corpse out there; sheep had grazed the field, and the short grass would have revealed a disturbance in the earth. The undergrowth that bordered it was marked with animal tracks diving into it, none wide enough to allow the passage of a man carrying a body. Jack returned to the lean-to, untethered his horse and led him back to the road. He stood looking up and down for a few moments, but there was no obvious place to hide a body in the village.

He mounted up and, trying to look on both sides at once, set off down the road in the other direction from the town. If *he* had been going to hide a body, he reasoned, he'd have headed away from the largest settlement in the area and not towards it.

But it was a faint hope, and one he found himself praying would remain unfulfilled. Young Henry was safe, he told himself, he'd gone haring off on the trail of some wonderful fact or supposition that he believed would reveal who killed Mistress de Lacey, and he'd probably never been anywhere near Trumpington and the old man found dead in the lean-to. Jack was just working out the precise words he would use to

issue the reprimand about not going off on your own and
always telling a superior officer – asking a superior officer
– before you act, when he saw the vixen.

The sight in itself was not unexpected on a warm summer
night. But her behaviour was, because instead of darting under
cover the moment she sensed Jack approaching, she stayed
where she was, her muzzle down, her shining eyes on Jack
and his horse, for several long moments. Then she twisted her
lithe body away and disappeared.

Jack slowed his horse until they were barely moving. Then
he jumped down and approached the dark object lying on the
far side of the ditch beneath the hazel bush.

The fox had not long discovered her meal, and the body
was barely touched. She had been lapping – with revulsion,
Jack pictured that busy pink tongue – and perhaps she liked
to consume the blood before going on to the flesh.

There was a lot of blood.

The blow had been to the back of the head. The skull was
crushed, the skin of the scalp mixed with the shattered bones.
He couldn't have seen the weapon coming. He'd have been
dead before he understood what was happening.

There was a small relief in that.

Jack knelt down beside the still figure, talking softly,
explaining what he was doing, his movements slow and steady,
his hands gentle.

'I'm going to wrap your poor head and cover your face,'
he said, 'look, I'll use your neckerchief. I've got my horse
there on the road, and you and I will ride back together. I'll
put you in front of me, astride like I am, and don't worry, I
won't let you fall. We'll get you back to the castle, and you'll
be cared for there.'

He was working as he talked, and now he was in the saddle,
the body before him, his arms around the chest and the torso
leaning back against him. It was like an embrace.

Which was fitting, because Jack had cared deeply for Young
Henry.

After a mile or so, Jack realized he'd been weeping.

He let the emotion run its course. He thought back to the

years he and Henry had worked together. He remembered how right from the start the lad had been eager, bright, quick to learn, and never anything but an asset.

And now he's dead, Jack thought.

Now he has interrupted the plans of some cruel, ruthless killer, and his life has been crushed out of him as if he was a fly on a wall.

Jack turned his face up to the dark sky and the stars.

Then, lowering his eyes to the road ribboning out in front of them, he said quietly, 'You are out there, whoever you are. You may be long gone. It may well be that you believe your secret is safe now. You have killed the three people who knew, or perhaps only suspected, what it was and why it was so vital.'

He paused, briefly dropping his head so that his cheek rested on the top of Henry's head.

'But you're wrong,' he continued. 'I do not know your secret yet, but I will. And when I do I shall make sure you *know* that I know, and when you come back to silence me too, I'll be waiting and I shall kill you.'

TWELVE

I dreamed vividly again.

I woke from images of darkness, fear and pain to warm sunshine, and for some moments simply lay letting my mind and my body adjust to the realization that I was safe; there was no immediate threat; it had been no more than a dream.

But it had been so very real.

Errita and I had faced each other and at the precise same moment we had both held up our right hands and pointed them straight at the other as if they held invisible weapons; as if, rather, the limbs themselves had been the weapons. And as if that concept had somehow travelled from my sleeping brain to the actions I was seeing, all at once the extended fingers of my outstretched hand seemed to turn into a long, narrow blade that glittered bright silver in the fleeting beams of moonlight. Then it seemed that she too had a blade, and that our two knives, or swords – I was not sure what they were, for they looked like nothing I'd ever seen before – were clashing and scraping against each other, sending wide arcs of brilliant, pale blue sparks flying up into the night.

It occurred to me as I lay there in the soft morning sun that the dream was a representation of a scene that had regularly taken place between Errita and me in life. Time after time she would challenge me, make it plain by word or action that she considered me an upstart, a usurper, a newcomer with an inflated opinion of herself, self-important because she had the favour of those great figures of power held in reverence in the settlement under the mountains and, perhaps more crucially, in the City of Pearl.

Figures such as Luliwa.

Her own mother.

To begin with I tried to deflect her hostility with a show of humility and even, at the start, understanding. But I learned very quickly that whenever I showed any sign of what she perceived as weakness, she attacked like a snake and I often got hurt. Thus I was able to salve my conscience and tell myself that when I met like with like, when I hit back as hard as she was hitting me, it was permissible because I was acting in self-defence.

I believe I knew all along that I held the stronger weapons; that I could crush her if I chose. But I sensed that the people among whom I lived, and whose good opinion I valued, would count it against me if I met Errita's increasingly cruel and cunning attacks with more violence than necessary. Besides, I knew that to do so was morally wrong.

I did not share with anyone – not friend or work colleague, not mentor or teacher – the unwelcome suspicion that had gradually been growing deep in my heart.

I had tried not to think about it myself.

But this morning I could not shut it out.

Get up, I commanded myself now. Get up and help someone.

My own instructions were joined by those of another, and I heard a stern voice in my head: *If you can't do anything but sit there feeling sorry for yourself, then go and do something for somebody else.* It was a standard saying of my mother's, and I sent her a silent word of thanks for the reminder.

With a briskness my mother would have grudgingly acknowledged, I set about my morning tasks, and only when both I and the little house were clean and tidy did I sit down on my folded bedding to eat a heel of stale bread softened and sweetened with a precious few fragments of honeycomb. Then I rinsed my fingers, picked up my satchel and went out into the sunshine.

I did not have to look far for people for whom I could usefully do something, because I knew of a houseful of them down on the quay. As I strode along towards the refuge, the river busy with early morning traffic down on my left, mentally I went through the contents of my satchel, assigning this or that remedy to a particular ailment. I would have to replenish some of my stores soon, and see if I could contrive some sort of workroom at Morgan's house so that I could replace the items I was fast using up. He'd had his own workroom, of course, although I'd checked in there and found little of use to a healer. Another idea occurred to me, but I was not ready to think about it and so put it away to the back of my mind.

Fritha greeted me with her usual laconic nod and jerked her head towards a room at the far end of the central passage. 'There's three cases of loose stools down there you might treat,' she said, and I increased my pace and hurried along to the source of the wailing babies and the stench.

My usual remedy was an oat-based medicine mixed with small amounts of herb bennet, blackberry and one or two largely experimental ingredients of my own, and when it was to be administered to babies and infants, I added honey for both sweetness and because it always seems to increase the efficacy of the other elements. I helped the three mothers dose their children – two boys and a girl – and then, when the patients were more comfortable and the crying had eased off, we all worked together to clean up the mess.

We were just finishing, and I was washing my hands and packing my satchel, when I heard raised voices from the doorway: someone – a man – was in great distress, and Fritha was barking out what seemed to be her idea of comforting remarks.

I hurried along the passage and saw, beyond Fritha's solid shape, Brother Aleric. His hands were clasped to his chest and his face was wrung with dismay. 'I cannot believe it is true!' he was saying.

'If that big lawman says it is, then I reckon you must,' Fritha said bluntly. Then, putting a surprisingly gentle hand on his arm and leaning close, she added very quietly, 'Look, I can see you're upset, brother, but I can't have you coming in and frightening my women with your tales of violence and your keening. It won't help them and I don't think it'll help you either.'

The big lawman. Jack.

Dear Lord, what had happened now?

I slung my satchel over my shoulder and said firmly, 'Come with me, Brother Aleric. We'll walk beside the water and find a quiet place to sit down.'

He'd clearly had a shock, and probably wanted more than

anything to share it with others and thus diminish its force. He had perhaps hoped for a larger audience, but he'd have to make do with me.

He came with me readily enough, and presently we were out beyond the last of the increasingly tumbledown old ruins at the far end of the quay, where the river ran on between fields and woodland. I pointed to a patch of grass in the full sun, and we sat down.

After a moment he said, 'You have come back and you've been treating the women?'

'I have.'

He didn't ask for any details, so I didn't provide any.

He did not speak for some time, so I prompted him. 'Fritha referred to violence?'

He turned his ravaged face towards me.

'Yes, yes, she did, for I had just told her the terrible news! He's dead, that poor, eager young man, hit over the head and his body rolled into a ditch.'

It could not be Jack, I told myself very firmly, because Fritha said *that big lawman* had been the one to say this death had really happened.

Eager young man . . . And known to Brother Aleric.

'Young Henry,' I whispered.

Brother Aleric had buried his face in his hands, but now he removed them and his red-rimmed eyes shot to mine. 'You knew him?'

'I did. I met him years ago, when he was first demonstrating the fine qualities that made him a good lawman.'

'Intelligence, compassion, enthusiasm, an aptitude for hard work,' Brother Aleric murmured.

'All of those,' I agreed. After a moment, I said gently, 'What happened? Are you able to tell me what you know?'

His face creased in distress. 'I can, and indeed I shall have to answer to a higher power, for I greatly fear his death is my fault.'

'Did you wield the weapon that killed him?' I asked softly.

He looked horrified. 'Of course I didn't!'

'Perhaps that is something you should keep telling yourself,' I said.

'But I told him about the old man who went calling so early at Mistress de Lacey's house!' he wailed. 'The man who I thought must be a friend, for her to admit him so readily!' He paused, gnawing at a knuckle pressed to his mouth. 'I told Henry I'd seen the man on the track up ahead of me, and that he'd crossed over the fields to the riverside path from the road that leads out to Trumpington. Don't you *see*' – he hurled the word at me as if he would hit me with it for my lack of perception – 'I told him where to look for the old man! *I sent him to his death! I*—'

'Enough,' I said very firmly. 'You help neither yourself nor Henry with this undermining remorse. Have you spoken to the lawman, told him what you know of Henry's likely movements?'

'Yes, yes, I have,' Brother Aleric said, sounding slightly calmer. 'He came to seek me out this morning – just now!' he exclaimed, eyes wide in amazement. 'And when he'd gone I came straight to the refuge . . . I can't believe it was such a short time ago!'

It is the way with shock and grief, I have often noticed, that time is distorted.

'What did he say?' I asked.

Brother Aleric screwed up his face as he remembered. 'He sought me out at the refuge late yesterday concerning the old man who visited Mistress de Lacey, and I said I'd told Henry about him, and he said the old man's body had been found' – *I know*, I might have said, *I overheard the conversation* – 'but he was worried because nobody seemed to have seen or heard of Young Henry for some time. He told me this morning that he rode back out to Trumpington to look for him – Henry – and he – he found him, dead, and he carried him back, and – and—' But he could not go on.

Oh, Jack, I thought, my heart clenching with pain for him.

Brother Aleric was weeping and sniffing beside me, and I tried to feel compassion for his distress. But I was thinking, *You barely knew him, whereas Jack worked with him, taught him, brought him on, encouraged him and helped him develop his natural ability, and now all that promise is gone. And Jack found Henry's body and bore him home.*

I didn't imagine Jack was sitting in the sun on the riverbank weeping.

I waited until I knew I would be able to speak without my emotion showing, then said, 'Brother Aleric, it will avail neither Henry nor you to sit here being sad.' Recalling my mother's voice of earlier that morning, I added, 'It will undoubtedly help you to feel better to do something for someone else, so—'

But he was already up and on his feet before I'd finished. 'Yes, yes, you're right,' he mumbled. He shot me an embarrassed look, and I thought he was probably already feeling ashamed of having allowed his sorrow to overcome him.

He was obviously desperate to be gone, but I said, 'It was the shock, brother. That's all.'

And as he hurried away, he sent me a grateful smile.

I waited until he was out of sight among the buildings along the quayside. I didn't know where he was going and I didn't really care.

He wasn't the only one grieving. As I'd told him, I knew Henry, and I was only then beginning to face the truth: I was never going to see him again.

I considered following my own – my mother's – advice and returning to the refuge to help out where I could. I considered going into the town and finding an apothecary's shop, where I could purchase fresh supplies and take them away to work up into remedies.

And that thought led straight back to the idea that had occurred to me earlier, when I'd been thinking where I might find a place to work.

It had greatly appealed then, and that was before I knew about Young Henry.

Its pull now was far, far stronger.

Even as I hesitated telling myself I was still making up my mind, I was already starting to walk. Slowly, reluctantly at first, then more quickly until, as I climbed up onto the road by the Great Bridge and turned towards the marketplace, I was all but running.

The place I was bound had one of the finest workrooms I knew. I had spent long hours, days, weeks there, learning,

experimenting, making mistakes, correcting where I'd gone
wrong and trying again.

I had longed to return there since I'd first got back to
Cambridge, and for very good reasons, I'd managed to resist.
But I had been fatally weakened by this morning's terrible
news.

The fierce woman who believed herself to be so strong that
she could withstand every onslaught had endured the discovery
of two brutally murdered bodies and the news that her adored
grandfather and her beloved aunt were dead, and managed to
stand up again and walk on.

But she – I – couldn't deal alone with Young Henry's death
and the image of Jack bearing his body home.

And so I made my way through the maze to the twisty-turny
house, climbed the steps and knocked on Gurdyman's door.

It opened with the creak and the grumble it had always had.

He stood there, bright blue eyes looking into mine, an
expression on his face that I couldn't read.

It was six years since I'd said farewell to him on the shore
below the settlement. Since, still unreconciled to what he had
put me through, I had watched as strong arms helped him
aboard *Malice-striker* and they'd sailed for home. He had aged
in those years – of course he had – but I knew even in that
first glance that this wasn't the reason he looked so different.

It was because his power had waned.

He had passed it on to me – willingly, he'd known he must
– and now as I stood before him I saw the result.

The shell was still much the same – a little more bent,
perhaps, a little more rotund, the smooth pink skin of that
lively face creased with new wrinkles – but his essence was
. . . diminished, was the only word that would do.

He was studying me as closely as I was him. After a time,
he opened the door more widely, stood back and said, 'Why
not come in?'

He preceded me along the passage to the sunny courtyard,
indicating the bench. I sat down, and he sank into his chair.

Presently he said, 'I am forgetting my manners,' and, leaning
sideways over to the little table next to his chair, he poured

out a mug of what proved to be cordial flavoured with lime and ginger.

'Thank you,' I said.

He was staring intently at me. 'Have you seen Jack?' he asked.

Instantly, not pausing to think, I said sharply, 'I do not wish to speak of or think about Jack.'

He went on studying me. 'It's strange, although I believe only to be expected,' he said presently, 'but I cannot look into your thoughts the way that once I could.' He smiled at me sadly. 'Oh, not for a long time,' he hurried on when I did not comment, 'and I had all but lost the ability by the time you and I said our goodbye on the shore beneath the settlement.'

'I rather hope you would have stopped trying by then,' I said coolly.

His smile widened. 'Oh, you are right, of course, and I ought to have done, but it was a habit I did not seem to be able to give up.'

A memory surfaced from our life together. 'You came up against my resistance when first I began to look into the shining stone,' I said softly, 'and you and my grandfather were determined to use my fledgling, new-born skills for your own ends and discovered you couldn't.'

He chuckled briefly. 'So we did!' he remarked. Then his face straightened. 'I am sorry that Thorfinn is dead, Lassair,' he said. 'I am right, am I not, in thinking that you do know?'

I nodded.

'And your aunt Edild . . .' he began, with an uncharacteristically enquiring and, I thought, slightly apprehensive look.

'I know about that, too.'

He shook his head sadly. 'Those were grievous blows to come home to, and I am very sad for you.' He paused, as if out of respect for the loss of two loved people, then said, 'In the case of your grandfather, I ventured out to Aelf Fen to attend his burial beside your grandmother on the little island. It was a fine occasion, child, and although there were many who grieved to see him go, all were in accord that his had been a long life well lived.'

I nodded. 'Thank you,' I whispered.

He sighed. 'The same comment concerning longevity cannot be said of your poor aunt, however.'

I sensed him watching me and looked up to see his bright eyes intent. 'She died in childbirth, Hrype told me.'

'Ah, so you have spoken to Hrype,' Gurdyman said. 'Yes, indeed she did, and let me assure you, as I am sure he did, that you could not have saved her.'

I nodded again, finding no words to say.

There was quite a long silence. Gurdyman broke it by remarking, 'I was all but sure you had come back, you know.'

'You were?' I was not sure I believed him. 'How could you know?' I recalled the moment when I'd stood in the alley outside his house and he'd walked straight past me without noticing my presence; remembered how proud I'd been that I could now hide from him. Had I been wrong? 'I didn't think you—' I began.

'Oh, you're quite right, I didn't see you. Please note, child, that I said *all but sure* and not *sure*.'

So he had.

'Well, then?'

He was smiling again. 'You used to have a habit, at the end of a long day when I had driven you hard and we had worked without rest, of coming silently to stand behind me and easing the pain that always stabs beneath my shoulder blade.'

I remembered. 'You – you felt my touch?'

'I believed so, yes. I told myself it was probably nothing more than my deep wish that you *had* returned.'

I thought about that. 'Why did you wish it so much?'

He studied me, his face grave. 'Think, child.'

But I didn't need to think; I already knew. 'You want to leave,' I said. 'You want to return to Spain, to the City of Pearl, where Salim and your old friends are waiting for you, because you have always known that only there will the circle of your life reach its close.'

'Yes,' he breathed. 'I have been very happy here in this town, and my life's work has been as fulfilling as any man could wish. But since I passed so much of my strength to you, child' – he said it without the least resentment, simply stating the fact – 'I have felt the cold far more intensely, and the prospect of yet another fenland winter dismays me.'

'You will go so soon? Before the sailings to the south begin to die down?' Oh, but that did not give us very long, for we were almost in August now and after August came September, and the autumn.

'I will,' he said softly.

I held his eyes. 'And Hrype will go with you.'

'He told you?' Gurdyman looked faintly surprised.

'He didn't need to.'

Gurdyman nodded slowly. 'Of course not,' he murmured. He stared at me, then his eyes glanced away. 'You are grown strong, Lassair,' he said. 'I do not believe that there is much Hrype could hide from you now. Or I, come to that.'

'I will not try to look into your thoughts,' I said quickly. He was still Gurdyman, still the mentor and the guide through the darkness, and I respected him far too much even to attempt such an intrusion.

He inclined his head. 'Thank you.'

After some moments, he said, 'She is close now.'

'Hrype could see her too.' I recalled how he had said he could see the dark shadow I'd brought back with me.

'She is full of malice towards you,' Gurdyman went on. 'As I am quite sure you are well aware.'

'I am,' I said shortly. Then, for in our changed relationship I no longer felt I must follow his lead, I said, 'There is a matter concerning which I would welcome your help, Gurdyman, if you will give it?'

He spread his hands. 'You have only to ask, child.'

'It concerns the brutal slaying of two people I believe were known to each other, and who possibly shared a secret, and also the murder of the young lawman who thought he had uncovered a valuable clue and did not hesitate to follow it up.'

Gurdyman's head jerked up and he made a small sound. But then, as if bringing himself back under control, he sighed and said, 'You speak of Eleanor de Lacey and Stephen leClerc.'

'Stephen leClerc?' Was that his full name, then? 'Was he a bent old man who dressed in worn-out clothes that were originally very costly and fine? Did he—'

'Stephen leClerc was one of the Conqueror's knights,' Gurdyman interrupted. 'He was, as you surmise, a man of wealth; also of power and influence. His life went awry, though.' He shot me a look out of narrowed eyes. 'He knew what he was doing, however, as I imagine did Mistress de Lacey, for they played a dangerous game and undoubtedly understood the risks.'

'Game? What do you mean?'

'They both agreed to be the eyes and ears for your Rollo Guiscard,' he said very softly.

I nodded slowly. I knew about Mistress de Lacey, of course, and it had hardly been a great leap of the imagination to surmise the bent old man – Stephen leClerc – had also been a part of Rollo's network.

I was about to push for more answers, to demand to know what secret those two dead old people had known that someone else wanted to keep utterly hidden, and I opened my mouth to speak.

But Gurdyman, his face suddenly fallen into grief, said, 'I was aware that Young Henry was missing.' He met my eyes. 'But slain! This is evil news, child.'

'It is,' I whispered.

'We must surely conclude that he was killed by the same hand that felled Mistress de Lacey and Stephen leClerc,' he murmured, half to himself. Then, raising his head, he looked straight at me and said, 'So I suppose I had better tell you what I know.'

THIRTEEN

'If you are expecting a detailed tale of secret plots involving the powerful and the wealthy of the land – and indeed your expression suggests that you are – then I fear you are to be disappointed,' Gurdyman began.

I had been anticipating exactly that, although on reflection, it did not seem very likely that even Gurdyman – inquisitive, interested in everything, sophisticated and very intelligent – would be privy to such intensely private matters. 'What *can* you tell me, then?' I demanded.

'Much of what I conjecture you could work out for yourself, child, as you may very well have done,' he replied. 'You knew perhaps better than anyone that Mistress de Lacey had dealings with your Rollo, and I imagine that by now you have collected whatever it was of his she had in her keeping for you.'

'Is that just a good guess?' I said harshly.

He smiled softly. 'I am sorry to remind you of that which causes you pain.'

'I'm not—' I struggled for the words to explain. 'Gurdyman, it is a long time since Rollo died and my grief has been dulled over the years. Mistress de Lacey's death is a far more recent memory.'

'Of course,' he murmured. When I didn't speak, he went on, 'I knew full well when we were on our travels in Spain that you had gold and coins in your possession – rather a large sum, I believed.'

'But I was always careful to—'

He sighed. 'Child, I never actually saw the money, I merely noticed – and very much appreciated – what you purchased with it.' He smiled at me very kindly. 'That pony and cart was the most welcome gift I have ever received.'

I returned the smile. 'It was for my benefit too, since I wanted us to reach our destination before we both died of old age.'

'I digress,' he said, his expression straightening. 'Such a vast sum of money could only have been given to you – left to you, I should say – by Rollo, and I did not imagine that even a large purse full of gold was the sum total of his bequest. For him to have left what else there might be for you in the keeping of someone who lived in the same town was the obvious choice.' He paused. 'Was there anything other than gold?' he asked very softly.

'Documents. A scroll bearing the King's seal. Notes about the state of affairs in Normandy and in France, comments about the King's brothers.' I frowned, a memory sparking. 'Mistress de Lacey mentioned Normandy too. She said the King had to find a new base across the water now that his brother the Duke was coming home, and that he would probably be looking to Poitou.'

Gurdyman was watching me with such intensity that I could all but feel it like heat on my skin. He said, 'I should very much like to see these documents, Lassair.'

I nodded abstractedly, for I had remembered something else that Rollo had written. 'There was another document that was a list of names, each with a place attached and many accompanied by several other comments and facts.' I met Gurdyman's bright blue eyes. 'Do you think if I went back to have another look I should find the name of Stephen leClerc and a note to say he lives in a lean-to behind the inn by the ford at Trumpington?'

'I should be surprised if you didn't,' Gurdyman murmured.

'You know who he is?' I asked.

'I have just told you,' he replied.

'But what did he—'

'Like many who endured the upheaval of the Conquest and the turmoil that ensued before the first King William took a firm hold on his new realm,' he interrupted, 'Stephen leClerc believed that the worst fate that could befall the land was to have two rival factions fighting for mastery.'

'Did you know him?' I asked when he paused for breath.

'I knew *of* him,' he replied. 'Stephen leClerc was an intensely secretive man. He was ashamed, I believe, that he had fallen so low, and he shunned company. Now where was I?' He shot me a frown. 'Yes. You might think it was easy for him to back the Conqueror wholeheartedly, but you ought to know that Stephen's heritage on his mother's side was Saxon, and the establishment of the new King's dominance was not without considerable sacrifice for him, as for so many others. Nevertheless, he chose a side and he stayed loyal to his King, as indeed he continued to do to William's son. He believed—'

Suddenly I'd had enough of this lecture on an old man's philosophy, his regrets, his beliefs; enough of these tentative remarks that hinted at so much and gave away so little. 'You said you're not going to reveal some involved secret plot, but what *are* you going to tell me?' I said angrily. 'That Stephen leClerc was a loyal supporter of the King, like Rollo and like Eleanor de Lacey? Well, they're all dead, Gurdyman, so that really is of very limited use!'

At first he looked shocked and not a little irritated by my outburst. Then he let out a long sigh, sat back in his chair and said, 'Well then, if you prefer it, let us speak of generalities. This matter does concern the powerful and the wealthy of the land, as I said, and what I fear is brewing could not be of greater import to those at the top of the tree.' He shot me a meaningful glance. 'But I cannot tell you precisely what the matter is, merely that I know it is approaching.'

I sat for a moment in stunned silence. 'Is that it?'

He nodded.

Slowly I shook my head as memory sparked realization.

'I know too,' I whispered. 'I have sensed it.' I looked at him.

He was smiling. 'I am not in the least surprised,' he replied. 'What have you seen?'

'*Seen.*' Slowly I echoed the word. 'I am not sure if what I perceived was actually visible, but there was a picture in my mind . . . It was when I crossed over from northern France, just as the coast of England began to fill the horizon. I thought I could see a dense blackness spreading over the land. And it seemed to echo the horror stories I'd been hearing on my journey from travellers from England, of demons and lakes of blood, and the focus for them all seemed to be the King. And then I spent a night in the New Forest, and I had such a dream . . .'

The dream had come to me again.

Two mornings ago I had woken with those same images in my head.

I stared at Gurdyman, my heart beating uncomfortably fast.

He read the question in my eyes. 'I do not know, child,' he said softly. 'I fear—'

But just then there was a loud banging at the door, and a deep voice called out, 'Gurdyman? May I come in?'

Both of us knew who it was.

Gurdyman was already on his feet, and I leapt up too. He grabbed my sleeve, started dragging me along the passage.

'I *told* you, *I can't see him!*' I hissed, frantically trying to prise off his fingers.

'*I know!*' he hissed back. 'I'm making sure you don't!'

We were at the far end of the passage now and the door to the alley was just in front of us. It vibrated as Jack thumped it again. 'Gurdyman? Are you all right?'

'He worries,' Gurdyman mouthed as he pushed me ahead of him into the corridor leading off to the left and down the first of the steps. 'Go on! *Hurry*, he'll let himself in any moment now!'

We were almost at the entrance to the crypt. There was nowhere to hide down there – I knew, I was familiar with every inch of it.

But still Gurdyman pushed me on.

We were on the steps that gave on to the crypt and the darkness was all but total. Gurdyman pushed in front of me and there was a sudden brief light, dim, flickering . . .

. . . and I was back in that exact same place seven years ago. The town had been under the terrifying power of a monster that killed under cover of night,[5] and I had been extremely worried for Gurdyman's safety. I had raced to his house to find him, and I'd come flying down the steps to the crypt. It had been in total darkness except for a brief dim flicker of light. In that instant of illumination I'd been sure I'd seen Gurdyman and Hrype, and possibly someone else as well,

---

[5] See *The Night Wanderer*.

down in the crypt, but only a matter of moments later when Jack had come to join me bearing a flaming torch, nobody was there. And later Gurdyman had reminded me that his old twisty-turny house held many secrets.

Now Gurdyman seemed to have vanished, but then he was back beside me, grabbing my hand and pulling me with him, across the flagstones, shoving me down, down until I was almost lying on the floor, and then he was pushing me, muttering terse instructions: 'Bend your body upwards, you have to *bend*, because the aperture is narrow!'

And I was so frightened, and for a horrible instant I was back in the tiny tunnels under the mountains of the south, but then I understood, this was not the same, it was a much larger opening, once I understood its construction, and my logical mind said scathingly, *Of course it's a decent-sized space! How do you think Gurdyman could contrive to negotiate it otherwise?*

Then I knew I was alone, scrambling on hands and knees up a very narrow, steep flight of stone steps which twisted round in a tight spiral. It was not quite so dark now, for a little light was permeating from above.

Dimly I was aware of voices, and guessed that Gurdyman had hurried back up the steps to admit Jack.

But I scarcely heard.

I had lived in this strange old house for years. It had been as much my home as anywhere. I loved every stone of it, and I'd thought I knew at least some of its secrets.

My head emerged into the large space that opened up at the top of the steps. The rest of me followed – I noticed that my legs were shaking – and I stood looking at what had just been revealed.

It was a room that was probably at least as large as the ground-floor spaces of the house that I was already familiar with. There was a heavy wooden shutter on the window over to my right, set at about my shoulder height in the wall. I worked out after quite an effort that this was the side of the house facing the tiny passage to the rear and not the broader one by which everyone approached the house.

I walked over to it.

The floor was of stone, beautifully crafted, smooth. The room, as far as I could see, was totally empty.

I noticed there was a narrow stone step set beneath the window. Jumping up on to it, I put my hands up to the shutter. It opened outwards. It was hinged at the top and fastened by means of a heavy wooden bar placed across it, slotted into three iron hoops fastened to the shutter and two more let into the stone walls on either side. I tried the bar, and it shifted readily. Very carefully, not making a sound, I placed it on the floor.

Slowly I pushed open the shutter, just a finger's breadth at first, and peered out.

As I'd thought, I was looking down into the passage behind the house, from a level above and to the side of the open court. I opened the shutter a little more – there was nobody about, and indeed the passage was so narrow that it could barely have been used other than by prowling cats – and leaned out. I could see the high wall of Gurdyman's inner courtyard over on my left. It would be relatively easy to clamber out through the aperture and let myself down onto the top of the wall, from where it was not too high a jump to the ground.

I could either wait up there until Gurdyman called out to tell me Jack had gone. Or I could use this surprising new exit, hoping that Gurdyman would understand and not mind that I'd left the shutter unfastened.

I gathered up my skirts, hitched my satchel out of the way and went out through the gap at the base of the shutter. My flailing feet discovered a little ledge at just the right height, and I paused, leaning back to let the shutter close. Then, swiftly before my courage could desert me, I edged across onto the top of the wall, paused briefly to gather myself and jumped down.

I edged along the passage, which wasn't as restricting as it looked, and soon found myself standing under a low arch, about to step out into one of the intertwining alleys behind Gurdyman's house. I looked back the way I had just come, but there was no sign of the courtyard wall or the shutter.

The secret room was *very* well hidden . . .

I wondered why it had been closed off.

I could see that Gurdyman had no use for it. He lived almost exclusively in the crypt, or he had done when he was still in possession of his full power, with only infrequent excursions upstairs to eat and breathe in the good fresh air. Was it simply that he'd shut it away and forgotten about it other than as an escape route?

I pictured the big, empty space with its one high window, placed just right to let in the bright sunshine. It reminded me of something . . .

I had it.

The room was very like a big treatment ward in the City of Pearl to which my doctor friend Fahim had taken me. We had spent quite a lot of time there, in fact, as he had been instructing me in the care of patients confined to their beds for days, or even weeks, at a time. The ward where we had worked had more windows, and even a little balcony with an iron rail where convalescents could enjoy the morning sun, but it had shared the same high-ceilinged sense of space.

A treatment ward . . .

The thought lodged somewhere in my mind.

Then I stepped out into the alley.

'You seem flustered, Gurdyman,' Jack said. 'Are you all right?'

'Yes!' Gurdyman replied brightly. 'I was engaged upon a task down in the crypt, and only latterly became aware of the knocking. Come' – he led the way along to the courtyard – 'sit down.'

Jack sank down onto the bench. Gurdyman moved between him and the little table beside his chair, but not quickly enough: Jack saw a jug and two mugs on a tray, one mug empty and one half-full.

'I will fetch a clean mug,' Gurdyman murmured. As he slipped inside, Jack noticed that the old man had the empty mug in his hand.

And he wondered why he should think it was significant . . .

'I heard about Young Henry,' Gurdyman said as he handed Jack a full mug.

Jack took a deep draught. 'In the marketplace, I suppose,' he said.

'It is appalling news,' Gurdyman murmured. 'That poor young man, so full of promise.'

'He was investigating Stephen leClerc's murder,' Jack said. 'Did you know him?'

'He was a recluse,' Gurdyman replied.

'And an agent of Rollo Guiscard, like Mistress de Lacey,' Jack said.

Gurdyman met his eyes. 'Really?'

'Really,' Jack echoed tonelessly. Then, impatiently, 'Gurdyman, there are dark depths here. I have an idea that these people, these agents of someone known to be a King's man – a King's spy – knew something, uncovered some secret, and they recognized it as their duty to pass this information on. It seems that it was Stephen leClerc, living as he did behind an inn by a fording place of the river, who was the more likely to have overheard some whispered comment as two exhausted travellers refreshed themselves over food and ale. Let us say that what he heard worried him, and so he went very early one morning to Mistress de Lacey, who was perhaps the next link in the chain of people like them. But someone else was determined that this secret matter should not be spoken of, and this man took the steps he deemed necessary to make sure it wasn't.'

'But I believe you told me that some efforts were made to try to force Mistress de Lacey to reveal information?' Gurdyman said. 'How does that tally with a killer who simply wanted to keep a secret?'

'I don't *know*,' Jack said. Then, his expression hardening, he added quietly, 'What matters most to me is that this man believed the secret was worth killing for, and as well as murdering the two people who really did possess it, he also slaughtered a young man who didn't but who simply got in the way.'

'Young Henry,' Gurdyman murmured.

'I intend to find this killer.' Jack's voice was unemotional. 'To do so I need to uncover this secret, or, rather, to make it very apparent that this is what I am attempting. I hope that the killer is watching, and notices what I'm doing and why. I hope that my actions deeply alarm him, so that he swiftly comes searching for me to silence me as he did my young lawman. When he finds me I shall be ready.'

'You plan to use yourself as bait,' Gurdyman murmured.

'I do,' Jack replied shortly.

He looked at Gurdyman, sensing the old man was weighing up whether or not to say something. 'What?' he demanded.

Gurdyman was staring at him. 'Oh . . . nothing,' he muttered, looking away, and there was something in his manner that suggested there was no point in trying to persuade him.

After a short silence, Jack said, 'I've been having alarming dreams.'

'You too!' Gurdyman exclaimed.

'Who else do you know who's been dreaming vividly?' Jack said quickly.

But Gurdyman smiled and said easily, 'Oh, almost everyone I speak to. Such is the nature of these wild times, Jack, when the talk is of frightening portents and rumours are circulating that tell of unease and strife in high places.' He paused. 'Are your dreams always similar in content?'

Jack stared at him steadily. 'My dreams, Gurdyman, feature a dark-clad, slim figure who hides and spies on me. From this person I feel such a sense of malevolence that when I wake I'm sweating and full of dread.' He waited, but Gurdyman made no comment. 'I do not fear a foe I can face up to and fight, for I trust the strength of my own body and I know I do not hold back in defence of myself or of those I love. But this—' He stopped, at a loss as to how to go on.

'Are you able to identify this figure?' Gurdyman ventured.

Jack raised an eyebrow. 'Why do you ask? Do you suspect that you know who it is?'

Gurdyman watched him. 'I am . . . not sure,' he replied cautiously.

'Not sure or do not want to put the suspicion into words?' Jack countered.

Gurdyman held his silence.

Jack stood up, placing his empty mug on the little table.

'Thank you,' he said. 'That was welcome on a hot day.' Turning, he headed off along the passage towards the door.

He heard Gurdyman coming after him and stopped. He waited.

'It sounds to me as if these dreams are a warning, Jack,' he said quietly.

'You think I'm in danger?' Jack said, not turning round.

'I do.'

'Yet you will not be more specific, even though telling me what you know, or suspect, might help me protect myself?'

There was a long pause. Then Gurdyman said in a whisper, 'I cannot. But please, Jack,' he added urgently, 'be on your guard!'

Jack threw open the door. 'I usually am,' he replied.

FOURTEEN

Jack cut through the alleyways on the west side of the market square, hurried over the road that bordered the town and struck out across the fields towards the river.

Eleanor de Lacey's house was already taking on the look of an abandoned dwelling. Grass was growing up between the front wall and the path, and several aggressive shoots of bramble were pushing their way across the walls, bright green veins on the pale daub. The door was locked, but Jack had the key.

He let himself in, shutting and bolting the door behind him. The stillness of the house closed around him, and for a moment he stood listening to the utter silence. He knew full well what had happened here such a brief time ago. He'd seen the body, smelt the metallic slaughterhouse stench. But already it seemed that Mistress de Lacey's presence was reasserting itself, for although there was dust on the surfaces and the formerly well-tended rooms still showed too many signs of the ransacking that had been carried out, the overriding smell was of rosemary.

And, as Jack had already noted, the house was peaceful.

Mistress de Lacey's body had been buried and the presiding priest at St Bene't's had said prayers for her soul. But that had happened elsewhere, in the church and the burial ground, and not in this place that the dead woman had made so very much her own. Obeying an order that seemed to emanate from somewhere within himself, Jack got down on his knees and said his own prayer for her.

He knelt on the hard flagstones until the pain in his knees told him to get up. He was sure it was only his imagination, but as he stood up again he sensed a small movement of air beside him and for an instant the smell of rosemary intensified. 'Go well, my lady,' he whispered to her.

Then he stepped back into his official self and began his search of the house.

* * *

His men had done a good job, and he did not uncover anything that they hadn't already found and told him about. Mistress de Lacey had lived well but simply, and before whoever killed her had wrought such damage in her house, everything there had been beautiful and of good quality, lovingly cared for. It pained him to witness the destruction.

He left the scullery till last.

Over in the corner was the moveable panel that hid the secret hiding place, and straight away Jack saw the scratches on the flagged floor that Cal had mentioned, where a tiny pebble or a piece of grit had lodged beneath the panel and dug into the stone. Bending down, he looked at it closely, mentally agreeing with Cal's suggestion that it had been made recently. 'Very recently, I'd say,' he said softly aloud, 'for the mistress of the house took care of every detail and would not have left this scratch here to mar the smoothness of her floor.'

He opened the panel and put his head inside the aperture it concealed. There, as Cal had described, was the clear rectangle marked out in the dust on the floor. Something had stood there, and it had been undisturbed for a long time. Mistress de Lacey's care of her domain hadn't extended to the inside of secret hiding places, Jack reflected; perhaps she had put the object away and then told herself to forget about it?

Until someone had come for it . . .

Out of memory came something Gurdyman had said, when Jack visited him the evening after Mistress de Lacey's body had been found. They had spoken of the object removed from the secret hiding place and Jack had surmised it had been taken by the killer. Then Gurdyman had commented enigmatically that there was another possibility, but Jack had been weary and in no mood to sit there satisfying the old man's whimsy by trying to guess what he might mean.

Now he thought he knew.

If Mistress de Lacey had been looking after the object – the chest, the box, whatever it was – for someone else, perhaps Gurdyman was suggesting it was this other person who had come for it? Eleanor de Lacey had been in the pay of Rollo Guiscard, so had the box belonged to him?

He was one person who quite definitely could not have come to collect it. He was dead, and Jack had stood in the place where his funeral pyre had been. He had interred the tiny fragments of his bones.

But if Rollo had bequeathed his chest to someone else, told that someone else where to find it and to go and claim it when the time was right . . .

That thought was dangerous, for it led straight to hopes and dreams that Jack worked hard to keep right out of his mind.

Slowly he wandered back into the room overlooking the river, sitting down on the seat beneath the window.

He fought briefly with himself, for the dying of hope was a process that was still going on, still causing the same pain after six long years, and he did not give in to the temptation to revive it yet again without a fight. But lately the past had been so vivid. He had seen that final scene on the shore many times, remembered the moment when she had leaned towards him and he had bent down to her so that their foreheads touched. She had said she would come home, and he had believed her. It was so little on which to place his hopes, but it was all there was.

Lately, too, there had been other, far less welcome reminders: his recurrent dream of that slim, dark figure that emanated more menace, promised more violence, than a fully armed enemy.

Jack knew quite well who she was, and, for all that neither of them had named her, he had no doubt Gurdyman did too.

Something was happening . . . Whether it was good or bad and would result in grief or joy, Jack had no idea.

He stood up, angry with himself for permitting the self-indulgence. He had a job to do: he must uncover the secret whose possession led to the murders of Mistress de Lacey, Stephen leClerc and, indirectly, Young Henry. He had found nothing in Eleanor de Lacey's house to give any clue as to what it had been. The chest – Rollo Guiscard's chest, it surely must be – had gone. If Gurdyman was right, then it might well be that it was in hands other than the killer's.

Filled with purpose, Jack strode out of the house, locked the door and tucked away the key. The fact that finding the chest might also lead to other discoveries of a very different nature was something he buried as deep as his mind and his memories would let him.

I remembered as I set off back to Morgan's house that one of my reasons for going to see Gurdyman at last was to ask if I might use his workroom to prepare some much-needed replenishments for the potions and remedies I always keep in my satchel. I did not dare return now, though, having no idea why Jack had gone to the house or how long he was likely to stay. *Tomorrow*, I thought; *I'll go tomorrow.*

I could always go back in the way I'd just left, I reflected with a smile, if I was afraid of encountering Jack.

He worries, Gurdyman had said. About Gurdyman, obviously.

Had Jack noticed too how diminished the old man was? Jack knew how and why that diminution had come about, and in his direct way he had probably opted not to judge, merely to do what was necessary to help and support.

Jack knew a lot of things, I thought as I trudged along. I'd thought of his nature as being all of a piece, but in the south, I'd learned differently. Luliwa and her son Itzal had observed him, and when I'd said to Itzal that Jack didn't have the sort of power that Hrype had, that my grandfather Thorfinn had, that Itzal had and that he and his mother were bringing out in me, his answer had come as a great surprise.

You are blinded by other emotions you feel for him, Itzal said. *When you look with clear eyes you will see it for yourself. You and your big fighting man are not as different as you have been assuming.*

And – oh, yes! – and I had seen it for myself. Hadn't I?

It had happened deep under those mountains that I now knew so well which run along the northern coast of Spain, in a place Luliwa took me to where the walls were painted with vivid images that came alive as I watched them; that moved and danced and parted to let me see through the veil – the membrane – that separates this world from the world of the spirits. As I moved among them I saw familiar figures: my spirit animal Fox; Hrype; Edild; Thorfinn; Granny

Cordeilla; all those I knew – and almost all of them my kin – who carried the power.

We had formed into a circle with many others of our kind, surrounding the still figure of someone – a woman – who was sick, who needed our power in order to heal and be made whole. As I sensed the force begin to stir and form itself, I had looked straight across the circle and seen another figure I had thought I recognized but not at first identified.

And then I had seen in a burst of joy that it was Jack.

I did not think then that he knew the truth about himself, and I wondered if that had changed.

Did he—

But I stopped the thought dead.

I was not ready to think about Jack. I must content myself with being pleased he'd seen the deterioration in Gurdyman and was keeping an eye on him.

I had stopped in one of the alleys off the marketplace as these disturbing thoughts ran through my mind, and now I forced myself to move. If I could not go and work in Gurdyman's crypt today, at least I could make sure I had the ingredients I would need all ready for when I did.

I turned left across the corner of the market and headed for the apothecary's shop.

It was very late, and I was on my way back to Morgan's house.

Earlier I had managed to find most of the ingredients that I required at the apothecary's shop, including in particular supplies of those rare and often costly substances that were not to be obtained locally. Sandalwood, myrrh, ginger; the poppy that gives bliss and deep, deep sleep. Some came from a very long way away, and as I always did I reflected as I held them in my hands on the vast distances they had travelled over land and sea.

I had carried my purchases to Morgan's house, leaving them carefully hidden away until I could take them to Gurdyman's crypt. I had developed the habit of leaving few, if any, signs of my temporary presence in the house. I still firmly believed that the townsfolk avoided it, but it was always possible inquisitive children might dare each other to peer inside.

As well as the items I'd purchased from the apothecary, there were also a number of fresh ingredients I was in need of, and these I could go out and collect myself. I had stuffed my old cloth collecting bag in my satchel, then set out again for the track that leads out into the fens.

The afternoon had passed in the sort of peaceful, quiet contentment I hadn't experienced for a long time. I rejoiced in my own company, putting my many anxieties and griefs to one side and concentrating solely on what I was doing. On finding a safe, dry spot to tread where I would not soak my feet; on discerning the precise place in a plant's abundant foliage to pluck the leaf; on taking care to detach the flower or the fruit or seeds that were in the act of forming.

Sometimes I was aware of a malicious presence, and occasionally it seemed very close. I dismissed it; dismissed *her*. She had invaded my dreams, and we had fought each other in that unreal world just as we had battled in life. But I was not going to let her malevolence spoil these precious moments of serenity.

I had lost track of the time, only realizing darkness was gathering when I noticed how hungry I was.

Now, at last setting out back to Morgan's house, I looked around, trying to work out where I was, and saw with faint surprise that my wandering steps had taken me far over to the west, so that now Cambridge lay almost due south, and two or three miles away. I calculated that I would be approaching the town from the area where the castle and the old workmen's village lay. I slung my sack over my back – it was full, but the contents were light and it would not be any great burden; I had borne far greater ones – and headed for my temporary home.

Jack was exhausted and dispirited. The long hours of the day following his visit to Mistress de Lacey's house had passed in an increasingly frustrating series of checks on all the places in and around the town that could be used as a hiding place by someone not wishing their presence to be known. He had already turned for home when he had remembered the little house beside the sacred well, where an old friend of Gurdyman's had been murdered along with a young assistant. Looking in through a gap in the wall, he had seen an orderly interior and not a sign of habitation.

Now, walking back across the grass, he felt as if his legs had turned to iron and every step was an effort. His extreme fatigue was, he was well aware, due in large part to the constant battle he'd been waging with himself not to think about the person he so much wanted to find.

I am allowing hope to drive out logic, he told himself as he crossed the Great Bridge. *I have put together a series of disconnected facts and vague suspicions and told myself they add up to something meaningful.*

They don't.

He was filled with a longing to be alone. He wanted more than anything to close his door on the night, eat, drink, then lie down and sleep.

It was late. As he walked swiftly along the tunnel-like path beneath the castle, he was hoping very much that there would be no crack of light between the shutters of the lean-to beside his house; that the door would not have been left ajar to allow the aroma of savoury stew to snake out into the night air. He'd told her over and over again not to prepare food for when he came home at night: 'I can never tell how late I'm going to be,' he had said, trying to keep his tone friendly and reasonable, 'and if I want anything when I come in, I'm content with some bread and cheese and I can prepare that for myself.'

'Not good enough for someone who works as hard as you do!' she had countered, bristling with indignation as if about to take to task anyone unwise enough to suggest it was. 'I like cooking, Jack, and I love to see you sit down at my table with a bowl of something tempting and tasty that I have prepared for you!'

He had bitten back the response that she had never seen him do that since he had always been so very careful not to. It was her way, he had been noticing with increasing dismay, to steadily insinuate herself; to create an image of closeness and interdependence. It was an illusion, as far as he was concerned. What worried him was that she clearly believed in the fiction. Either that or she pretended she did, which was perhaps even worse.

He was almost at the far end of the dark passage.

'Please let her be fast asleep,' he muttered.

He emerged into the little village.

And an extraordinary sight met his eyes; so strange, so incomprehensible, that for a few moments he simply stood and stared.

A brilliant blue flame lit the scene.

It was focused on one spot and the intensity of the blue light threw everything else into deep, impenetrably black shadow.

There was a strong smell of smoke, and the great white cloud billowing high up above the fire was lit blue from beneath. Jack had never seen anything like it. And those flames . . . they were powerfully seductive. Jack could not tear his eyes away. His mind – his capacity to think, to reason – seemed to have frozen.

And then he thought: *My house is on fire.*

He hurled himself forward, through the thick haze of smoke, straight towards the fire. He felt its searing, agonizing heat from ten paces away but he kept running.

Then hands were grabbing at him, grasping hold of his arms, his leather jerkin, his thick belt, and he heard people shouting right in his ears, making them hurt.

'*Stop!*' came a man's bellow.

'Jack, you can do *nothing!*' another man said in a voice tight with alarm and anguish.

Jack tried to go on, and for another couple of paces dragged the men behind him.

Then someone else was right behind him and two huge arms were wrapped round his waist. He was lifted off the ground and borne back away from the fire, then dumped on the blessedly cool ground, where his head banged back so hard on the impacted earth that for a moment he was dazed and dizzy. He screwed his eyes shut, and brilliant points of light spun and fizzed behind his eyelids.

When he looked up again he saw Big Gerald bending over him, his face distressed, black smuts on his cheeks and a bright red burn on his forehead.

'Sorry,' he muttered. 'But you'd have died if you'd gone any nearer.'

Jack struggled to sit up, to wrest himself out of the hard grip of the hands still holding him. Turning, he saw Walter crouching beside him.

'Chief, Gerald's right,' he said gently. 'That fire's not natural. Your neighbours are all here watching it, as well as us' – he jerked his head towards Big Gerald, and now Jack could see Luke and Ginger behind him – 'and not a one among us has ever seen anything like it.'

Jack looked beyond him to where a clutch of villagers stood, some of them smoke-blackened like Gerald, all of them looking shocked and frightened, their pale faces taking on a blueish tinge in the light of those extraordinary flames.

Flames . . . Jack could still hear the hungry roar and now, as the horror of it flooded through him, he couldn't think why the people all around were not trying to arrest the fire's progress. With a huge effort, he wrested himself out of Walter's grip.

'We have to put it out before it spreads and we all lose our homes!' he yelled, trying yet again to get up.

'Do you think we haven't tried?' a tall man standing behind Gerald yelled back. He lived in the village and he was a carpenter. People called him Wolf. 'We've thrown bucket after bucket of water at it, and for all the good it did we might have been fanning the flames!'

'But what about—'

'It's not spreading, Jack.'

He didn't understand. It was a fire in a settlement of timber-framed, thatched dwellings, most of them ruined but some of them restored and once more the treasured homes of the people who dwelt there. They ought to be drenching every unburnt roof and every wall facing the fire to halt it when it leapt up into the night sky to find new fuel . . .

But someone had just said something about that.

Walter.

Jack turned to look at him. 'Not spreading?'

'No, chief. That's what's making us all think it's not natural. According to your neighbours, it was the noise of the flames that disturbed them, and when they came out to look they felt the heat and saw that weird blue light. And—' He stopped abruptly, shaking his head, apparently unable to go on.

The tall man at the back shouldered a way through the crush of people. Crouching down beside Jack, he said harshly, 'It's concentrating itself on your lean-to. It's not spread out to the right, which it should have done given the wind direction.' He paused, breathing hard. 'And the last time we could get near enough to see through the smoke, your house wasn't burning either.'

Jack did not believe it.

Roughly he pushed Walter, Gerald and the tall carpenter away and finally managed to stand up.

He moved through the small gathering, impatiently brushing off the hands that tried to detain him.

He walked forward, and as he advanced it seemed that the bright blue flames died down; almost as if whatever force powered them was reacting to Jack's approach.

The smoke was rapidly dissipating. It was once again possible to breathe, even when he was quite close to the dying fire.

He stared up at the lean-to. Looked to the left, at his house, and saw that the tall man had told the truth. The side facing the lean-to – that formed its wall, in fact – was singed and blackened but it still appeared to be intact.

He turned back to the lean-to.

The stout door had burned away, leaving the iron hinges reaching out into empty air. The wooden shutter over the small, high window had fared little better.

He went to stand in the open doorway.

Various objects within were still burning, but now there were only these numerous small fires. With unnatural swiftness, the fierce main blaze had died away to nothing.

In the far corner lay two shapes huddled together.

He stepped carefully across the floor, his heart pounding in dread at what he was going to find.

A heavy blanket covered them. The smoke was still thick in that corner, and he began to cough. Bending down, he touched the blanket. It felt hot, and one corner was smouldering. He seemed to recall its colour had been a pattern of soft shades of blue. Now it was unrelieved black.

Very gently he drew it back.

Leveva lay there, and Aedne was in her arms. In death, the mother's touch was kinder than in life. One of Leveva's arms was curved beneath her child, one hand rested lightly on the dark hair.

He pulled the blanket right off them.

They were unmarked. Their garments were not even scorched, and their flesh was unblemished.

'Reckon it was the smoke got them,' a quiet voice said behind him. Briefly turning, Jack saw Wolf. 'It was terrible, that smoke. It was what drove us away, even more than the heat. Straight away, soon as we breathed it in, we all started to cough and then choke, two of the lads passed out and we realized we'd die if we didn't back off. Sorry,' he added.

Jack replaced the blanket, drawing it right up over the two pale faces, then followed the carpenter out through the door. 'I don't imagine you have any cause to apologize,' he said. 'You tried, and you were forced back by the smoke.' He paused. 'If you're right and the smoke quickly caused unconsciousness, then—'

'Then they'd have been dead well afore the flames came,' the tall man finished for him. 'From the looks of them, I reckon that's about right.'

Jack nodded.

'It's a comfort,' the carpenter murmured.

'Yes,' Jack said.

Side by side they walked back to the small group watching them.

Approaching the town from the north, my most direct route back to Morgan's house was to cut through the workmen's village and take the tunnel-like passage that ran beneath the castle hill. But I made up my mind not to go that way but to take the longer route, passing the castle on its north side and approaching the Great Bridge down the road that led away towards Huntingdon.

Walking through the workmen's village felt like cutting at

my flesh with small, very sharp blades, and I didn't want to put myself through that again.

But then something caught at my attention, sparking a sudden alertness that bordered on fear. I stopped, smelling the air.

And I caught a faint smell of smoke.

It came from over to my left: the direction of the workmen's village below the castle. Looking over that way, I could make out a blueish glow in the darkening sky. Even as I watched, wide-eyed with horror, one or two long tongues of brilliant blue flame snaked up through the glow.

My heart thundered in my chest. Now the fear was there in force, and a part of me wanted to flee for my life. I forced it down.

I recognized those blue flames, for I had seen them before. Then there was no question of avoiding the village and I was running towards it, pelting along the narrow track, my mind filling with horror at what I was going to find.

I burst into the open space in front of the little chapel and was met with a wall of backs, belonging to those who had already been alerted by the sight, smell and sound of the blaze. I tried to wriggle through the knot of people to the front, to see what was happening, but the moment I pushed forward into a gap between two tall and bulky men, the intense heat made me cower away. '*Get back!*' one of the men shouted furiously, turning towards me with a face full of horror.

'But there must be people in those houses!' I yelled back, frantically pushing against him. 'We must save them, we should—'

Anger turned to compassion. 'Won't be anyone left to save, lass,' he muttered, and turned away again.

I was shivering and trembling with shock. With the awful sense that I had just received a mortal blow, and that my mind hadn't yet realized. Hadn't even begun to take in the implications.

Because in the brief glimpse I'd had, I had seen that the brilliant blue flames were soaring up from Jack's house.

There was a sudden commotion. Someone else had arrived – someone big and powerful – and was forging a way through the onlookers like a battering ram. He broke clear and started to sprint towards the fire, and I thought I would tear myself apart as I struggled with those hemming me in so tightly, so desperate was I to run after him. But then the tall villager who had spoken to me and another, equally large man who I belatedly recognized as Big Gerald dashed after him and one of them lifted him right off his feet, bearing him back to relative safety and throwing him on the ground. There was shouting: the man was struggling, trying desperately to get up and dash out to the fire, but the others managed to hold him back.

I crept round the rear of the crowd and risked a glance at the man.

I didn't need to see him to know who he was, for I already knew.

He was in my blood.

It was Jack.

The rush of relief took all the strength out of my knees. On wobbly legs, stumbling and twice falling, I staggered over to the chapel. With my hands against its cool walls for support, I moved back until I reached a spot where I could see out but nobody in the crowd could see me.

In the instant of supreme elation when I saw Jack alive and unharmed, there had been no time for anything else. But now, peering out at the dying fire, realization was coming hard and fast. For I had not been quite right in thinking it was Jack's house that was on fire: in fact it was the lean-to next to it.

I stood with my back against the wall of the chapel, staring at the house and the lean-to, trying to understand. The fire had all but consumed the lean-to, leaving only the sturdy framework and the beams that had supported the roof still standing. Yet Jack's house – right next to it – seemed undamaged.

Of all those gathered there, I was the only one who had seen anything like this before. It had been in the City of Pearl, where a row of low buildings had been set on fire, and the flames, rather than spreading to surrounding structures, had burned all the more greedily on no more than the original source. If Gurdyman had been standing here beside me, he too would have recognized the blue flames. He had been there in the City of Pearl, and in addition he knew of another occasion when they had materialized, although that time he had not seen them for himself but had only the accounts of others to go by: those men and women who had witnessed the terrifying ferocity of the fire that had burned down his parents' inn and killed all within.

The person who had started tonight's fire was neither the woman who had started that blaze nor the man who had fired the row of buildings below the City of Pearl. But I knew who she was, as well as if she had been standing there before me admitting it. That brilliant blue fire was their trademark, and I guessed it was a skill passed down through their family, generation to generation, and that they probably guarded it very strictly; for sure, I had never seen it anywhere else. But Luliwa and her son Itzal could make those bright blue flames that consumed only what they were commanded to consume, and I had every reason to think that Luliwa's daughter Errita could too.

But why had she done it?

Why had she burned the lean-to? Had she not known that there might be people inside, or did she not care? My mind had shied away from thinking about them, but I comforted myself with the thought that, from what I'd seen, the woman and the child only used the lean-to for food preparation and cooking and would sleep in the main part of the house.

Had Errita set the fire out of a desire to hurt Jack, then, and by doing so hurt me?

No. I did not believe she had reasoned in that way.

I forced my mind back, making myself recall why Errita's mother and her brother had made their special blue fire before.

Your child used your trademark blue flames to attract my attention, Gurdyman had said to Luliwa.

And Itzal had replied, *I did not mean there to be victims*, but even as I'd heard him I'd sensed he hadn't really cared if there were or not.

And Luliwa – what had Luliwa said to Gurdyman?

I was so angry and I wanted you to know that I was there and see the power I had, and I started the fire to show you.

Was that it? Was Errita using the precise method that had worked so well for her mother and her brother? Had she broken cover at last, finally decided to make me aware of her presence and done so in a way that only I would understand?

Yes. That was exactly what she'd done.

She had declared war.

I stood very still, absorbing that, while time passed . . .

I came back to myself, with no clear idea of how long I'd been mentally absent.

I was still staring out at the lean-to. The main force of the blaze had died down now, and there remained only a few small residual fires. Then suddenly there was movement out there and I saw Jack stride over to stand in front of the ruined building, the big villager who had shouted at me hurrying behind him.

After a few moments Jack went inside the lean-to, and the villager followed. He crossed to the far corner and crouched down. It was hard to see, but I thought I saw a huddled shape lying there. He made some small movement – perhaps drawing back a cover – and then stayed very still. The villager peered over his shoulder. Then Jack straightened up and the two men came out into the open space before the house. They spoke quietly together, then slowly re-joined the watching group. The villager, in response to a muttered question, shook his head.

So the woman and the child had perished in Errita's fire.

Jack's woman – his wife – and his daughter.

I could not take my eyes off him.

I did not understand, and, intensifying my concentration until it hurt, I sent my awareness out to him.

I stood there in utter stillness for what felt like a very long time.

It had seemed wrong, right from the first moment. I had expected him to hurl himself repeatedly at the burning building. I had been so very afraid he would throw himself inside, even though he knew it would kill him, because he was Jack, and that was what a man like him would do.

He had tried. I'd seen him. But Big Gerald had picked him up bodily and carried him to safety, and he hadn't tried again. Yes, they'd all have told him it was useless, and he must have known the woman and the child were already dead and he'd be giving his life for nothing. But for people he loved Jack would have gone in anyway because he couldn't have stopped himself.

For people he loved . . .

I'd been gazing at the lean-to, but now my eyes shot back to Jack.

He was standing with Walter and Big Gerald, and the other villagers were slowly moving away to their own dwellings, still looking shocked and uncomprehending. One or two were making for the chapel, presumably to give thanks for a miraculous delivery, and I crept deeper into the shadows as they passed close by. Then I moved so I could watch Jack once more.

He was talking to Walter. I could make out the rumble of his voice, although I was too far away to hear the words. He made a remark that caused Walter to smile briefly, and for a moment Jack smiled too. Then he looked across at the lean-to, said something and Walter answered.

They were walking slowly towards me now, and I could hear what they were saying.

'. . . can come and bed down with us if you like, chief,' Walter was saying.

'It's kind of you, Walter, but I'll stay here,' Jack replied. His voice was hoarse from the smoke, as was Walter's, but otherwise he sounded just as he always did.

'Did she have kin?' Walter asked. They had stopped again, only some five paces from where I stood.

'No, only the child,' Jack said. 'Tomorrow I'll see about burial, and—'

'We can do that, chief,' Walter interrupted. 'Luke's cousin and her daughter will take care of them.'

'Thank you, Walter, I'd be grateful,' Jack said. He looked out over the little settlement.

'Reckon you'll find out what happened?' Walter asked. 'How it began and what exactly it was?'

Jack shrugged. 'I'll have to try, but . . .'

He left the sentence unfinished.

Walter turned to leave. 'Night, chief,' he said.

'Goodnight, Walter.'

Walter trotted off up the narrow passage. I went on watching Jack.

Presently he sighed, rubbed a hand over his short hair and then with sudden impatience strode across towards his undamaged house. Briefly he went into the lean-to – perhaps he was checking that the last of the flames really was out – and then, emerging again, he went inside his own house and closed the door.

I leaned against the wall of the little church.

I could hear voices from within, raised in fervent thanks for the villagers' narrow escape. I wanted to cry out in heartfelt gratitude too, but mine had a very different cause.

I'd been wrong. So wrong.

Jack would mourn the woman and her child, for they had been neighbours, living in his lean-to, and he'd probably have known them quite well.

But he was not broken with grief, for he had not been married to the woman, he did not love her and her little girl was not his child.

I *knew* that, as well as I knew my own identity.

I closed my eyes and prayed for the souls of the woman and the child. I was devastated that they had perished, and I was already feeling a powerful stab of guilt because I was certain who had brought about their deaths.

But even through all that, part of me was singing with joy.

FIFTEEN

I slipped into the darkness behind the little chapel and made my way across to the passage leading under the castle, hurrying along it until I emerged onto the road. I trotted over the Great Bridge, my sack bumping up and down on my back, and turned off the road to cross the field to Morgan's house.

For the first time in days I had a clear purpose, and I was filled with new strength. I let myself into the house and quickly gathered together my possessions, bundling them up in the wool blanket I'd bought from the market and careful to pack my purchases from the apothecary's shop so that nothing would break. I rolled up the old mattress and stowed it back in the corner where I'd found it, then swept out the room that had been my home for these past few days, all the time picturing Morgan and Cat and thanking their gentle spirits for having taken me in and protecting me.

Finally I went through into the dark little storeroom, kneeling down in front of the shelf in the damp corner and unearthing Rollo's chest. I filled in the empty space and trod down the earth, then returned to the main room.

It was time to go. I said my goodbyes to Morgan and Cat and stepped outside into the night, closing the door after me.

I arranged my various burdens about my body, leaving my arms free for the chest. I was going to be very heavily laden, but this would be a risky journey, even by night, and I didn't want to have to make it twice. Bracing my shoulders, I set off across the field.

Thankfully I hadn't far to go. Up to the road, over it and by the shortest route into the market square. Across it, keeping to the shadow of the buildings that surrounded it, and then into the criss-cross of alleys leading off it. I had neither seen nor heard a soul, so I didn't bother with doubling back but again took the most direct route.

And, feeling as if my arms were about to be wrenched out

of my shoulders, I put the chest down on the steps to Gurdyman's house.

It was very late, but I knew it was his habit to work far into the night. I raised my hand and, making a fist, thumped softly on the door. After only a brief time it opened.

He stood there smiling at me.

'I thought you would come,' he said very softly. Then, standing back, he beckoned me inside. 'In! Quickly, now, before anyone sees you!'

I dragged my packs and bags into the passage and put the chest down at his feet. 'Is it all right if I stay?' I panted.

'Of course!' He sounded surprised that I should ask. 'The house is all ready,' he added.

I wasn't sure what he meant. Did he mean he had carried out a spot of tidying because he was expecting me?

He eyed the sack of leaves, flowers and roots I had gathered that afternoon. 'That is to go in the crypt, I imagine from the heady green aromas emanating from it?'

'Yes, and I have a package of supplies from the apothecary's shop as well . . .' I reached inside the bundle and extracted it.

'Come along, then.' He preceded me into the side passage and down the steps. 'I have cleared the work benches for you,' he said over his shoulder.

I jumped down the last steps into the crypt. I hadn't had time to notice much when we'd come through here earlier, my attention having been grabbed by the secret stair up to the hidden room. Now, however, in the good light from the lanterns and the torches on the wall, I saw that the room where he had worked for so long was unnaturally tidy. So tidy, in fact, that not one object was visible on the long benches or the wide shelves that rose up the wall.

'Where are all your things?' I demanded. Turning to him, full of sudden fear, I whispered, 'Gurdyman, what's wrong?'

He drew a deep breath, letting it out in a sigh. Then he said, 'Child, you knew this would happen. When we spoke earlier of my return to Spain, it was clearly no surprise to you.'

'No, it wasn't.' I tried to steady my voice. 'I— It's just that— Oh, Gurdyman, I hadn't thought it would be so soon.'

Because when he left, he wouldn't be coming back. The

moment he walked out of the twisty-turny house for the final time would be our last goodbye.

And I didn't think I was ready for that.

He put his hand on my arm. 'It is time, child,' he said kindly. Then – and I could clearly hear the effort he was making to sound bright and cheerful – 'I have cleared away my materials to make room for yours, Lassair, and here you are, laden with a fine supply! Let us begin to stow them, shall we?'

My heart wasn't in it, but I knew he was right. The crypt's purpose had been taken away, but it was about to be given a new one, and the sooner I marked my presence, the better. I placed my purchases from the apothecary on the bench, and together Gurdyman and I arranged them on the shelves. I put my sack of plant matter under the lowest shelf. The items I had brought with me took up only a very small amount of the available space, but we had made a start, and that was what mattered.

Straightening up, I saw that Gurdyman's low bed was still in its accustomed place against the opposite wall, the blankets neatly folded, the pillows smooth. Following the direction of my gaze, he said, 'A few more nights yet, child.'

Then he turned and hurried up the steps, and I followed.

I knew without asking that he was finding this as difficult as I was.

He had stopped beside the dark, low-ceilinged area where we stored and prepared food, out of which the ladder leads up to the little attic where I used to sleep. With a smile, Gurdyman pointed to it.

'Go and have a look,' he said. 'It is not quite as you are probably imagining.'

I had been told what Errita had done when she was here in the town before. Jack had described a malign power that tore through Gurdyman's house, breaking and destroying the place where I slept. But I hadn't really been seeing it in my head as he told me; on the contrary, I'd tried hard not to. I had always loved that little room.

But I trusted Gurdyman. He would not now be telling me to go up if I was going to be distressed by what I saw.

I went up the ladder. My head emerged into the space, and, happiness flooding through me, I looked at what he had done.

The room had been freshly cleaned and the surfaces shone. Had Gurdyman clambered up here and done it? It seemed a demanding task, for a fat old man who easily became breathless.

Then I stopped puzzling about that and at last took in what I'd unconsciously been staring at.

The narrow bed had always seemed the height of luxury to me; or perhaps it was the extraordinary combination of my own bed and a room to sleep in by myself. But there was no sign of that old bed now; undoubtedly it had been the first object to feel the force of Errita's fury. In its place was a bed so large and generous that it took up most of the floor space. On top of the wooden frame was a thick mattress, and spread on that were sheets, blankets and pillows.

It was a bed fit for a king. A king and his queen, in fact, for it was so big that—

I stopped that thought before it could develop.

But as I clambered back down the ladder to give Gurdyman a huge hug of thanks, it occurred to me how strange it was that, had I seen this bed a matter of hours before, it would have plunged me into the most profound unhappiness, whereas now . . . well, now everything was possible.

'Thank you,' I said, my arms round Gurdyman's stout body. 'You have worked so hard.'

I felt him vibrate as he chuckled. 'Not I, child,' he said. 'I told the carpenters what to make, and explained to the lads who brought the goods from the merchant where to put them, but there my involvement ends.'

I stood away from him so I could look at him. We both knew he was being modest; that this wonderfully generous gift had been his idea and that he had paid for it.

'Now,' he said, rubbing his hands together, 'what about that chest you deposited inside the door? Shall we look through it straight away?'

I heard the eagerness in his voice, but I was aching with fatigue and any resolve I might have had to sit up deep into the night with Gurdyman and talk until we ran out of words had been utterly undermined by the sight of that beautiful bed.

'I'll take it down to the crypt,' I said firmly, determined not to be swayed by the way he was looking at me, 'and I'll unlock it. Gurdyman, I'm exhausted and I need to sleep, but I would love it if *you* would go through the contents, and then we can discuss your conclusions in the morning.' I hesitated, then said in a rush, 'If Jack comes back you can show it to him too. There are documents in it that may be relevant to his hunt for whoever killed Mistress de Lacey, Stephen leClerc and poor Young Henry.'

The very act of saying the names – particularly the last one – brought the shock and the horror flooding back.

Gurdyman opened his mouth to speak, but then, perhaps recognizing I wasn't going to give way, he nodded. He must have picked up my sudden surge of emotion, for briefly he put a kindly hand on my arm.

Back in the crypt, I put the chest on the bench and unfastened the padlock. As I threw back the lid, Gurdyman said, 'Why now, Lassair?'

I turned to him. 'What do you mean?'

'You came to see me this afternoon and gave no hint that you were about to move back in. Yet here you are.'

I paused, thinking how to answer.

Then I said, 'I am tired of fleeing from her, Gurdyman. I have remained in hiding, kept away from you and – and from people I care for, out of fear that she would attack me by hurting those I love.' I hesitated, for I had been going to wait until the bright light of morning to tell him what had just happened. But my inner voice said, *Tell him now.*

He was staring at me, his eyes intent, and I realized he knew full well something bad had happened.

'She can use that blue fire too,' I said quietly. 'Just like her mother and her brother, she has the skill. She's just set her flames in the lean-to attached to Jack's house, and it is destroyed.'

He had gone pale. Leaning against the bench for support, he whispered, 'And those within? I know Jack is unharmed,' he added quickly.

Because of how I am, I thought. Because if Jack had died, I would be—

But I didn't even want to think about that.

'A woman and her child are dead,' I said. 'I thought she was his wife – that he'd married her and they had a child. But I was wrong and he hadn't.'

He was slowly shaking his head. 'Of course not,' he murmured. Then, his expression changing – hardening – he said, 'You know for sure this was Errita's doing?'

'Yes.'

'And this attack has led to your decision to return to this house?'

'Yes. I am going to emerge into the open and let her do her worst. I will keep away from Jack until – for now,' I amended, 'but I believe that you and I together are a match for her. At least, I hope we are?' Suddenly it occurred to me that I ought to have asked him what he thought before making this decision . . .

But he said, 'Good. *Good!* I am glad to hear you say this, Lassair.' He studied me, eyes narrowing in concentration. 'You are not the same,' he said very softly. 'When I look at you I see the Lassair I knew, but you have . . . *grown.*' He smiled wryly. 'You have a great deal more power now.'

I have, I wanted to reply. *I have much of the power that was once yours and Luliwa's.*

But he knew that as well as I did, so I didn't.

He was darting little glances towards the chest and its contents, and I didn't like to keep him from it any longer. I murmured a good night, and he grunted in reply.

By the time I was on the first step, he was bent over the chest and had probably forgotten I was there.

'It's no good trying to bully me, I'm not going to tell you how it came to be in my crypt,' Gurdyman said, not for the first time. 'I can't,' he muttered.

It was the next morning, and Jack had gone round very early to Gurdyman's house to tell him what had happened the previous night. It was odd, he thought, because as he was describing the sinister blue flames, he had the distinct impression Gurdyman already knew about them.

In exchange for those unwelcome tidings – Gurdyman had looked grieved when Jack told him about Leveva and Aedne – the old man had said, 'I have something for you,' and taken him down to the crypt, where an iron-bound wooden chest stood open on the worktop.

'I believe,' Gurdyman said as Jack stared open-mouthed at

it, 'that among the contents may be the clue you are chasing. The means to uncover what the secret was that your young lawman died for.'

'Is it the chest from Mistress de Lacey's house?' Jack demanded. But he knew it had to be, for as far as he could see, its dimensions were the same as the space marked out on the floor of the hiding place behind the panel.

'Yes,' Gurdyman said.

And no matter what persuasive arguments Jack employed to make him say more, he would not.

'May I at least be allowed to examine the contents as much as I need to?' Jack said angrily.

'Of course,' Gurdyman replied. 'And if you come up with any notions that you would like to discuss, I am at your disposal.'

'Thank you,' Jack said grudgingly.

'I will go and fetch us some refreshments,' Gurdyman announced, 'for the day is hot already, and I am sure a cool drink would be welcome.'

He was gone for some time. When he returned, bearing a tray with a jug and two mugs, he said, before Jack could comment, 'The woman and child who died – you must have mentioned their names but I do not recall them. They had been living in the lean-to for a while, I believe, but were not friends or relatives of yours?'

Jack looked up from the piece of parchment he was studying. 'No, they were neither. Leveva had been widowed, and the death of her husband meant that she and her little girl had been thrown out of their cottage. She came to the town hoping to find work, but without success – although I hesitate to speak ill of her, she was not an easy woman – and I came across the pair of them begging down on the quay. They were both filthy and starving, and Leveva was desperate. I said she could stay in the lean-to beside my house for a few days until she could find employment and lodging.'

Gurdyman was watching him intently. 'And since you did not specify how long *a few days* amounted to, you discovered that she wasn't in any hurry to move on.'

'Yes. She – oh, it became awkward. She acted as if I wanted to— As if I viewed her as—'

'She pretended that she thought you wanted to bed her and with any luck wed her,' Gurdyman supplied. 'No doubt you were hard put to stop her mending your shirts and preparing a hot meal for you when you returned home in the evening?'

Jack grinned briefly. 'I managed to keep her hands off my linen, but I never did work out how to dissuade her from cooking for me.' He stopped, frowning. 'There was never any question of courting her,' he said firmly. 'She was not a kind woman. I dare say life had treated her cruelly, and knocked the gentleness out of her; it's common enough, and it's always the women who suffer the worst, and, of course, the children. I could have understood aggression and a self-serving attitude towards the world in general, but Leveva had no tenderness even for her child. Aedne was a skinny, timid little girl with a perpetually runny nose, and I don't believe Leveva cared for her much. She certainly took no pains to try to feed the child up with tempting foods, even when she had the—' He stopped.

'Even when she had the means to go out and purchase them?' Gurdyman suggested. 'Provided, of course, by you.'

'Others helped as well,' Jack protested. 'Old Father Edmund – he's the priest of the church in the workmen's village – was in the habit of dropping a coin in her hand whenever he could.'

'She couldn't marry an elderly priest,' Gurdyman pointed out. 'Whereas you . . .' He left the sentence unfinished.

'*I* wasn't going to marry her.' Jack was repulsed by the idea, then immediately felt guilty because the poor woman was dead.

'Blue flames, you said?' Gurdyman asked presently.

'Yes.' Jack looked at him. 'You sounded as if you were familiar with such a phenomenon?'

Gurdyman didn't answer for a moment. Then: 'Yes,' he said slowly. 'I have heard about this sort of fire, and once I saw it for myself.'

Jack waited, but he did not elaborate.

And Jack decided it was time to stop holding back and say what he was quite sure they were both thinking.

'It's her, isn't it?' he said. 'The daughter. Luliwa's other child. The one who was sent here to arrange your summons. She knows the town – she spent a whole winter here – and she has come back.'

He thought Gurdyman wasn't going to answer. But eventually he said, sighing, 'Yes.'

'Why?' Jack asked bluntly.

'She—' But he did not go on.

'Gurdyman, she set the lean-to next to my house on fire last night and two people died.' Jack heard his voice rise in anger and he tried to control it. 'If this woman, this—'

'Errita,' Gurdyman supplied.

'If this Errita has come to the town with the intention of starting fires and otherwise posing a threat to the people who live here, then it's my responsibility to stop her.'

'Oh, you are not responsible for the malice that controls Errita,' Gurdyman murmured.

Jack groaned in exasperation. 'Why is she here?' he repeated. 'What does she want?'

But Gurdyman looked up at him, his expression blank, and said, 'I cannot say.'

'Cannot or will not?' Jack countered. 'Gurdyman, you must—'

But then the old man seemed to reach down within himself to some hidden source of power. When he replied – 'I must *not*,' was all he said – the three words emerged with such power that Jack actually took a pace back.

'You have other matters to attend to!' Gurdyman said swiftly, and Jack had the impression he was trying to hurry Jack away from what had just happened. 'You told me you want to set a trap for whoever killed Mistress de Lacey, Stephen leClerc and your poor young lawman. Well, believe me, Jack, that is a far better use of your time, your talents and your strength than trying to work out what Errita's intentions are.'

Jack found himself staring straight into Gurdyman's bright blue eyes. For a moment he couldn't look away. When he felt himself released – and that, he reflected, was exactly what it amounted to – he wanted nothing more than to get back to the documents in the chest.

And, as if eager to facilitate this wish, Gurdyman pulled out a stool from beneath the bench, indicated to Jack to sit down and murmured, 'I will fetch more cordial.'

*   *   *

He was gone for even longer this time, but Jack, totally absorbed, barely noticed.

The chest was ancient, and Jack recognized Saxon workmanship. The iron hoops that bound it were strong, and the two locks would have needed a craftsman to pick open. The lid folded back in some clever fashion to form a flat working surface, so that someone unpacking the contents of the chest had a convenient place on which to spread the documents out.

Jack felt himself drawn into the world of Rollo Guiscard.

Once he had undone the numerous carefully tied and tightly packed leather bags full of gold and coins that formed the top layers, the first object that really stunned him was a rolled parchment covered in beautiful script and decorated with the King's seal. So it was true, Rollo really had been a spy for the King. Jack put his personal emotions aside and thought about that.

He wondered if the King had been told of Rollo's death. Had the news filtered back up through some secretive web of spies and informants until it reached the outer and then the inner circles of the court until, finally, someone told King William?

Jack had been unrolling other parchments as he contemplated this, and one in particular caught his attention. Perhaps it was because he had been thinking about the King, and this document had a beautiful little illustration of a crown at the foot of the parchment, right in the middle. A series of lines were drawn from the crown up over the page, stretching out to right, left and centre with smaller lines coming off them, like the increasingly fine branches of a tree that all stem from the main trunk.

If the crown represented the south of England, Jack mused, then the left-hand branch went to the west, the central one due north and the extreme right-hand one led to the fens, the most easterly part of the kingdom. It terminated in a single fine line, and at the tip of this line were tiny letters in the same small, even hand that featured in many of the documents and that Jack assumed to be Rollo's. The initials were a large *E* followed by a small *d* and a large *L*.

He traced the line back in the direction of the crown and came to its first branch, at the end of which was inscribed *SlC*.

If the tip of the line marked *EdL* represented Cambridge and the first branch off it marked *SlC* was Trumpington, then the next one, close to it over to the left and up a little, must be . . .

Jack looked up, puzzled. If his interpretation was right, then the branch terminating in the initials *HdV* was in a place where there wasn't a town, a village or even a hamlet: the only habitation in the vicinity that Jack could think of was a long, low, semi-ruined old building that had been a Saxon hall before the Conquest, when it had been given to one of the Conqueror's knights whose line had ended with his son. Nobody had heard of him for years and it was assumed he'd taken sick and died.

And, as if in confirmation, the inscribed *HdV* had a small but heavily marked cross beside it.

Jack thought hard and came up with the name. The father had been William de Varaville and his son was called Herlvin.

Supposing Herlvin de Varaville was not dead but simply living a quiet, solitary life, deliberately – and for reasons of his own – keeping himself and his doings beneath the notice of his few neighbours?

Jack stood up and paced to and fro across the crypt, thinking.

If he was right – and he had only the thinnest grounds for believing he was – then the killer was moving in secret through the area quietly dispatching agents in the King's spy network who had happened across something that was not meant to be known. Eleanor de Lacey had been at the end of the branch that led into the fens, and it had been the next person down the line, Stephen leClerc, who had brought the dangerous secret to her. The killer had tracked both of them down and dispatched them.

Who had told Stephen leClerc?

If it had been this HdV, then was it possible he – or she – had managed to hide away better than the other two? Jack only knew of the dilapidated longhouse by merest chance, and to the casual observer it looked abandoned.

If Herlvin de Varaville had managed to evade the killer who was hunting for the link in the chain that preceded Stephen leClerc, and if Jack could somehow reveal his location to the killer, then anybody waiting at the old Saxon dwelling with a sword and a couple of loyal fighters to back him up would have the advantage . . .

And the man who had killed Eleanor de Lacey and Stephen

leClerc, and bludgeoned Young Henry to death simply because he got in the way, would find himself having to answer for what he had done.

Jack went back to the chest, rolled up the documents and stowed them away, covering them with the bags of gold. He closed the lid and put the hasp over the loop.

He stood staring down at it for some moments.

It had belonged to Rollo Guiscard, who had left it with Eleanor de Lacey. It had been removed from her house, but not by the killer, for if that had been the case, how had it ended up here in Gurdyman's crypt?

The alternative explanation – that Mistress de Lacey had given it to someone else before the killer got to her – had to be the right one.

Jack felt a fierce flare of hope.

Could it be?

He reached out his hands and laid them on the top of the chest. He closed his eyes, concentrating all his attention into the flesh of his palms. For the briefest of moments he sensed something – something he did not dare to examine or even think about – then it was gone.

He drew back his hands, slowly rubbing them together. It was folly, he told himself firmly, to believe he'd just picked up the essence of the last person to examine the chest. 'It's Gurdyman who has just been going through it,' he said aloud. 'That is the plain truth, and anything else is pure imagination.'

With a very deliberate effort, he forced his mind back to the plan to snare his enemy.

Was he right in what he had surmised? If he was, could he justify putting this HdV in mortal danger in order to catch the killer?

He will find Herlvin de Varaville sooner or later, he told himself.

If you reveal his whereabouts, it'll be sooner, his conscience answered.

But we will be there to protect him, he replied.

Then the argument seemed to fade away. It had become pointless, because he knew he was going to go ahead anyway.

SIXTEEN

I had slept blissfully in the big bed in my attic room. As I lay drowsing in the morning light, I wondered idly how long it was since I'd slept on anything but hard ground, with only an inadequate old mattress at best between me and the earth.

Then my reverie was interrupted by the sound of the door opening and male voices.

Jack was back.

I heard the deep rumble of his voice, then Gurdyman said, with such careful enunciation that I guessed he meant me to overhear, 'I have something for you.'

I lay very still, as if Jack could possibly have heard some small movement from down there in the passage that led down to the crypt. For that was where they went: I heard Jack's boots clattering down the steps.

Gurdyman was going to show him Rollo's chest.

I slipped out of bed, washed and dressed, and I was pulling on my boots when Gurdyman's head appeared at the top of the ladder.

'Jack's in the crypt going through the chest,' he panted. There was a faint look of enquiry on his face.

I smiled. 'It's all right, I said you could show it to him.'

He nodded. He was looking intently at me.

'What is it?'

Slowly he shook his head. 'Oh – nothing, I'm sure. But . . . Lassair, the sun is pouring into this room, and there you are with your bright hair shining like new copper, yet I perceive a darkness around you.' He put out a hand as if to touch me but I was out of his reach. 'It seems unlikely, now, that it is I who should warn you, for I know full well your sight is far keener than mine. But nevertheless I say, be careful.'

Then he was gone.

I sat utterly still for some time after I had heard his footsteps shuffling back along the passage. Darkness . . . There was darkness around me.

I did not have to think for long to find its source.

I reached beneath my pillow for the leather bag in which I keep the shining stone. I unwrapped it and was just curving my fingers round it, as I always do when I begin in order to re-establish our connection, when it seemed to leap in my hands and almost out of my grasp. Desperately I clutched it, and for a heartbeat or two it felt burning hot and I thought I smelt my flesh singe.

Then I brought all my mental powers together and fought back.

This does not belong to you! I thundered silently. *It was my grandfather's and he passed it on to me, and it is mine by the ancient rites of the blood!*

There was a tense moment of fierce, violent struggle, and in the stone's black depths I saw bright flashes of green, gold and white, and twisted through their streams of brilliance was Errita's face, horribly distorted so that it looked like a jagged length of ribbon, her eyes black slits and her mouth an animal snarl.

With a huge effort I rolled up the ribbon that held her image, crushing those hate-filled features until her furious face faded to nothing. Inside my head I thought I could hear a long, despairing howl, tailing away to a sob.

The shining stone was quiet again, its black surface reflecting only my own features.

I was trembling with exhaustion, the right side of my forehead throbbed with agony as if someone had driven an axe into it and I thought I was going to be sick. I closed my eyes and dizzying zigzags danced down the screen of my eyelids. I took a breath, then another, and presently I began to feel slightly better.

The shining stone was cool – cold – in my lap. Obeying an impulse, I picked it up and rolled it slowly across my forehead, back and forth, back and forth. Then I looked into it again. I could see Thorfinn, and Granny Cordeilla was standing beside him. At first they looked old, as I had known them in life, but then by some sort of magic the years rolled off them and they stood young, straight of limb, their long hair twining together in the wind off the sea and their eyes bright. It was a beautiful image, full of love, full of joy.

And then, of all the unexpected things, suddenly there was something else, something very different: I thought I felt shame emanating from the stone.

It was surely quite impossible, but it appeared that the shining stone was ashamed of having let Errita in . . .

I cradled it gently in my hands and held it to my heart.

'She is powerful,' I murmured, raising it to my face, my lips against its hard, smooth surface. 'Her strength is fuelled by hatred, and I was not ready for her. That's why she managed to find a way in.' I paused, for from somewhere – from some power outside? from within myself? – suddenly I was receiving a strong, powerful message: *She will not do so again.*

Then, as if the image of Thorfinn and Cordeilla in their proud prime had sparked off some element in me, all at once I too was filled with joy. Perhaps it was the work of those two wise old souls whom I had loved – still loved, would always love – but it seemed as if all the good things in my life were shown to me in a series of rapid flashes. My parents and my siblings, all of them surviving the many years of my absence, safe and well and waiting in Aelf Fen for me to go home to them. My own survival, through the perils of my time in the south and the long journey home. The power that Luliwa and Gurdyman had given up that was now within me. Gurdyman, waiting patiently here in this very house for my return, *knowing* I was coming back and, what was more, that I would be requiring this splendid bed in which I had just enjoyed such a wonderful night's sleep.

Jack, who had not got tired of waiting for me, given up and married someone else. Who was even now down in the crypt.

Now that I knew the truth, I allowed my body's response to his nearness to flow through me unrestrained.

I had been standing up, gazing absently through the little window down into the courtyard, but my legs had gone trembly and I had to sit down on the bed again.

Smiling, gently I put the image of Jack aside and concentrated on what else lay before me.

There was struggle and the threat of death ahead. That was clear from what the shining stone had shown me. My future was in the balance. Errita had thrown everything into the fight; I knew that because it would have taken all that she had and more to insert herself into the shining stone. She was coming for me, and when we finally faced each other it would be for the last time.

As I had already uneasily recognized, it was not possible for both of us to survive. I had finally admitted it to myself that morning in Morgan's house, when I'd been shaken awake from the terrifying dream in which Errita and I fought each other with imaginary weapons that turned into blades resembling nothing ever seen in reality.

Either she would kill me or I would kill her.

I was holding the stone loosely in my lap now, my palms cupping it. I looked down at it, following some prompt whose origin I didn't pause to work out. I saw an image of the track that leads out of the town to the south-west, and Jack was walking along it, an indistinct figure beside him. Both were armed. As I watched they turned off the track, down a path that dipped in and out of the trees through a stretch of woodland, and, on the far side, they took a narrow trail that looked like an animal's track through scrub and undergrowth. I caught a glimpse of a long, low, dilapidated building in the distance.

Then I saw that someone was following them.

And I went cold all over.

Jack leaned over the workbench, intent on his task. He was making a copy of the chart with the crown that he had found in the chest. He knew it had to be accurate, so he could not hurry, yet as he drew the lines with their branches and their markings he felt as if someone was standing right behind him, urging him to get on, make haste.

Very carefully he drew the line leading out to the west of where Stephen leClerc had been slain, and then he inscribed the initials *HdV*.

He left out the heavily inked cross beside the name.

*   *   *

He had finished. He stared down at his work, satisfied, then looked up to see that Gurdyman had returned.

'How long have you been standing there?' he demanded.

'Oh, a while,' Gurdyman replied. He nodded to the piece of parchment Jack had been copying. 'You have found your bait?'

'I believe I have.'

'You have a plan of action?'

'I hope so, yes.' But it was fraught with uncertainties, Jack thought. Herlvin de Varaville might be dead. He might have been dropped a long time ago from the chain of agents who were kept informed of happenings in high places. The killer might already have paid him a visit, and left him as dead as Eleanor de Lacey and Stephen leClerc.

But you have to do something, a quiet voice said – it sounded very like Gurdyman's, although he was standing there smiling gently, not speaking – *and there is logic to what you propose.*

Logic, Jack thought. Was it going to be enough?

'Good luck,' Gurdyman said.

Jack covered the ground from Gurdyman's house to the castle at a near-run. He went first to his house, where, to his great surprise, the smell of burning had gone, and all that remained to show what had happened was the blackened shell of the lean-to. The bodies had been taken to the little chapel last night, as soon as they were cool enough to move, and would be buried today.

Jack would have liked to stop and say a prayer, but the sense of urgency was even more powerful now and he could not afford the time. Inside his house, he unlocked the hidden recess where he kept his sword, buckling on his sword belt and sticking the long, thin knife in its holder. He felt behind him for the broader-bladed knife he carried in its sheath beneath his leather jerkin. It was where it always was; the touch was more from superstition than the need to verify its presence.

Then he raced back down the passage and went up into the castle.

He knew they would be there, Walter, Luke, Ginger and Big Gerald, and they were. They had worked with Young

Henry just as he had, they had grown to like and admire him and they grieved for him. Jack was fully aware that their urge for revenge was as fierce as his.

He looked round at them, meeting four pairs of eyes. 'Is it time, chief?' Walter asked softly, nodding at Jack's sword.

'Yes.' Jack turned to Luke. 'You're the fastest runner, Luke. I want you to take this—' he handed him the copied parchment – 'and hide it in the shed where Stephen leClerc was killed.'

Luke looked down at the folded document. 'When you say hide it . . .'

'Somewhere not too obvious, but where someone looking for secrets would check.'

Luke frowned. 'But won't this person have searched already?'

Jack grinned briefly. 'That's what I mean by not too obvious.' Then, as Luke nodded his understanding, he added, 'If I'm right – and God knows, I have no idea if I am – then the killer will be looking for something like this.'

'Right, chief' – Luke was already at the doorway – 'I'm off.'

'When you've finished, come and catch up with us. I'll need to know you've managed it. Take the lane that goes cross-country roughly south-west. You know the old Saxon longhouse, out on its own beyond the woods?'

'That old ruin? Yes, but it's falling down, there's no one—' But, noticing Jack's expression, he stopped. 'Right, chief.' He hurried away.

Jack and his companions were roughly halfway to their destination when Luke came running up behind them. He was scarlet in the face, sweating and panting hard, and Jack called a halt while he rested and took a long drink from his water flask.

'Well?' Jack demanded.

'I found a good place, chief,' Luke replied. 'There was a scooped-out recess in the floor under the bed with an off-cut of timber at the bottom to form a solid base – to keep the moisture out, I imagine, the shed's stinking with damp and mould – and I put the parchment underneath that.'

It was as good as anything, Jack thought. Once again, he crushed the doubts that kept nagging at him. 'Good. Anyone see you?'

'Yes, that old woman.'

'Agathe,' Jack supplied.

'Yes, her. Reckon she camps out there so she can keep an eye for the next exciting thing that happens.'

'And?' Jack was impatient, itching to get on.

'She says there's been someone watching the shed.'

'Description?'

'Medium height, athletic and slim, dressed in black. Furtive-looking. She said it was hard to spot him, and even when she had, he kept slipping out of sight again.'

Jack nodded. It was encouraging. Or so he hoped.

'Very well,' he said. He glanced round at them, at Walter, Ginger, Big Gerald and Luke. 'Come on.'

The old longhouse looked as if it was slowly sinking back into the earth. As if the timbers, the reed thatch, the clay, dung and straw from which it had been made were in the process of being reabsorbed into the ground. A thin trickle of smoke rising up through a large hole in the roof was the only sign that it was inhabited.

'Not much of a living out here,' Walter observed, scratching his chin as he gazed around him. 'Someone's dug a vegetable plot, and I can smell goat. But the place is on its knees. It's a lot worse than when I last passed this way,' he added. 'Mind you, that was probably five, six years ago.'

'Walter, you and I will go and see if anyone's at home,' Jack said.

He'd known there would be a protest from the other three, and it was Ginger who voiced it. 'What about us, chief?' He hadn't managed to hide his indignation. 'We should all go, it's much better if—'

'No,' Jack interrupted firmly. Ginger stopped, glaring at him, then opened his mouth to resume his objections. 'Ginger, *listen*,' Jack said, impatience making his voice sharp. 'We know of one killer but there may very well be others with him. If we all go inside, that leaves nobody to watch. That's your job, yours, Luke's and Big Gerald's. Spread yourselves out and keep your eyes open.'

After the briefest pause, Ginger gave a curt nod and the three of them turned and moved off.

With Walter close behind, Jack led the way across the filth of the open space between the vegetable plot and the door, stepping over ridges of mud that had dried as hard as stone. There came the yelping bark of a hound, and a cracked voice said harshly, 'Stop that.'

Jack tapped on the door, arousing more barking and a yelp of pain as someone aimed a curse and a kick at the dog.

The door was opened about a hand's breadth and a foul stench of stale urine, sweat, rotten food and general decay billowed out. Faded brown eyes stared up at Jack out of a thin, pale face. Hanks of greasy hair so dirty that it was impossible to tell the colour partly concealed the forehead and the sunken cheeks. The hand gripping the door was bony, the long nails like claws and foul with dirt.

'What?' the same hoarse voice demanded. 'You can't come in!' the man added.

With only the merest pressure from Jack's shoulder, the door opened wide. 'I *am* coming in,' he said calmly. Walter filed in after him, and closed the door again. 'Jack Chevestrier, lawman of Cambridge,' Jack said. 'This is Walter.'

The man's attitude was a mixture of fear and aggression. He was cowering away from Jack, but his face was full of belligerence and his eyes were narrowed in anger. 'What do you want with me?' he demanded.

'Are you Herlvin de Varaville?' Jack asked.

'What if I am?' the man snapped back. 'This is my house, and my father's before me, given to him in thanks for loyal service by the Conqueror himself, God rest his bones, and no man can turn me out!'

'I'm not going to try,' Jack replied mildly. 'I wish to talk to you, however, and—'

But Herlvin de Varaville didn't appear to be listening. His eyes roamed from Jack to Walter and back again, and Jack, watching him intently, saw fear and confusion slip away, replaced by what seemed to be condescending arrogance.

'You'll be wanting food and fine wine, and beds for the night,' he said, a smile stretching his lips to reveal a few ruined yellow teeth and foul-looking gums. 'Such is our reputation that everyone wants an invitation! They all say this is one of the best halls for good hospitality, and many's the time we've had a dozen, *two* dozen and more, and no one ever goes hungry! I could tell you a tale or two of the high old times we've had, and—'

'Who comes here now?' Jack said, cutting ruthlessly into Herlvin de Varaville's reminiscences.

'Now? *Now?*' The man looked confused. 'Oh, they don't come now, not any more, they *used* to, mark you, because they knew I was important, a man of influence, and that my loyalty to the King was as true and reliable as my father's to *his* father, the Conqueror, God rest his bones, and my father fought with him, side by side with the knights of the household, charging and charging again until the ground was red with blood and—'

'They came here to pass on secret information, didn't they?' Jack said. 'The King's spies, keeping an eye on what was going on out in the countryside, passing on the things they heard and saw along the branches of their network, and always watching out for the King's interests.' He was guessing, hoping the old man would agree but fully expecting him to clam up and refuse to say any more.

But Herlvin de Varaville threw out his narrow chest and said proudly, 'Oh, yes, and I was one of them, back then.' His face fell into sorrow. 'But they stopped coming here. They cut me out, that's what they did, said I got confused and wasn't to be trusted any more.' Two fat tears fell from his reddened eyelids and traced tracks in the filthy cheeks. Then suddenly he leaned close to Jack and, looking slyly up at him, whispered, 'They think I don't know anything any more, but I *do*. They're not as clever as they think they are and I found out, that's what I did, I followed him and I listened, and I *know* what's going to happen, and even though they think I'm not capable I'm keeping watch, because the killer's got to get here somehow from over the water and he may well come in to one of our ports, so I'm manning my post, dawn to dusk, I go out there

every day and – is it day?' he demanded, grasping Jack's
arm. He looked wildly out through the tiny window, and it
seemed he only noticed then that it was full daylight, the sun
climbing high in the sky.

And Jack, looking down at him with a stab of compassion,
wondered how on earth he was going to distinguish the truth
from the swirling fantasies of the old man's madness.

I felt weirdly disorientated.

I was walking along the path in the real world. I knew that,
for I could feel the heat of the sun-warmed earth beneath my
feet, and smell the rich green smell of early August. Yet
my actions so perfectly copied the images I'd seen in the
shining stone that I kept getting confused. Was I really here
or was I in the middle of a vision?

I was following the track that leads out of the town to the
south-west. Jack strode out ahead of me, and Walter, Ginger
and Big Gerald were with him. All of them carried weapons.
There was a strong sense of purpose about them.

Then I heard running footsteps pounding the path, coming
up behind me. I jumped off the track into the undergrowth,
crouching down low, and I saw Luke dash past. I peered out
and watched as he caught the others up. They talked for a
short while, then Jack led them on.

I crept out of hiding and followed.

They turned off the track, down a path that dipped in and
out of the trees in a stretch of woodland, and, on the far side,
they took a narrow trail that looked like an animal's track
through scrub and undergrowth. I caught a glimpse of a long,
low, dilapidated building in the distance and I drew back, using
the last of the cover before the land opened out.

Jack had paused and was saying something urgently to
the others. After a short time, he and Walter went on to the
house and the other three spread out and melted away into
the surrounding trees and undergrowth. He'd ordered them, I
guessed, to keep watch.

I leaned against a birch tree, watching, calculating.

She was here: I knew she was. I had seen her clearly in the
shining stone and it never lied to me. And now, although I

couldn't see her, I could *feel* her, and that was far worse. For she was blackness, malice, chill and cold, and wherever she was, she was making my skin crawl.

What was she doing out here, hard on Jack's trail?

I'd had to recognize the fact that she knew full well how I felt about him. For all that I'd kept away from him, she had seen us together in the settlement under the mountains, watched us on the shore as we said farewell. And, although she might not be capable of receiving or giving love herself, witnessing it in others roused her to fury.

Last night she had fired up her terrible blue flames and burned down the dwelling that adjoined Jack's. Snuffed out the lives of the woman and the child within for no greater reason other than to shout out silently to me, *I'm here! Look what I can do! See how puny you are, how powerless to stop me!*

'I *will* stop you, Errita,' I said quietly.

The shining stone was in its leather bag inside my satchel. I put my hand over the place where I could feel its round hardness, and I felt strength flow into me.

I stepped out onto the path.

SEVENTEEN

J ack could not isolate the moment when he realized events were running away from him.

Herlvin de Varaville had rapidly descended into some sort of madness, talking very quickly in a harsh whisper about being brought to the longhouse when he was a boy of ten and how he and his mother were repeatedly told by his father how lucky they were to be so favoured by the new king, for this gift of a fine dwelling and the surrounding acres was a sign of the esteem in which the senior de Varaville was held by the Conqueror. It was not easy to tell from the drawn-out, disjointed discourse, but it appeared Herlvin's mother had not long survived her uprooting from Normandy, and had withered and died in the new soil.

Then he had started telling them how proud he was that, just like his honoured father, he too was of great value to his King. He seemed to have forgotten he'd just said he had been cut out of the network of informants and intelligence-gatherers, and now he was proclaiming loudly about the many secrets he held in his keeping.

Abruptly he had sunk down onto the filthy floor and buried his face in his hands. His shoulders shook with weeping, and presently a high keening sound emerged from him.

'Go and fetch him some water,' Jack said to Walter. 'He seems to be having some sort of fit.'

Walter went through a low arch that led into a dank little room which appeared to be a scullery, his feet crunching on small animal bones and mouse and rat droppings. Jack heard the sound of water being poured, then Walter called back, 'The only mug is thick with slime so I'll have to rinse it.'

'Very well, but be quick,' Jack called back.

He went to crouch beside Herlvin, his back to the arch through which Walter had gone. 'Do you live here alone?' he asked gently as the keening briefly paused.

Herlvin nodded, then shook his head, so violently that Jack heard his neck crack. 'No! No, of course not! Can't you *see*, you dolt? My father's household are loyal and they care for me as they cared for him!'

He stared up at Jack. Just for an instant his mouth turned down in a wry smile, as if to say, *I am deceiving myself, am I not?* Then the wildness in his eyes returned, and he started humming quietly to himself.

Jack stayed where he was, unsure whether it would help or hinder if he put his arm round the thin, trembling body in its dirty, ruined clothes.

Then he noticed that the sounds from the scullery had stopped.

He felt a chill run through him and, very slowly, began to straighten up, turning round to face the arch as he did so.

Walter was standing between him and the arch. There was an arm around his throat and a short, thin knife pressed against his neck, just beneath the ear. The brilliant glimmer of its blade was an indication of its sharpness. Very close behind him stood a slim figure dressed in black, a hood thrown back to reveal a sallow-skinned face with small, dark eyes and black hair slicked with oil.

Jack was on his feet now, fighting the powerful urge to hurl himself at Walter's captor.

'Not a good idea, lawman,' said the man in a calm voice. 'Perhaps you move more quickly than your size suggests, but are you willing to take a chance on being faster than I am?' The blade moved fractionally, a bead of blood appeared on Walter's neck and Jack forced himself to relax. 'Very wise,' commented the man.

Watching him intently, Jack saw his eyes flick to the door and then to the tiny window. 'You are but two,' he said.

'There are more outside and I—'

'Do not lie,' said the man coldly. 'I have searched all round the house and I know there is no one here but the three of us.'

Amid the peril Jack felt a brief stab of triumph: the killer hadn't spotted Ginger, Luke and Big Gerald. But then, he realized in dismay, it appeared they hadn't spotted him either, for if they had wouldn't they be here?

The man glanced down at Herlvin. 'Four of us, I suppose I should say, if you count him, but I do not advise it. Apparently it is some time since he has been of any use.'

'Then why have you come here to kill him?' Jack asked, careful to keep his voice level.

'Because I do not like to leave untied ends,' the man replied sharply. 'I knew there was another one of them somewhere in this vicinity, for they were always spoken of as a trio.'

'Spoken of by whom?'

The man eyed him for a few moments, then said, 'One faction watches the other. It is always thus, is it not? The great matters of state and country are high above the everyday concerns of the mass of the people, yet always there are those who elect to involve themselves, who are prepared to take the risk of failure and ruin in return for the slim chance of rising on the tail of the star they follow. Such a man ran a network for the King, efficiently and ruthlessly, and it has been my task to – ah, to *tidy away* the vestiges of it in this area.'

Rollo Guiscard, Jack thought. 'And you think it the work of a warrior, a brave fighting man, to beat and kill an elderly woman and to slay a lost old man in the hovel he was forced to live in?' He remembered Young Henry's dead body leaning trustingly against him as he rode back to the town. 'To slay my officer when he got too near?'

'He saw me,' the man said dispassionately. 'What else could I do?'

'You killed him as you killed the others.' Again Jack fought the urge to go on the attack. 'With no more thought than a man crushing a beetle.' His fists were clenched so tightly that his arms trembled.

The dark eyes flashed in anger. 'I do what I must,' the man replied tersely.

'What harm did you imagine Mistress de Lacey and Stephen leClerc could do?' Jack pressed on. 'What weapon did they possess?'

'Knowledge!' the man shot back. 'The network was too efficient – that old man you speak of was Stephen leClerc, and he was once a man of great influence and wealth, until a spectacular fall from grace forced him to hide away in

Trumpington. But he did not lose his intelligence along with his position – he had once been valued for the subtlety of his mind, and the fact that he retained this made him dangerous.' He paused. Jack, alert for any sign that he was about to relax, was disappointed, for the man did not move a muscle. 'It was necessary to dispatch him. There was a leak, you see, and for a time it seemed as if that which must not be known was spreading out of control, as one person whispered to another, and that person passed the information on to yet another. But then it was discovered, to the great relief of – to our great relief' – he corrected himself smoothly – 'that there was only one network along which word was being passed, and this is it. These little whisperers had to be stopped. You see, don't you?' he asked, and his tone was reasonable, as if to imply that any sane person would understand and approve of what he had done.

'You followed Stephen leClerc to Mistress de Lacey's house,' Jack said neutrally. 'You saw him tap at her door early in the morning, when there was nobody about – or so you thought – and you watched as Mistress de Lacey admitted him like the old friend he was. You realized why he was there and you knew the secret had been passed on.'

'She had something I wanted,' the man said softly. 'I had been informed that she was one of the select few who kept gold hidden away for the person to whom she passed information. I persuaded her to tell me where the hiding place was, but what I sought was no longer there and she would not tell me where it was.'

'She could not tell you,' Jack spoke harshly. 'She did not know.'

'Didn't . . . Of course she knew!' For the first time an instant of doubt flashed across the man's face.

'She had given it to the person to whom it rightfully belongs,' Jack went on – all at once he knew it was true – 'and it had gone out of her knowledge.'

The killer's expression twisted cruelly as realization dawned. 'You have it,' he whispered. 'Don't you?'

'No, but I know where it is.'

'And . . . yes, of course! You found the document, didn't

you? Was it the original that you placed so carefully where I would find it, or did you copy it?'

'I copied it.'

The man nodded slowly. 'Well, it has served its purpose, for here I am. I do not know what *you* hoped to achieve, lawman, for as you observe, I hold your companion, and you cannot make a move while my blade is poised to cut his throat.' He watched Jack closely, smiling slightly. 'I move fast,' he murmured. 'Faster than you can know, and I am afraid that you will only discover the truth of this when it is far too late and you too are dying.' He glanced down at Herlvin de Varaville, now huddled on the floor with his thumb in his mouth. 'As will he. There is a plan, you see, lawman,' he added in a murmur, 'and it *will* come to pass – we have seen the unfolding of the future, and the way is set for us.'

Jack stood utterly still. Then, holding the killer's eyes, he said, 'What is this secret that you have been at such pains to keep?'

The man narrowed his eyes slightly. 'What day is it?' he asked.

Taken aback by the inconsistency, Jack said without thinking, 'It is the first of August. No, the second.'

A smile spread across the killer's face. 'And they are far away, and there is no more time. Ah, what joy – all this comes too late, and it does not really matter any more. Nevertheless, why not?'

And, faster than a striking predator and still maintaining his hold around Walter's neck, the killer flung aside the short knife and drew a long, thin blade from a sheath at his belt. Lunging forward and leaning down in one swift, smooth movement, he plunged it into the side of Herlvin de Varaville's neck, just beneath his ear.

Before Jack could react, he was back precisely where he had just been standing, Walter held against him, the longer blade now at his throat. Jack could have thought he had imagined the sudden devastating flash of movement, except for the fact that Herlvin's blood was rapidly forming a pool on the dirty floor beneath him as his life's force pumped out, quickly at first and then more and more slowly with the dying beats of his heart.

'The last of the de Varavilles, or so I believe,' the killer said matter-of-factly, staring down dispassionately at the corpse. 'He was not the man his father was, or so they say.' He met Jack's eyes. What he saw there – shock, surprise, perhaps – made him smile faintly. 'I told you I was fast,' he said.

I crept up the track, keeping to the shade of the trees where I could, my eyes trying to see everywhere at once, my ears alert to every small sound, my skin tingling with the sense of Errita's nearness.

I was close to the old building now, and it became clear that it was on the point of collapse.

What was Jack doing here? Why had he brought his four most loyal followers? What could have led him to this lonely, desolate spot?

I didn't know, had no way of discovering. But it was not my first concern. Jack was in danger, for without a doubt he was hunting down the killer, holding him to account for the deaths of Mistress de Lacey, Stephen leClerc and Young Henry. I knew he would not stop until he had found him.

But Errita was on his trail, and I was quite sure she meant to kill him. She knew I loved him, had never ceased to love him, and it was perfectly possible that she had felt an echo of my joy at discovering he had not given up on waiting for my return and married someone else.

We were linked, Errita and I, and I suspected she picked up my feelings as I did hers. I stopped, leaning against the broad trunk of an oak tree, and, slowly and deliberately, drew every one of my tender emotions back into my heart, locking them away from her probing intrusion.

She felt it: I knew she did. I sensed her slight jolt of shock, and I felt a moment of triumph.

I walked slowly on.

'Where are you, Errita?' I said softly. 'I know why you are here, and I am going to stop you.'

I was nearing the house now.

I could hear voices from within. I crept up to the door and, positioning myself on the hinged side, peered through the gap between it and the frame. Jack was standing with his back to me. A shabby, dirty figure lay curled on the floor in front of him, a thumb stuck in his slack mouth like a baby seeking comfort. But then I saw the pool of blood spread out beneath his head and neck and I realized he was dead.

Beyond Jack, Walter was standing very still, and the man dressed all in black who held him in a tight grip was pressing a knife to his exposed neck.

And then, at the very instant when I needed to focus my full attention on what was happening in that filthy, shadowy room, I saw Errita.

She was no more than a flash of muted brown on the edge of my vision, over at the other end of the long building, where I had spotted a second door. She was clad in her habitual dull colours, hood pushed back to reveal the hair that was so like her brother's, with the same silver streak through the brown.

She was there and gone again in a heartbeat. But I had seen where she was and, perhaps through the strange link between us, I knew what she was doing; knew how she planned to get into the house and reach her quarry.

I also understood that she knew what was going on inside the house, and that she did not intend anyone to take Jack's life but her.

I waited, trying to make out what Jack and the killer were saying. But almost all my attention was directed at Errita, and I missed much of it.

It was, as I had already decided, not my affair.

I saw a tiny movement in the arch that led off the main room into the dark space beyond. To the kitchen, or perhaps the scullery. Mapping the building in my mind, I realized Errita had gone in through the other door and was planning to creep up behind Jack.

I felt the stab of fury as she took in the positions of those within the room. Jack was standing facing the arch, and it would be impossible for her to advance any further without him seeing her.

I knew what she would do next.

I looked round hastily for somewhere to hide, and saw a large water butt with a broken lid standing beside the door.

Quietly, moving soft as smoke, I moved round behind it and crouched down.

I waited.

I sensed her approaching. She too moved in utter silence, but she brought with her some sort of disturbance in the air that seemed to make it crackle, although I didn't think anyone but I could have heard it. Looking down, I saw the hairs on my forearm slowly rise up.

I sensed a diminution of the light, and, very carefully, I peered round the side of the barrel.

She was standing exactly where I had just stood, looking through the gap between the door and the frame. The murmur of voices continued uninterrupted: Walter and the killer hadn't seen her, just as they had failed to see me.

Errita and I were both very good at remaining unobserved when we needed to.

She made no sound, but I knew the moment when she gathered herself to act. I felt the sudden sharp increase in tension, and, praying that I had judged right, I hurled myself out from my hiding place just as she flew into the room.

It was as if her irruption – our irruption – into the room had broken a tableau that had been frozen into immobility. Even as Errita launched herself through the air to fly at Jack, he had moved out of the way, his hand up behind him to draw out the dagger he kept under his leather jerkin. Errita, with the target she had aimed at suddenly no longer there, landed heavily and a great scream of fury shattered the air.

Jack did not even look round. Grasping the killer's arm just above the wrist that held the blade, he shoved Walter out of the way with his free hand, so hard that Walter stumbled and fell, cracking his head on the stone floor with a sickening thud.

Jack and the killer engaged. I heard muffled oaths, heard the clash of steel as one blade thrust and the other parried.

And then Errita threw herself into the fray.

Jack stood a chance against the killer. But with a second foe suddenly materializing at his back – one who, I now saw with horror, had drawn two short, sharp, matching knives from a double sheath at her belt – it was going to be a very different matter.

Even as she flew towards him, I screamed, '*Jack! Behind you!*'

He turned for just a second, saw me – and even in that desperate instant the expression that spread across his face made my heart sing – and then his eyes shot to Errita.

She must have heard my cry but all her focus was on Jack. The killer, instantly understanding that Jack now faced two attackers, gave a snake-like twist of his lithe body that somehow got his knife arm out of Jack's grip.

I knew what I must do.

I shouted to Jack, 'Leave her to me!' And, even as he responded and turned his full strength onto the killer, Errita spun round at last and faced me.

We stood staring at each other, neither of us moving but for the rise and fall of our chests as we panted.

I thought she would attack. I balanced my weight on both feet, hands out to parry her move. She held the knives out before her, and their blades caught the sunlight.

I remembered those knives. She used them for everything from slaughtering and skinning small animals to paring her nails, and she honed them every day. They were as sharp as the keenest razors. She was so familiar with them that they were like extensions of her hands. Her mother had given them to her when she was emerging from childhood into girlhood, and I don't think she had been parted from them for a single moment since.

Now they were aimed at me.

I had no weapon, but my satchel hung across my shoulder and down over my hip. It contained remedies, the shawl my beloved sister had given me . . . and the shining stone.

The shining stone was heavy and hard as rock.

I grabbed the satchel's strap, swung it violently upwards and caught Errita under the jaw. There was a loud click as her teeth crashed together, and she howled in pain. I threw myself towards her but she shot sideways and I only managed to grab hold of her sleeve. I heard the fabric rip, then she was free and running for the door.

She was running away from me.

I felt the implications of that sweep through me.

Then I ran after her.

*   *   *

More than he had ever wanted anything, Jack wanted to turn round and see if his eyes had told him the truth. If Lassair was really there in that ruined room, her long copper hair spilling out from under the white cap and her bright blue-green eyes alive with ferocious courage.

But he couldn't, for the killer had wrested his knife arm free and the tip of his dagger was coming straight for Jack's eyes.

I will not die now, he thought in an instant of cold, calm fury. *The woman I have waited for through all these long years has come back, and it is no time to let this bastard with his secrets and his murderous habits take my life.*

Finding a strength he hadn't been aware he possessed, he pushed his forearm up against the killer's wrist and heard a snap as a bone gave way. The killer grunted in pain, but came straight back on the attack and once again the knife point was right in Jack's face.

Enough, he thought.

He grabbed the killer's damaged wrist – with one hand then with two – and turned the knife towards the man's chest. Jack was taller by almost a head, and the height advantage made the crucial difference.

The killer's eyes, wide with horror, watched as his own knife drove down into him. Through the black cloth of his tunic, through skin – a spurt of blood – and down, down into his flesh towards his heart.

Jack went on driving the knife downwards, and slowly the killer sank on to the floor.

Sprawled at Jack's feet, dying, a smile stretched his sallow face.

'The day after Lammastide, you said?' The words were no more than a faint whisper.

'Yes.'

He laughed, and the action coughed up a great gout of blood from his fatally damaged body. 'Then none of this matters' – the words were barely audible now – 'for he is already dead.'

EIGHTEEN

E rrita was fast. At first I thought she was going to outrun me and I would lose her, but then I found my rhythm, my breathing steadied and, as we both settled down to a comfortable jog, I was able to maintain the gap between us.

The ruined longhouse was some three miles out of town to the south-west, with Trumpington maybe a couple of miles to the south-east. The track we were on was little used, and the only people I saw until we neared the town were distant figures bent double in the fields.

I felt very alone.

The track emerged onto the road to Trumpington, and then we were entering the town. I increased my pace, for all at once we were among houses, carts, horses and, after the isolated longhouse and its desolate setting, suddenly people seemed to be crowding in on me. I kept Errita in sight, although I told myself it didn't matter if I lost her for a moment because I reckoned I knew where she was going. She had spent a whole winter in the town once, when she had fallen ill late in the autumn and had no choice but to put up in the cheapest type of accommodation down on the quayside until the boats started running again in the spring. She'd have found a similar place to stay now, because every type of traveller found lodgings down there and nobody asked awkward questions.

She had slowed to a swift walk now and was striding up the road. I could see the slight rise of the market hill up ahead to the right. She would go on towards the Great Bridge, I thought, and turn off down to the right on this side of it along the quay. I could—

But then she wasn't there.

I stopped dead, then, realizing that pausing for even a few moments would squander any chance of finding her again, I broke into a run, evading people when I could and elbowing them out of the way when I couldn't, and pounded on.

She surely hadn't turned off to the left, for that way there were open fields leading down to the river. Construction work was going on there – new churches were being built – but they were some way away from the road, and Errita couldn't have got right down there into the cover they provided in such a short time unless she'd grown wings.

She must, then, have taken a turning on the right.

Oh, dear Lord, there were so many of them! Winding alleys, narrow little passages and dark tunnels between buildings seemed to my desperately anxious eyes to form a spider's web, and Errita could have disappeared down any one of them and by now be so deep in the maze that I would not find her.

Making a lightning-quick decision, I opted to pause for the briefest glance down every exit off the road and, if I could spot neither Errita nor an obvious place where she could be hiding, run on.

And, after checking perhaps half a dozen – and agonizing each time my eyes did their rapid rake in case I was missing something – I came to a junction. The road that came in from Trumpington and led up to the Great Bridge went on, bending gently round to the right as it enfolded the market square, and the road that went past St Bene't's dived off to the right.

I stood panting on the corner, leaning forward, my hands on my knees, catching my breath, staring down the road. And there, some twenty paces ahead and slinking along in the shadow of a row of low dwellings, was Errita.

Finding her again sent a great surge of renewed energy through me. No longer caring if she saw me now, for more than anything it was crucial that she didn't evade me again, I ran after her.

I was only a dozen paces behind her when abruptly she turned into the churchyard. She ran across the grass as lightly as a girl, and I marvelled at her energy; I was flagging now, my throat raw from panting, and I was desperate for water.

But it would have to wait.

She had reached the church door. The tower rose up high above us, and its deep shade was very welcome. She danced up the low steps and disappeared into the gloom inside.

I followed her.

Straight away I felt uneasy. I had been here once in pursuit of a monster which was slaying its victims by tearing their throats out, and I'd seen a young priest lose his life in the most horrible way. I'd been with Jack, and we—

No. Don't think about Jack. He is strong, he won't be harmed, he—

Ruthlessly I wrestled my mind back to my own battle.

The interior of the church was chilly after the hot sunshine outside, and I felt the sweat grow cold and damp on my skin. I paused to let my eyes adjust to the dim light.

The tower dominated the building. The nave consisted of little more than the large square space that formed its base, with modest extensions to either side.

The tower soared up into the heights. About a third of the way up there was a timber gallery running round all four walls, with an opening on one side where the narrow, steep little steps gave access from below. Above it, on a platform reached by a series of ladders and right at the top of the tower, was the open space where the bell hung. Gracefully arched openings let the light in, and there were round holes that allowed the owls to make their nests up there in safety.

It was a place of serenity and sanctuary, mysterious with the perfume of incense, and I should have found simply being there a comfort. But my eyes seemed to see that dead young priest, and my skin crawled in anticipation of some horror that I knew lay ahead. I told myself repeatedly that these fears were unreal; the priest was long gone, buried and probably forgotten, and my strength was equal to Errita.

Such was her power, however, that the phantoms persisted.

I heard her feet tapping on the steps. Turning, I saw that she was starting to climb.

I muttered a prayer and walked over to the base of the tower. I put my hands on the sides of the steep flight of steps and raised my foot to put it on the first one.

The ascent seemed to go on for ever. My body felt increasingly heavy, and the effort to raise each leg in turn made me wonder if flesh and bone had turned to lead. I fought off her malign spell and pushed on.

By the time I clambered out onto the gallery she was already halfway up the succession of ladders that went up at adjoined angles right to the top of the tower. And as I followed, there was a swirl of her skirts and she disappeared into the belfry.

I took the last few rungs slowly, deepening and steadying my breathing, calming my mind. Part of me knew what was ahead and welcomed it. I could not escape it – did not want to escape it – and the urge for confrontation was powerful. The other part of me was simply scared; very scared.

By the time I stepped off the ladder and ducked under the low arch that gave onto the space where the bell hung, my breathing and my heartbeat were utterly steady.

She stood with her back to the west window. She was silhouetted against the light, and although I could see her outline in sharp definition, I could not make out her face.

But I *felt* her evil, clouding out of her in a cold, clutching miasma, reaching to envelop me. I summoned my strength and imagined I had a bubble around me that held me untouchable. She knew; I could tell she did, because she let out a hiss of fury.

She did not speak. I stared at her intently, trying to judge her mood, trying to read her intention. She was a slight figure against the window, which formed a rectangle topped with two elegant curves that met in a smooth cube of stone. Behind her the lowering sun painted the sky a rich, deep blue.

It was time to break the silence, and I knew it must be I who did so.

'You have come a long way to find me, Errita,' I said, pleased to notice how calm I sounded.

I felt her surprised displeasure as she noticed too.

'You left without saying goodbye, Lassair,' she said, her voice thin and harsh. 'And the two of us as good as sisters, for my mother was mother to you as well as to me!'

I might have guessed she would mention Luliwa the moment she spoke.

'I loved your mother,' I said. 'It grieved me to part from her, but both of us knew it was time.'

'Yes, because you had stolen from her everything she had to give!' The hot, furious words echoed round the tower.

'If you choose to express it that way, I cannot stop you,' I said coolly. 'But you know as well as I do that is not a true interpretation, for what Luliwa gave me was in recompense for a moral debt that she had incurred, and she bestowed it freely.' She bestowed it with love, I could have added, but I did not want to provoke her further.

'She should have given what she had to give to *me*,' Errita said, and there was a sob in her voice. 'I am her child, I always did as she bade me, I followed her orders and carried them out immaculately.'

'You went beyond what she commanded, Errita,' I replied. 'You killed where there was no need, purely because you could and you saw no value in the lowly life you took.'

She shrugged. 'So?'

I loathed her in that moment.

But for her mother's sake who I loved, I tried one last time.

'Can we not put this behind us?' I said, trying to smile. 'We have suffered the consequences of a deep-reaching conflict that was not of our making. Have we not endured enough? You just said we were as good as sisters, you and I, so may we not start to act as if we truly are?'

She moved slightly so that just for a moment the light fell on her face. I knew then that this was hopeless, for she had changed from the woman I had known, and now her flesh seemed to have fallen away, leaving holes for eyes and mouth and an impression of snarling teeth reaching out for me like those of a savage predator.

And, as if to underline the impression, she said icily, 'No. It is far too late.'

She was staring at me, the clear brown eyes with the golden lights fixed on mine, compelling, controlling, and, glancing down as I caught movement, I saw her hands go to the sheath on her belt where she carried her pair of knives and unfasten the flap that hid them from sight.

I gathered my strength and stepped towards her, closing in on her, pinning her arms to her sides.

We were locked in an embrace like lovers, and my cheek was against hers. I felt the rasp of her rough, dirty hair. She stank of foul things: of bodily waste, of old sweat, of bad teeth and rotting flesh.

The thought flashed through my mind: *I think she is dead already.*

But then she began to fight me.

At the outset I thought in horror that she was trying to wrest me round so that it was I who stood in front of the window, my back to the vast space. But then I realized with equal dread that she wasn't.

She was trying to get out of my grasp, and already she was leaning backwards, her spine curving over so that her head and shoulders were out there in the empty air above that awful drop.

I tightened my grip, arm and shoulder muscles starting to cramp as I held her to me, her panting gasps right in my ear deafening me, dizzying me when already my head was swimming. '*No*, Errita!' I cried, 'please, you must not do this!'

'*I must!*' Her words were a wail of despair. 'I have set myself against you, persuaded myself that one of us must overcome the other, that there is no other way than that you recognize me as the stronger, the greater, the more worthy.' She began to weep, great wracking sobs bursting out of her, her entire thin, enfeebled, filthy body shaking and trembling. '*But I'm not!*'

Then the struggle began in earnest. I knew she was already seeing herself falling backwards out of the window, tumbling and turning towards the unforgiving ground, smashing herself to pieces when she hit it. I could *see* the images, for in that moment our consciousnesses merged and I saw what she saw, felt what she felt.

And the depths of her despair struck me like a knife blade.

'Please, Errita,' I cried, 'I can help you! There is a way for both of us to survive and thrive, and you must not—'

She had wriggled her arms out from beneath mine, and now I was grasping her round her thin waist. Moving with desperate speed, she delved down into the sheath at her belt and with unbelievable strength, raised her hands again.

But now her hands were lethal, for each gripped a short-bladed, deadly sharp knife.

She stared straight into my eyes.

I waited for my death.

But then she whispered, 'Sorry.'

I did not know at first what had happened.

I felt as if I'd been hit, simultaneously in two places at once, and suddenly I was grasping at empty air and there was a whistling sound and then a thump. And the late sun came pouring unimpeded through the window.

Trembling, shaking, I leaned forward and looked out.

She lay half on the path, half on the grass. One leg was bent right out to one side, the other was crumpled under her. Her hands still held her knives, and the blades were red. Her head lay at an angle to her body, and her eyes were wide open.

Although a pool of blood was already forming beneath her, she was smiling.

What a lot of blood.

And it was odd, but I could *feel* the blood, smell it, hear it drip-dripping on the ground.

Wasn't that strange, when she was all that way down, far, far below me?

I leaned back against the cool stone of the wall, my legs weak, dizzy and sick. I let myself slide down until I was sitting on the floor.

Then the pain began and, faster than I could have imagined it could, the last darkness stealthily stole over me.

Jack was almost exhausted. He had reached the town far ahead of Walter and the others, but then Walter was still recovering from having knocked himself out, and he wouldn't have been moving at all were not Ginger, Big Gerald and Luke taking it in turns to support him.

Jack's concentration was all on finding Lassair and Errita.

I cannot search for them alone, Jack thought as he ran. *I have no idea where Errita would lead her – where she has been hiding.*

He must go first to the castle, to gather together a band of men to hunt for them. He was filled with the urge to tear the whole town apart with his bare hands till he found her, but his logical side told him he couldn't do this alone.

He pounded up the road that lead towards the market, shoving people out of the way and earning shouts of indignant protest and raised fists. He was running past the turning that led to St Bene't's church when he heard voices.

A woman screamed.

And he felt as if his heart had stopped.

He flew along the narrow lane, the church up ahead, its tower like a raised, admonitory finger.

The woman screamed again and a man shouted, 'They're fighting, and they're right in the window! Oh, God, oh God, *oh God*, they're falling!'

The cry was taken up by others, someone was wailing and a priest appeared, still chewing, looking round anxiously for the cause of all the shouting.

'Up in the tower!' a young woman yelled at Jack. '*Look!*'

He looked.

They were poised on the windowsill, the figure with her back to him leaning right out, the other with her arms wound tightly round the first one's waist. *If one goes they both will*, Jack thought, and he felt ice-cold with horror.

'Someone get up there and stop them!' an old woman cried.

Jack spun round, about to race into the church, but then the screaming started up again and he caught a flash of movement.

There was a thump and the sound of a crack.

Very slowly he walked over to the body.

It lay in the deep shadow of the tower and at first all he could see was a dark gown and a white cap. The long hair had come unwound and it was rapidly turning dark red.

But what still remained unsullied was not copper but brown, with a streak of silver running through it.

He turned to the priest, who was right beside him. 'I must go to the other woman,' he said, and the priest, already dropping to his knees, nodded.

The steep flight of steps up to the gallery was hard enough, but as he made his way up the successive ladders to the belfry, Jack thought his strength was going to run out. He was gasping for breath, chest heaving, soaked in sweat. He made himself go on.

He bent down under the arch and emerged into the sunlit space.

She was slumped beneath the west window. She was covered in blood. Her eyes were closed.

He thought she was dead.

He went over to her, knelt down, put a hand to her face. She was cool.

He said, 'Lassair.' It was all he could manage.

An eternity passed.

He thought of the time they had spent together. Of growing to love her. Of their one night together, straight after which he had been so badly injured that everyone, including him, had thought he would die. Of how she had nursed him, then gone away. Of how, when she came back, he told her he didn't want her.

Of how every single day since he had regretted it.

He sat down beside her and bowed his head.

'Jack?'

It was the tiniest whisper, and he thought at first it was his imagination, refusing to believe she was dead and providing proof she wasn't.

Then it came again.

'Jack, I am hurt.'

He leapt up so swiftly that his head swam. Then he was bending over her, taking her face in his hands, laughing and sobbing at the same time and only able to say her name, over and over again.

Then, with a huge effort, she raised her hand to touch his.

And he realized hers was drenched in blood.

'Be still, rest now and I will look after you,' he said, fighting to keep his voice calm and low, to reassure her. To reassure himself. 'Let me see.'

Mutely she put her hands, palm uppermost, in her lap.

And he saw what Errita had done.

Lassair had been holding on to her, stopping her from taking her plunge down to the hard ground.

And she had cut herself free.

On the inside of each of Lassair's forearms, carved into the pale white skin like a mason's incisions, were two long, deep cuts.

Both of them were pouring out blood.

Some inner wisdom took over. Jack pushed aside Lassair's gown and grabbed hold of the white underskirt, tearing into the fabric with his teeth and ripping off length after length. Then, taking hold of her left hand first because that cut was the more severe, he bound the forearm as tightly as he could, winding the cloth round and round and trying to ignore the way the blood kept welling out and staining each successive layer.

More fabric tearing and more binding. Then at last, when her left forearm was so heavily wrapped it was at least twice the normal size, he turned his attention to her right arm. This cut was not so deep but it was longer, and it clearly hurt much worse than the left arm. He sensed her trying to bite back her cries, but in the end the pain was too much and she howled like a wolf in a trap.

It all but broke him.

When he had finished he took her in his arms, for he felt both of them needed a brief rest. Because the next challenge was to get her down from the tower.

He heard the grunting and the muttered exclamations of people on the ladders outside. Turning towards the arch, he watched as Luke, Big Gerald and Ginger came into the bell room. Big Gerald was carrying something.

'Walter wanted to come up but he's still sick and dizzy from where he fell,' Luke panted. 'To be honest, chief, we reckoned we'd be safer without him.' He stared at Jack, frowning. 'Is she – has she—?'

Jack glanced down at Lassair. He was holding her tight against his chest. Her eyes were closed and he suspected she had fainted.

'She is alive,' he said softly.

All three men muttered words that were probably prayers. Ginger crossed himself.

'She's been badly hurt, though,' Jack went on. 'Deep cuts to both forearms.' He glanced at the arch. 'I don't know how we're going to get her down.'

Luke knelt down beside him. 'We've thought of that, chief,'

he said. 'We thought maybe – that is, if she'd been— Well, it's like this, we brought a thick blanket with us' – he nodded at Big Gerald, who smiled tentatively and held up the bundle he was carrying – 'so we could take a – take her down if she wasn't able to get down on her own.'

Briefly Jack closed his eyes as his devastating grief of only a very short time ago, when he had thought she was dead, returned. These men of his had thought the same thing, and they had come prepared to bear a corpse down out of the tower.

He was filled with gratitude for their practicality and, looking at their concerned faces, their kindness.

'How do you think we can manage?' he asked.

Ginger spoke up. 'Gerald here says he can carry a woman over his shoulder,' he said. 'I know it sounds dangerous, chief, what with all those blasted ladders, but he's done it before.'

Jack looked enquiringly at Big Gerald.

'Aye, I have, and more than once,' Big Gerald said. 'Trick is to wrap them in the blanket and fasten the ends tight, then if they take fright and try to get out of your grasp, they can't. Then you tie the blanket round you because you can't hold it with both hands. You need at least one for the descent, see, chief,' he added.

Two thoughts ran through Jack's head. Then first was that the process sounded fraught with peril, and the second was that if anyone was going to carry her, it should be him.

And Big Gerald leaned down and whispered in his ear, 'I know what you're thinking, chief, and course it should, only I'm stronger than you.'

To which there wasn't really a reply.

The descent seemed never-ending. Big Gerald, calm and steady, made his slow way down each of the ladders, most of the time only holding on with one hand and with the other around Lassair's waist. As the distance to the ground steadily decreased, Jack, leading the way, began to believe it might be all right . . .

But then just as Big Gerald began on the steps leading from the gallery to the safety of the ground, Lassair came out of

her faint, realized where she was and gave out a scream. Jack,
already standing below, moved in a flash so that he was standing
right beneath her.

But Big Gerald was equal to it.

'Steady there, my lovely girl,' he said, his voice warm and
kindly. 'I have you safe, and very soon we'll be back on the
ground. You'll see!'

Jack waited, barely even breathing, until Big Gerald stepped
off the last rung. Then, with a quiet 'Thank you' that didn't
even begin to express the depth of his gratitude, he took Lassair
from him and, with the others either side of him, walked out
of the church.

'Where to, chief?' Luke muttered as Big Gerald and Ginger
went ahead to forge a way through the crowd, Walter staggering along in their wake.

There was only one place to go. Jack gave directions, and
the men and the women who had witnessed the whole horrific
episode stood in silence to watch as they walked away.

NINETEEN

I woke with a start. I wondered where I was. It was dark, I was lying on something soft and I was warm.

Was I really awake?

I wasn't at all sure.

I had been dreaming vividly, and I had a horrible memory of screaming in pain. Gurdyman had been there, and Hrype of all people, although I could not at first recall what he had been doing . . .

I think I slept again then.

I woke with that particular memory restored. Hrype had been sitting beside me, bending over each of my arms in turn as they rested on his lap. Gurdyman had held me still while Hrype stitched me with tiny, careful stitches. It had hurt so intensely that my throat was raw with screaming.

I sent sensors through my body.

Was I still in pain?

I wasn't sure.

There was something else: I kept slipping from reality to dreams, passing in and out of visions and illusions, and I knew from the bitter taste in my mouth that Gurdyman or Hrype – Gurdyman probably, he was the more humane when it came to other people's pain – had given me some of the precious, peril-fraught poppy. Being Gurdyman, however, he'd have judged the dose with absolute precision, and I had no cause to be concerned.

Something else felt . . . not painful, not even uncomfortable, but strange . . .

Again I slept for a while.

When I woke again, I understood.

I was in my bed in my little attic room. I was lying on my left side, and my arms were crossed over in front of my breast. I felt totally, utterly safe, and the reason for that was because I wasn't alone. Someone was lying deeply asleep behind me, someone big and strong and exuding a wonderfully comfortable warmth. What felt odd was that he had his arms around me, so that he held me close to him, and his hands were over mine, gently restraining me and making sure my damaged forearms didn't move as I slept.

I sent my thoughts back to the events of the day. My memory seemed to run out when Errita threw herself out of the tower, and how I came to be here in my bed with my wounds tended and a draught of poppy keeping the pain at bay, I did not know.

It didn't really matter.

I don't think I had ever in my life felt more safe.

Everything else could wait until the morning. I leaned into Jack and went back to sleep.

When I woke again it was bright morning and I was alone in the bed.

The initial instant of panic swiftly dissipated when I heard steps on the ladder and Jack appeared, a mug of some hot, steaming liquid in his hand.

'An infusion made with the ingredients Gurdyman left beside the hearth,' he said. 'He told me you were to have it when you woke up.'

'How did you know I was about to wake up?'

He didn't reply, just smiled at me.

He put the mug down on the floor and came to perch on the bed beside me. Moving very slowly, he helped me sit up and propped me up with pillows.

He looked anxiously at me. 'That hurt. Didn't it?'

I nodded. 'But I imagine that infusion will help.'

He picked it up and, sitting beside me, one arm round me, helped me to hold it while I sipped. My hands felt stiff and I could see they were very swollen. My fingers didn't have their usual flexibility.

I tried not to think about the implications of that, but Jack must have realized what was on my mind. 'It won't be easy at first,' he said quietly. 'The cuts went deep, and Hrype said there was a lot of damage to the sinews, especially on your left arm.'

I nodded. 'I'll just have to give it time,' I said, trying to sound bright and cheerful. 'I've told enough patients to do precisely that, so now I'll have to take my own advice.'

'It's good advice,' Jack said, helping me to tip up the mug so that I could drain the dregs. Then he took it from me and changed his position so that now we were looking at each other.

I drank him in.

'I can't believe you're really here,' he said huskily, putting into words exactly what I was thinking.

'No. It's like a miracle,' I agreed, 'particularly when you consider that only yesterday both of us were face to face with someone who had been doing their best to kill us.'

He nodded but didn't reply. Then, after a moment, he said, 'Are you back?'

I didn't even have to think about my answer. 'Yes.'

He looked straight at me, and I saw the love in his eyes. 'Then I—'

But I couldn't let him go on. Not yet.

'Jack, there is something I must tell you,' I said.

His expression changed. His eyes wary, he said, 'Yes?'

Even in that single word I heard his slight withdrawal. But I had to go on.

'When we – when we lay together, that time just before Gaspard Picot wounded you so badly, I – I later found out I had conceived a child.' He went pale but did not speak. 'When I went away, as you were starting to get better, I had only just realized and I did not know what to do.'

'You could have told me,' he said dully.

'I couldn't,' I said very gently. 'If I had done, you would have said we should marry and I would have agreed because I loved you – love you – but I didn't think I was ready because I had a very strong sense that there was something I had to do, and when Rollo asked me to go on his mission with him I thought perhaps it was that, but it wasn't, it – the thing I had to do – was going off with Gurdyman afterwards and living in the City of Pearl and in the settlement on the coast, and being taught all that the people there had to teach me.'

He was no longer looking at me, but down at the floor. 'Where is the child?' he asked, in a voice that didn't sound like his.

I felt the tears prickle behind my eyelids. I took a breath

and said, as steadily as I could, 'I lost it, very soon after I got back to my village when I'd left you.'

Now I too was staring at the floor. I didn't think I could bear to look at him.

For several moments time hung completely still.

Then I felt him move, and suddenly his arms were round me, holding me to him, even in that moment being so careful not to hurt my wounds, and I leant against him and let his being absorb mine.

'I am so sorry,' he whispered. 'You came back, after everything you had been through, and I told you to go away.'

I'm going out now, he had said when I went to his house to find him. *When I get back, I'd like you not to be here.*

I could still hear him saying the words.

I thought he probably could too, for he gave a sort of a moan. 'I didn't know about the baby,' he muttered.

'I know why you turned me away,' I said through my tears. 'You believed I was grieving for Rollo, and if you'd let me come back to you, you thought you'd just be helping me get over the loss of someone else. I *was* grieving, because Rollo and I had once been very close, but that was a long time in the past, and when we spent that time together, it was he who was helping me get over losing you and the baby. So when he was killed, I lost a good friend, and it was—' But I couldn't go on.

Jack reached up a hand and very gently stroked the hair back from my face. 'And then you went to Spain for half a dozen years,' he said, and a very faint smile twisted his lips.

'Yes,' I agreed. 'You came to find me, and I told you I would come back.'

'You did, and here you are.'

His hand on my jaw, very gently he turned my face so we were looking at each other. I stared into his eyes, and saw the question that still lingered.

'I shall not go away again unless we go together,' I said. 'I have known for a long time that the place I want to be is here, with you, if you'll have me?' I had asked once before and he had rejected me, but this was no time for pride.

'I would be on my knees before you asking you to stay,'

he murmured, 'only I'd much rather be sitting here holding you.'

Then he bent his head and kissed me.

The hours of the day passed in a strange mixture of elation when visitors clambered up the ladder to see me, and sudden annihilating fatigue that had me falling into deep sleep within moments so that I was only vaguely aware of Jack or Gurdyman quickly ushering out whoever had come to call. But I would not have missed the visits for anything. They served to show me, if I needed showing, that I had friends here, that I had a role in the community, that I belonged.

Big Gerald brought me a bunch of rather battered flowers – his hands were a little too large and unsubtle for holding delicate blooms – but I was very pleased to see him. Jack had told me how he had carried me down the tower, and I knew I wouldn't rest easy until I'd thanked him. The others came too, Luke, Walter, Ginger, and we took a quiet moment to share the thought that we all wished Young Henry was there too.

Fritha and Mattie came from the refuge, and Mattie brought her little girl with her. They both looked healthy and contented, and I realized how much prettier Mattie was when she smiled. As she negotiated her careful way back down the ladder, I beckoned to Fritha to wait for a moment.

'May I come and talk to you once I've recovered?' I asked quietly.

'Of course.' She looked at me enquiringly.

'I have had an idea,' I said. 'I've discovered that there's a large room hidden away in this house, at present with no purpose. I think it might serve as somewhere safe and secure where girls and women and their children who are sick and wounded, and perhaps trying to escape from some brutal man, can be tended. Please don't think I'm being critical of the refuge,' I added hastily, for her expression had changed and I thought she might have taken offence, 'I think what you do there is invaluable.'

Slowly she shook her head. 'I didn't think that,' she said. She grinned. 'Well, maybe I did, but I'm the first to admit conditions down there on the quay aren't ideal.' She caught my eye, raising an ironic eyebrow. 'They'd let you do it, whoever's

house this is? Let you open up this hidden room as a place to
care for people?'

The predictable and innocent question raised matters I
didn't want to think about. Not yet; not till I had to.

So I just said, 'Yes.'

She nodded. 'I like your idea. Come down to the refuge, soon
as you're fit again, and we'll talk.'

She was descending the ladder, intent on what she was
doing, when she raised her head and said very quietly, 'You're
not going to let Jack Chevestrier go, are you?'

'Oh, no.'

She grinned. 'Very wise. See you soon.'

Late in the afternoon, while Jack had gone on a quick visit to
the castle, Hrype came up to the attic room.

I looked at him as he stood at the foot of the bed. He was
still gaunt-faced, pale and too thin, but now there was a hint
of excitement in his silvery eyes.

'You look better,' I said softly.

He nodded. 'How about you? In pain?'

'It's manageable,' I replied. 'I believe I am in your debt.' I
raised my arms.

'We'd better have a look before you start thanking me,' he
said gruffly.

The unwinding of the bandages was as unpleasant as I'd
anticipated. Hrype fetched a bowl of hot water, with which
he softened the crust of dried blood and yellowish fluid that
stuck the layers of cloth together, and that helped a little. All
the same, by the time both my forearms lay bare, I was in a
lot of pain and sweating all over.

Together Hrype and I looked at his work.

The cut on my right arm was long and quite shallow, and
he had only stitched it together at one end, where Errita's
knife had driven in hard. The wound on my left arm was more
worrying, for it was much deeper and now it hurt far worse.
Hrype touched the surrounding flesh with gentle fingertips.

'No heat, so far,' he observed. 'The weapons were sharp
and the cuts cleanly made, which is all to the good.'

I pictured Errita and her knives. She had looked after them

with great care, always keeping them sharp. She had also been in the unlikely habit of plunging them each morning and evening into a pan of boiling water and leaving them bubbling and bouncing for the length of time it took to boil a couple of eggs. When I had asked her why she did this, she had scowled at me, turned on her heel and stalked away. It was Luliwa who had explained, when I mentioned it to her. 'It is something they do in the City of Pearl,' she said, and subsequently I had seen for myself. Nobody really explained the reason; merely that flesh cut with a clean blade was far less likely to fester and turn putrid than if a dirty blade was used.

'She washed her knives in boiling water,' I said to Hrype now. He looked at me quizzically. 'It's good practice,' I added.

His expression said as loudly as words, *I'll wait and see before I try it for myself.*

He picked up my left arm, turning it this way and that. I said when I could no longer hold the question back, 'Will it get better?'

He looked up at me. 'Provided infection does not set in, then yes, of course. You are young and fit, and it is the body's main mission to heal itself.'

I hesitated, for the answer to the next question would mark out the path I took for the rest of my life.

'Hrype, I can't move my fingers very well. Is that – will that improve?'

He examined first my right hand, then the left, pushing at the puffy skin, moving the joints, curling up the fingers as tightly as he could. Dear God, it hurt. Then he said, 'The swelling is because of the severity of the wounds. See how the left hand is the more affected?'

I looked. He was right.

I met his eyes and he smiled: such a kind, understanding smile.

'Keep moving your fingers,' he advised. 'Stretching and bending your hands will encourage the fluid to dissipate.' He leaned closer. 'You know this, Lassair! You do not need me to tell you, for you have treated many injuries such as these of yours.'

I managed a smile. 'It's different when it's yourself.'

He laughed. 'The perpetual complaint of the healer.' Then, his expression growing serious, he added, 'You are a fine healer, Lassair. Better than I, for you engage with those you treat where I stand detached.' He paused, then, his face working, he said very softly, 'Your aunt would be very proud of you. You are Edild reborn.'

He couldn't have said anything that pleased me more. That moved me more. I wiped away a tear, and I think he probably did the same.

My last visitor of the day was Gurdyman.

'I have stayed away,' he puffed as he clambered up into the attic room, 'because you have had so many well-wishers insisting on seeing you, and in the intervals between callers it was important that you rest.'

'Jack has been making quite sure I do,' I replied.

Just saying his name made me glow.

Gurdyman sat down with a grunt on the end of the bed. He was watching me, his bright blue eyes moist. 'He loves you,' he said.

'I love him.'

'Enough to stay? To make your future here in the town? No more sailing away to outlandish destinations like Iceland and Spain?'

'Not unless Jack and I go together,' I replied, just as I'd said to Jack.

Gurdyman's gaze was even more intent. 'Will it be enough? Do you truly see your life bound to his?'

I hesitated. Not because I was in any doubt but because I wanted to find the words that would make Gurdyman understand.

'Jack and I have much to discuss,' I said slowly, 'for I have not spent the last six years – and, indeed, much of my life prior to that – learning so much from so many deeply wise, knowledgeable and skilled people simply to give it all up now. But Jack knows this,' I hurried on as Gurdyman opened his mouth to speak, 'and also that what I do is what makes me the person I am.'

'You are quite sure he knows this? You've asked him?' His tone was urgent.

I smiled. 'I don't need to.'

There was silence for some time. Then Gurdyman stirred and said, 'This house is yours now, together with everything in it. I shall pack a small bag with my personal belongings, but there is nothing else I want.'

I had known this moment was coming. I had tried to prepare for it, to brace myself for the pain I knew it was going to bring, but it seemed that preparation hadn't done much good.

'The heat of the south will be good for your aching muscles and joints,' I said after a while, trying to smile.

'Yes.' He reached out and took my hand. 'Thank you for not even trying to deter me,' he said quietly.

'Would it do any good?' I asked.

'Not the very least.' Now he smiled too.

'I have no right,' I said after a moment. 'Besides, you told me what you were going to do, ages ago.' I frowned. 'Or at least I think you did . . . Anyway, it is your decision. They will be very pleased to have you back.'

He inclined his head in modest acknowledgement. 'The pleasure will be mutual.'

There was something I very much wanted to ask him, but it was not easy.

'When you see Luliwa . . .' I began, but found I could not go on.

He waited, but when I still did not speak, he gently squeezed my hand.

'I believe she will already know what has happened, child,' he said. 'I imagine she said her farewells to her daughter when Errita left to come chasing after you.'

'But now Errita's dead,' I whispered. 'I tried to hold on to her, Gurdyman, truly I did. I didn't want her to die and right at the end, when she looked at me and said "Sorry", I thought just for an instant that she had suddenly changed, that we'd be friends, close friends. She even said we were as good as sisters and—'

'Stop,' Gurdyman said softly. 'You knew, I think, that you could not both survive. Luliwa had given to you what Errita believed should have been hers, but even had it been she who lived and you who died, those powers would still not have been bestowed upon her. Luliwa knew – we all knew – that in Errita they would have become corrupted. Whereas in you they will flourish and grow.' His eyes twinkled. 'Especially with Jack to remind you what's right and what's wrong.'

Greatly surprised, recalling our exchange of only a short time ago, I said, 'So you *do* think Jack and I will make each other happy?'

He chuckled. 'I've always known you would, child. I was only waiting for the two of you to realize it too.'

It had grown dark outside.

Gurdyman fetched water for me to wash my face and hands, and helped me prepare to settle for the night. When I was lying back in bed, both arms throbbing with pain, he fetched me an infusion. 'I've made it strong,' he said. He grinned as I drank it down. 'There won't be any enjoying of your beautiful bed just yet, my girl. You'll sleep soundly this night.'

I smiled as I watched him disappear down the ladder.

He was right, but it didn't matter.

There was plenty of time.

I was already drowsy when Jack came back. I watched through half-closed eyes as he peeled off his jerkin and dropped his dagger in its sheath on the floor, then dragged off his boots.

He sat on the side of the bed, looking down at me. His face seemed to glow and his eyes were full of love. I'd never seen that expression on his face before.

'How are you?' he asked.

'Lonely,' I replied.

'Even after all those visitors?'

'They weren't you.' I moved over and he got in beside me. 'They weren't going to be here with me and keep me safe through the night.'

He put his arms round me, very carefully drawing me to him. 'Is this all right?' he asked quietly.

I crossed my hands and pulled my arms in close to my chest, the way he had done the night before. Either Gurdyman's infusion had suddenly taken effect, or Jack's closeness and love were driving out the pain, but all at once it was all right; far more than all right.

So I just said, 'Yes.'

TWENTY

t did not take long for the extraordinary news to reach Cambridge.

When Jack came hurrying home from the castle to tell me, I did not need to hear the details because I had already seen the whole event in the vision I'd had in the New Forest. I saw him die, although I did not know then who he was.

And very soon afterwards, as we absorbed what had happened, finally we understood the nature of the secret that Eleanor de Lacey, Stephen leClerc, poor, bemused Herlvin de Varaville and even Young Henry had died to keep: there had been a conspiracy to murder the King, and word of it had leaked out.

I remembered the image that had filled my head of the fierce fire burning and the dangerous little trails of flame creeping out from it across the dry grass, only to be ruthlessly stamped out.

And so they had died, those three old conspirators and that likeable, cheerful young man whose life had held such promise.

As shock and amazement faded, in the aftermath the questions began.

Who had killed the King?

Quite a lot of people, especially the monks and the priests, claimed it had been divine retribution. I understood their point of view, but I preferred to think that Jesus told us the truth when he said his God is a God of love, and such a deity surely did not take that sort of vicious revenge.

A man called Walter Tirel had shot the fatal bolt, or so it was said; he was someone of high status in France and he was a companion of King William and his guest on the hunting trip. The story went that he had been dazzled by the setting sun and sent his arrow at the stag, not seeing the King standing between him and his quarry.

Had it been an accident? Of course, people said; a terrible

accident, and this man Tirel must be devastated, crushed with
guilt at having killed his friend the King, desperate to explain
what had happened and that it really wasn't his fault. But then
the rumour began to be whispered that he had fled straight
back to France immediately after the King died.

So was it in fact murder, carefully disguised to look like
accident?

As Luke remarked as we all sat in Magnus's inn on an
evening a day or two later, this Tirel was either a rotten shot
or a very good one.

None of us could understand why Walter Tirel wasn't
instantly under suspicion. Why he hadn't been stopped,
arrested, questioned. He'd just killed the King, even if it was
an accident. Did everyone just take Tirel's word for what
happened? We learned that they had greeted him back in his
native land like a hero and feted him for what he had done.
The French king himself was said to have embraced and
congratulated him, but surely that had been no more than
gossip . . .

Another factor that threw suspicion on Walter Tirel was
that he was married to a woman whose family enjoyed the
patronage of Henry Beauclerc. And Henry was our new King.

He had been with William on the fateful hunting trip. For
all any of us knew, he might have been right there in the
clearing at sunset and seen his brother die. Whether he had
or not, he wasted no time in racing to Winchester to lay claim
to the royal treasury, after which he hurried on to Westminster
and was crowned on the fifth of August, a mere three days
after his brother's death.

Poor William, they said, had had an ominous dream the
night before he died. He dreamt he was being bled, and a great
spurt of blood shot up out of his body like a fountain. Perhaps
he would have been wiser not to go out the next day, but kings
have to demonstrate that they are not afraid, and so he went.
And as soon as he was dead, he went from the most to the
least important in the land, his body slung on a cart that
bounced and jounced it to Winchester for swift burial.

I knew all about it. I'd seen that, too.

There was speculation that the earlier, very similar death of

Duke Robert's illegitimate son Richard, back in May, might have been what gave the conspirators the idea for how to kill the King. By all accounts Duke Robert's son really had died in an accident. Was it not rather too much of a coincidence for exactly the same accident to have killed the King three months later?

If it had been murder and not accident, why should somebody want him dead? Discussing it in Magnus's tavern as we all did, the best suggestion was that word had spread of King William's planned mission to Poitou to carve out for himself a base in France – the mission for which I'd seen the fleet being prepared as I came home – and that some powerful factions over there decided they'd really rather he didn't proceed with it. It was an answer, of sorts.

The death of the King was all anyone talked of for days. Then, as so often happens when something momentous occurs, slowly and steadily the excited chatter lessened and people discovered that gossiping about their neighbours and the ruinous price of a loaf of bread was actually more interesting. We had a new king, who might or might not prove to be a good monarch. Since there was nothing any of us could do if he didn't, most of us turned away and got on with our lives.

I was healing rapidly, already able to do simple tasks and rejoicing that the stiffness in my fingers was easing so quickly. My wounds did not fester. Hrype was staying in the town, in Gurdyman's house, and as I showed him the swiftly mending scars I remarked that maybe there was something in Errita's belief in the beneficial effects of cleaning a blade in boiling water after all. He didn't comment other than to give me an enigmatic look out of his silvery eyes.

I had moved into Jack's house. I did not feel comfortable taking up residence again in the twisty-turny house while Gurdyman was still there. I felt, I believe, that he ought to be free to enjoy his last days there without the presence of the person who was to take over its occupation. My beloved Gurdyman would soon be gone, and I dreaded the day.

But in compensation, there was so much to make me happy. To make *us* happy, for Jack and I had given each other our promise and we would be wed in the autumn. In the meantime, there was his small but perfect house, a bed, an ardent, fiercely loving man and a woman whose wounded arms no longer pained her. I watched him glow with joy, and I knew I looked exactly the same.

We went out to Aelf Fen as soon as I was sufficiently healed to ride a horse. Jack waited with our mounts under the tree that stands on the higher ground behind the village, and I went down to my parents' house alone.

I had not known, but my mother was on her way back from a visit to my sister Goda that day.

When I pushed the door open and looked inside, my father was alone. He was sitting beside the hearth, and he was carving a piece of wood into a little statue. He didn't hear the door open, and it was only after a few moments that he seemed to sense me looking at him.

Very slowly he raised his head and turned to me.

He let out a soft breath and just said, 'Lassair.'

I flew across the little space between us and into his arms even as he rose up and stepped towards me. Neither of us said a word. I felt his body shake with silent sobs, and my own face was wet with tears.

After quite some time, he said in a surprisingly normal voice, 'Your mother will be home soon. She said she'd be back by midday, and I promised to get the fire ready for the pot.'

I dried my eyes and said, 'That's good, because I have something to tell you.'

By the time my mother came home – she greeted me with a brief hug, a nod and a muttered, 'You've come back, then,' but I was wiser now and I could read her love for me like words on a page – my father had built up the fire and put water on to boil and I had summoned Jack down from beneath the tree. My parents took the news of our betrothal each in their own typical way, my mother remarking she was pleased I was to settle down and stop 'all this roaming aimlessly about', my father saying the right words but nevertheless giving Jack the sort of look that a father who dearly loves his daughter always bestows on the man she is going to marry.

But I had no doubt that it would be all right. I knew Jack, and I knew his quality. My father was a decent and honourable man, and once he too understood Jack's nature, he would, I believed, appreciate that I had chosen wisely.

My mother succeeded in making a meal for two stretch to one for four, employing her usual efficiency and skill so that anyone would have thought that was what she'd been planning all along. And, as we were sitting back after the food, the conversation flowing well and a happy atmosphere in the little house, I caught her looking at me. Her eyes fixed on mine, she gave a small nod and sent me a private smile.

It was good to be home.

I left Jack listening to a lecture on eel-catching from my father while my mother, having refused my offer to help ('Those wounds of yours won't heal if you keep getting them wet, as you ought to know without me telling you'), cleared away the meal. I slipped out of the house and went to the burial ground behind the church, where I knelt by my dear aunt Edild's grave and said goodbye to her.

I didn't know why she had been lain to rest there and not out on the little island with others of our ancestors. Had it been her choice? Hrype's choice? I could have asked him, but somehow I knew I wasn't going to. She was dead, and that was hard enough to overcome. Where she was buried didn't really matter to me.

A week went by, then another. The wounds on my forearms were improving daily. Hrype had removed the stitches from the deep incision on my left arm but, although the skin had knitted itself together again, the wound was still lividly pink and quite sore, and I kept it padded with protective bandaging. But now, thankfully, I was able to leave the shallower cut on my right arm uncovered. The scar would always remain, but the incision had been straight and true, and it was not too unsightly. Jack, when he saw me staring down at it one morning, must have seen some echo of dismay in my face, for he took my hand, turned my arm so the scar was uppermost and put a trail of very light kisses all the way down it. Which, given how new our physical closeness was and the vast delight we took in each other, of course led to intimacy of a different kind and delayed him, so that when he finally arrived panting in the guardroom, Big Gerald – patiently waiting because he and Jack had a task to see to that day – had started to wonder where he'd got to and innocently asked what had held him up. To the huge amusement, Jack confessed to me, of everyone else present.

I kept busy that day.

I was gathering together the items I would need when I moved into Gurdyman's house, amassing ingredients for remedies, potions, balms and ointments, purchasing the implements I required to go about my craft. It was an extraordinary novelty to have money; to be able to enter an apothecary's shop – any shop – and buy what I needed. I was already feeling embarrassed about my wealth, and I had tried very hard to pass much of it on to my family. My parents would accept absolutely nothing – I'd anticipated as much – and my dear sister Elfritha, being a nun, had no use whatsoever for money. My brother Haward and his wife Zarina accepted a little, but only because they needed more space for their growing family, and I promised to reserve exactly the same sum for my younger brothers Squeak and Leir. It wouldn't be long until they were husbands and fathers too, and few in that position turn down the offer of money.

My sister Goda would have taken the lot if I'd let her, but I only gave her the same amount I'd presented to Haward.

I was thinking about my brothers and sisters, smiling with the sheer pleasure of knowing they were less than a morning's ride away and I could go and visit whenever I liked, as I went about my tasks that day. I needed to think of happy things, needed to keep occupied, because, late in the afternoon, I was going to have to say goodbye to Gurdyman.

Jack was back early. He knew what this parting meant to me, and, as I was quickly discovering to be typical of him, he showed his support and his understanding just by being there. I was often reminded of the way he'd lain behind me the night after Errita had wounded me so gravely, just there, holding me close, keeping me still so that I didn't disturb the stitches and the bindings.

Now, as we sat down to food I'd prepared but didn't feel able to eat, he looked up and simply said, 'Shall I come with you or would you rather go alone?'

I was quite surprised that he should ask; that he didn't know how much I needed him there with me. But then I thought, *He understands that Gurdyman and I have a long history, one which began before he and I met, and he's giving me the chance of having a private farewell without the awkwardness of asking for it.*

It made me love him even more.

I reached across the little table and took his hand. 'I would like you to come with me, please.'

And, yet again, the expression on his face filled me with joy.

We were on the quayside next to where *The Maid of the Marsh* lay alongside when Gurdyman and Hrype arrived. Both were dressed for travel, with cloaks that would provide warmth as well as keeping off the worst of the weather and the sea spray. They would not have been too warm, for the late afternoon had a chill to it. Autumn was on the way.

Gurdyman carried a bulging leather bag, but Hrype had no more than his habitual small pack. Jack and I waited while they exchanged words with the boat's master, paid their fares and briefly went on board to stow Gurdyman's bag and reserve their space on deck. Then they returned to the quay.

Hrype stepped towards me and gave me a quick, intense hug. 'Goodbye, Lassair,' he said softly in my ear. Then he held me at arm's length and looked straight into my eyes.

I returned the stare, although it was not easy. It seemed as if everything that had ever passed between us, the good and the bad, flashed through my head, and I suspect it was the same for him. After a few moments he nodded, gave a wry smile and murmured, 'You will do fine.'

Then he let me go, jerked his head in farewell to Jack and hurried back up the plank, to dip down behind the boat's rail and out of sight.

I turned to Gurdyman.

He made no brave attempt to hide his emotions. His bright blue eyes were full of tears and his face was working as he tried and failed to smile. My heart aching, I wrapped my arms round him and simply leant against him. He returned the hug, and I felt him gently patting my back.

'Don't be sad, child,' he whispered, the words just for me. 'You have such a life ahead of you! You have so much to give, and this town will benefit greatly from all that you and your man there will do for it. He is respected and admired because he is honest and just, and you will be treasured because you cannot see someone sick, wounded or in trouble without rushing to help. Use your inheritance wisely' – he gave me a little shake – 'and open up the old house so that it can provide the safe haven you have in mind for it. It is high time,' he added enigmatically.

'I will, I promise,' I replied, tears streaming down my face. 'And you, oh, *please* take care, dear Gurdyman! Don't keep on and on till you're worn out but take a day or two's rest now and then, and once you reach Spain and settle in the City of Pearl, don't try to do too much, remember to—'

But he put a gentle finger to my lips and stopped the flow of words.

'You forget, dear child, that you learned the good, wise advice you are so freely giving me from the very people among whom I shall be living,' he said gently. 'Be calm, for I shall be in good hands, and I shall find contentment and happiness down there in the sunshine. There is no need to worry.'

We stood in silence, eyes on each other's, then he leaned forward and kissed my cheek. 'Farewell, child,' he said, and his voice broke on the words.

'Farewell, dearest Gurdyman,' I whispered.

He turned and held out his hand to Jack, then, with Gurdyman leaning rather heavily on Jack, together they edged up the short length of the plank and, just as Hrype had done, my friend and mentor disappeared from view.

Jack came back and without a word took me in his arms.

The Maid of the Marsh was ready to sail. We watched as ropes were released and drawn up, as the sailors pushed off with their poles, as the boat found the current and slowly began to move off. All around us those seeing people off or who had had business with the boat were swiftly dispersing, and presently Jack and I stood there alone. We went on watching as *The Maid of the Marsh* slowly rounded the first long, shallow bend, until the final moment when at last we couldn't see her any more.

Then we went home.

I felt Gurdyman's absence keenly. I had a dire need of some big task to get on with, and happily I had one: I took over the twisty-turny house the day after he left.

Jack helped me whenever he could, as did every one of the close group of his companions. They too needed something purposeful to occupy their thoughts, for all of them mourned Young Henry and were still sore and angry at the waste of the promise of his life.

Big Gerald said modestly that he was quite good with a sledgehammer, and he proved to be even better than his word as together we set about opening up the hidden room. I'd entered it via the tiny, narrow, twisting flight of stairs, but that would be no good for people coming to the house because they were sick or wounded, and our first task was to make a new access off the passage that ran through the house from the door to the courtyard at the back. I thought at first that it was going to be too much; that my enthusiasm far outreached what could be achieved; but I'd reckoned without my dependable and capable band of helpers. All of them were good at something, some of them were good at everything, and, most importantly, all of them were always willing, turning up when they had promised to even when they'd had a hard day, were exhausted and would far rather have gone home to eat and rest.

Jack proved to be an excellent handyman – not that this surprised me – and it was he whose artistic eye and skilled hands turned the hidden room into a large, light, bright ward with whitewashed walls and a floor of dark, glossy oak. Less than six weeks after Gurdyman had gone, we were ready for our first residents, and Fritha brought a procession of eight

women, two of them pregnant and one very near her time,
four children and two babies from the quay. The first baby
was born in the twisty-turny house's new ward a day and a
half later.

The hidden room quickly became loud with the voices of
women and children, and already I was planning to instruct
other women in the skills needed to care for mothers in childbirth and infants in the tender early hours and days of their
lives. Fritha and I hoped that our reputation would quickly
spread, and, as we prepared to take in more people, the next
task would be to turn the dingy little space under the attic
room into a proper kitchen.

I had created my workroom down in the crypt. I'd had a
window installed up near the ceiling so it was no longer the
dark and secret place where Gurdyman worked and wove his
magic, but a place that smelt of sweet herbs and fragrant oils
where the sun crept in to brighten the darkness. As I worked
down there I very often felt Gurdyman's presence and he
always seemed to be smiling his approval. I had spent rather
a lot of Rollo's gold on furnishing the new accommodation,
as well as on buying in my store of preparations, ointments,
remedies, oils and infusions, and, although I never actually
sensed him with me, I had an idea he too would have approved.

I had never been quite sure of the source of Rollo's wealth,
but I had a strong suspicion it might not all have been honestly
earned. There was nothing I could do about that, and it wasn't
for me to pass judgement on how Rollo had elected to spend
his life. I was happy to think that money was money, when
all was said and done, in itself neither good nor bad; and to
hope that, however it had been acquired, there could be no
doubt that now it was being put to very good use.

The crypt had another purpose. It was the place where I
could be quite alone, and that was very precious for sometimes
the pull of that other world, which Luliwa and the others
in the south had shown me how to access, was very powerful.
Her teachings had been a revelation, and although much of
what I learned seemed somehow to have become a part of me,
at times I felt drawn to enter the trance state and slip back to
that strange place of dreams, visions and possibilities. I was

the only person like me that I knew, just then. It would have been lonely, except for two things. First, I only had to reach the margins of the world beyond the membrane to be aware of all the others, and I could see them as clearly as I did that first time, when, deep under the mountain, I became a part of the circle standing around the sick woman and restoring her to health. They were all there, the dead and the living too.

I knew that the living were of their company, and that was the second thing. Apart from the fact that I was there myself – and I had never felt so vibrantly alive – I always saw two people whose company I enjoyed every day. One was Fritha, and her presence through there in the spirit world confirmed what I had long thought: she had the power in her. I was watching out for a means to make her aware of this, but I did not worry unduly for such powers tend to make their own way.

The other person was, of course, Jack.

I knew already that he too had the power, for hadn't I recognized that unexpected spirit version of him that time beneath the mountain? I sensed he knew it too, and I had the strong sense it would not be long before it was openly recognized between us. It seemed like yet another gift to us both.

Gurdyman's house, then, was where I worked on my healing remedies and preparations; where, with Fritha, fast becoming the friend I'd known she would be, I did what I could to improve the lot of the women who came to us in need. The work was hard, sometimes harrowing and often reduced both of us to tears, which we always saved for when we were alone and never allowed our women to see.

But neither of us would have wanted to do anything else.

The house was not, however, where I lived.

I lived with Jack, in his house in the former workmen's village. Amid all the other demands on him, Jack had found the time to rebuild the lean-to, and now there was an opening between it and the house, making our living space more generous and considerably more comfortable.

Which was just as well, for even as we celebrated our October wedding I suspected I was with child, and now, a month later, I am in absolutely no doubt.

Jack has been acting as I suspect most men who know they are to be fathers act – the good ones, anyway – and he worries when my days are too long and I come home exhausted. But since I have the same concerns about him, it balances itself out. He is always busy, for he is sheriff in all but name, although I believe that being officially appointed would make very little difference. He is the man the townspeople want, because they trust him and they like him. He says modestly that coming after Sheriff Picot, even a pig would be popular, but those of us who know and love him make up our own minds.

I did not think it was possible to be as happy as we are. I try to remember to give regular thanks for my many blessings, but to be honest I'm usually too busy enjoying them. Sometimes I fetch the shining stone from its little secret place in a gap in the wall beside our bed, but it's more for old times' sake than anything else, and usually it reveals to me nothing more than its customary and beautiful swirls of gold and green light.

Once, however, I did see a vision of the future, or so I took it to be. I saw Jack and me, together, his arm round me as I leaned against him, and I had a baby at my breast. This child wasn't the one I am now carrying, however, for as the image broadened out I saw that already two – no, three – small children were clambering over their father's legs and hanging off his free arm.

If that is indeed a true picture of the future, I shall not complain.

ACKNOWLEDGEMENTS

The final book in a series seems a good time to express my thanks to some clever and talented people who have contributed so much to the Lassair stories and without whom my life (both professional and personal) would be that much harder.

At MBA, first Laura and lately Sophie have been the very best of agents, always there when I've asked anything of them, knowing when to leave me alone inside my head with a myriad characters and then, when presented with the resulting manuscript, ready with wise words and excellent advice which inevitably puts right everything I've got wrong. Thank you both for your steering hands, your professionalism, your friendship and your kindness, which are very much appreciated. Still with MBA, my grateful thanks also to Tim, who does the sums so efficiently and reliably.

At Severn House, Kate has taken hold of each one of the manuscripts and employed her particular skills to turn them into the finished article, always coming up with the perceptive comment and the spot-on amendment with skill and diplomacy. Rachel picks up the smallest of nuances and suggests subtle amendments I wouldn't even have thought of. Nicholas, who undertakes the copy edit whenever he is free, does a brilliant job, and I really appreciate his meticulousness and his sharp eyes (and I still have the photos of how to load a crossbow). Natasha and the whole team at this excellent publishing house are highly efficient and don't hang about, and I am lucky to be with them (and I love the latest jackets).

Lastly (and perhaps he should have been first since it is always he who initially reads every manuscript) my thanks and my love to my husband Richard. We have been together through the writing and the publication of more than forty books, and over the years he has honed the particular demands made on someone who lives with a writer to a high degree of

precision (plus he makes a mean cup of tea and a fine bowl
of soup, and also manages to remind me to take a pause and
MOVE without making me want to throw something at him
. . . usually). We've travelled together to so many locations in
the interests of research, signing sessions and library talks,
usually enjoying it far more than we should given that it's
meant to be work (and even the disconnected bottom hose in
Southport had its upside).

Thank you all. I couldn't do it without you.

Alys Clare
October 2020